ADVANCE PRAISE FOR *IT HAPPENED ONE CHRISTMAS*

"With its charming setting, addictively sweet love story, scene-stealing dog and all the fun, festive feels I could ask for, this adorable novel ticked every box on my Christmas romance wish list. A delightful read that's guaranteed to add sparkle and joy to your holiday season!"
MARISSA STAPLEY, bestselling co-author of
Three Holidays and a Wedding

"A grumpy Christmas tree farmer versus a relentlessly optimistic film producer, a picture-perfect Canadian town at Christmas—Chantel Guertin checks all the boxes in this delightful holiday romance."
JENNY HOLIDAY, *USA Today* bestselling author of
So This Is Christmas

"*It Happened One Christmas* is the perfect holiday treat! With warmth and wit, Chantel Guertin celebrates everything we love about the season: charm, coziness, and especially love. Readers will adore this fun and fresh small-town romance as Guertin spins a novel escape behind the scenes of our favorite holiday film franchises—and the result is binge-worthy."
COURTNEY KAE, author of
In the Event of Love

IT HAPPENED ONE CHRISTMAS

It Happened One Christmas

CHANTEL GUERTIN

DOUBLEDAY CANADA

Doubleday Canada and colophon are registered trademarks of
Penguin Random House Canada Limited

Library and Archives Canada Cataloguing in Publication

Title: It happened one Christmas / Chantel Guertin.
Names: Guertin, Chantel, 1976- author.
Identifiers: Canadiana (print) 20230237576 | Canadiana (ebook) 20230237584 |
ISBN 9780385697989 (softcover) | ISBN 9780385697996 (EPUB)
Classification: LCC PS8637.I474 I82 2023 | DDC C813/.6—dc23

This book is a work of fiction. Names, characters, places and incidents
are products of the author's imagination or are used fictitiously.
Any resemblance to actual events or locales or persons,
living or dead, is entirely coincidental.

Cover design and illustration: Emma Dolan
Cover art: (snowflakes) kornkun/iStock/Getty Images

Printed in the USA

Published in Canada by Doubleday Canada,
a division of Penguin Random House Canada Limited,
and distributed in the United States by Penguin Random House LLC

www.penguinrandomhouse.ca

10 9 8 7 6 5 4 3 2 1

Penguin
Random House
DOUBLEDAY CANADA

For Chris—
I'll stop the world and melt with you.

CHAPTER ONE

Friday, December 19, 9:30 a.m.

Michael Bublé was right: It *was* beginning to look a lot like Christmas everywhere I went. Metallic silver and gold balls dangled from the baskets of petunias that hung from the streetlamps. Tiny white lights wrapped the trunks of the palm trees that lined the sidewalk, and the billboard on top of Epic's Burbank offices featured the current number one flick in Holiday Movies on Netflix. I hummed along to Bublé's version of one of my favorite holiday songs in my AirPods, taking it as a good omen for all Canadian things to come as I pushed through the front door of Epic Productions, which had been wrapped to look like a Christmas present, and tried to banish Tomas from my mind. I hadn't thought about him in days.

Dumped. Why did the word have to be so dirty? *Dumped,* like a *dumpster.* It was bad enough that someone didn't want to date you anymore; now you were supposed to *feel* like garbage, too? When you got "fired" it wasn't *so* harsh. "Lost your job" was as though you'd forgotten to scatter bread crumbs from the office to your home, and now you just couldn't go back. Not the worst thing in the world. If we could figure out other ways of saying you were fired, why couldn't there be a nice way of explaining the end of a relationship? One that didn't involve refuse?

I didn't want to be thinking about Tomas, or the fact I had no plans for Christmas. But getting the call to confirm the spray tan appointment this morning had brought him back to the forefront. I'd made the appointment months ago in anticipation of the trip since the California sun did nothing for my pale Irish skin thanks to the SPF 45 I wore every day.

I popped my oversize black sunglasses onto the top of my head, and my AirPods into their case, then into my black cross-body bag, which was slung over my jeans and coral boyfriend blazer, and continued through Epic's bright atrium.

The space featured Persian rugs, secondhand couches, distressed antique furniture. The frat-house decor persisted not because of a lack of success; no, success we had in spades—we had the top-streaming Christmas movie on Netflix for the third straight year. Hiring an interior decorator to overhaul the vibe of the place was on someone's task list, somewhere; it was just that no one ever got that far down on their to-do list. There was actual work to be done if we wanted to maintain our position as the country's biggest holiday movies production company.

I waved at Misha, who sat on a tall stool at reception. "Hey, Zoey!" she called after me, leaning over the edge of the slab of salvaged wood. "Ooh, nice shoes," she said, eyeing my kitten heels, which gave me just enough extra height to be eye level with my boss, Elijah. "Sitter just confirmed. I'm a baby-free lady. Cocktails at Azure?"

"Let's do it," I said to one of my best and oldest friends.

I headed down the hall, past the lunchroom, where I ducked in to fill my water bottle, then by the first of the writers' rooms, where I said hi to Bethany before hanging a left and going down the hallway with the scratched paint. I knocked-then-walked into the office of Roberto Diaz, problem solver, solution wrangler, the vagueness of whose actual title (production assistant) served as an accurate description of the way he seemed to fix any film-related snag.

"How's it going on the permits?" Even talking about something as procedural as permits brought a smile to my face and made me forget all my troubles, Tomas and a solo Christmas included. I couldn't wait to get going on this holiday movie—*my* holiday movie, a friends-to-lovers romantic comedy about Ruby Russo and Jacques Pelletier, the fictional heroine and hero.

Roberto flipped his shaggy sand-colored hair away from his face and fixed his blue eyes up at me. He nodded to the script on the pile opposite his monitor. "Done," he confirmed with a confident grin. "Last location came through this morning."

"That calls for a fist bump," I said, pushing up the sleeves of my blazer. Roberto gave an overexaggerated nod.

"Oh Zoey, you know I live for the fist bump." Roberto's love of fist bumps was the *only* reason I'd suggested it.

I extended a clenched hand to receive one. "Really nice work, Roberto," I said sincerely.

"Some caveats," he said, running a bronzed hand through his hair. He picked up the sheaf of papers and flipped to the locations form, where my list occupied the right-side column: *Tudor-style house. Convenience store. Snowy walking path.* There were probably a dozen locations in all. Based on my descriptions, Roberto would have spent several weeks using Google Street View to find perfect facsimiles. He'd have contacted the owners and arranged a per diem price for however long we needed to shoot there. I knew exactly how much work that could be because I'd formerly had Roberto's job—along with most of the others in between.

"I know you wanted a Tudor-style house," Roberto said. "I couldn't find something exactly like that but I got a couple who are in a Georgian brownstone to agree to using their place. We actually used it when we shot *It Takes Two* a few years ago. The space is gorgeous—high ceilings, crown molding—and they already know the routine. Plus, they winter in the Cayman Islands so they won't be there anyway."

I frowned. "Georgian brownstone? Georgian's a long way from Tudor, stylistically speaking," I said. "But it also doesn't sound like Chelsea to me. And wasn't *It Takes Two* set in New York?"

He flipped through to the actual location permit, and as he did, I caught a glimpse of a familiar logo: Film perforations on the first pillar of the capital *N*, followed by the bold black *Y* and *C* of the New York Film Office, which issued any and all shoot permits for the five boroughs.

I pointed to the page with my freshly polished nail (shade: OPI's You Don't Know Jacques, in honor of Ruby's love interest in the film). "That's from the *New York* Film Office," I said, my eyes wide. It felt like I had just been fist-bumped in the stomach—hard.

"Right," he said. "Like West Twenty-Fourth and Ninth. Do you want to see the other agreements? I've got a bodega on the corner of West Tenth and West Thirtieth, and I'm pretty sure the High Line is going to come through for the 'snowy walking path,' provided we film on a Monday, which I think is totally doable for the schedule."

"I wanted Chelsea, *Quebec*," I said, my voice rising slightly. I tugged at my long brown hair, which I'd quickly thrown back in a ponytail on my way out of the gym this morning.

"What do you mean?" he said, confused.

"The little town. In Quebec. *Canada*."

"What about it?"

"That's where the movie is set, Roberto! Didn't you read the script?"

Even before I finished asking the question I knew the answer. Of course he hadn't read the script. I never did, either, when I had his job, back when I was first starting out in the industry. There was no time for reading scripts, just for getting permits.

"Does it matter?" he asked. He looked puzzled.

"What's going on?" Elijah's voice echoed in the hallway moments before he stuck his head through the door. He was wearing a blue blazer over a fitted white shirt, and a gold chain—that he thought was tasteful (debatable)—gleaming between the points of his casually unbuttoned collar. A weathered leather portfolio was tucked under his arm, and a pen was in his left hand. My boss, Epic's executive producer, always looked like he'd been professionally styled, right down to the accessories. Which he probably had been—his girlfriend was a stylist on a morning talk show.

"Nothing," I said quickly. "Small problem. Nothing we can't solve." I forced a smile at Elijah, then turned back toward Roberto. "Okay, let's just figure out how we're going to get the right film permit."

"*Right* film permit?" Elijah said. "What's the wrong one?"

"Misunderstanding," I said. "Roberto did a great job sewing up Chelsea, New York, but I wanted Chelsea, Quebec."

"We're not shooting in New York," Elijah said, his own voice going up an octave. "We don't have the budget for New York."

"I know that." More important, we *couldn't* shoot in New York because the setting for my screenplay was the snowy, rural Laurentians. Poutine. Maple syrup. Céline Dion. Long walks in white woods. *Not* the bustling streets of Manhattan.

"Didn't we get a permit for Vancouver?" Elijah barked at Roberto.

Roberto's hair swooshed up and then landed back on his forehead again as he nodded. "Yep."

"So we'll just use that." Elijah looked at me and shrugged.

I shook my head. "We can't shoot this film in Vancouver," I said firmly. "The story is set in Quebec. It has to be in Quebec."

He squinted at me, like what I was saying was fuzzy. "They're both in Canada. How different could they be?"

"It's not the same," I said. I'd been to Vancouver enough times to shoot holiday movies, ski with my sister, go to that surf school in Tofino with Tomas—*dammit, why did I have to think about Tomas?*—so I knew it was nothing like Quebec. "It's called *A Very Chelsea Christmas*. People say things in French. There are crêpes and maple syrup. It's a small town," I said, looking from Elijah to Roberto and back again. "Vancouver's a big city. It won't feel right. The whole point is that this story is set in Chelsea, Quebec. We have to film it in Chelsea, Quebec."

"All right," Elijah said, and I exhaled, realizing my shoulders had been glued to my ears for the past five minutes. I arched my back, cracking my spine. Then my mind started racing. What did we have to do to make sure we got the film permits we needed from Chelsea in Quebec? We had to figure that out soon. We were supposed to start filming in less than a month, just two weeks into the New Year.

Elijah finally stepped into the office. He tapped the distressed leather portfolio with his pen, a tick I associated with him thinking deep thoughts. "We'll just have to shoot *I'll Be Home for Christmas*."

It was as though a bucket of ice water had been dumped on my head. "What?" I asked.

"If your movie needs to be in Nowheresville, Quebec, and you don't have a permit for Nowheresville, Quebec, then let's go with the other holiday movie we have a script for, in a place where we know we can get a permit." Elijah shrugged, and looked at Roberto, who nodded in agreement.

My heart pounded. I'd spent months writing my script. It had come from the heart, and it was *good*, and it had been greenlit all the way to the networks. *A Very Chelsea Christmas* was my big chance.

"*I'll Be Home for Christmas* is . . ." I lowered my voice in case anyone in the office was friends with the freelancer who'd submitted the script. "It's fine. It's Christmassy, but it's the same story people have seen a billion times."

"You sound bitter," Elijah said with a smirk.

Not bitter, exactly. I'd read the script. I knew audiences would love it. And the truth was, as much as I hated to admit it, I knew *I'd* love it, because I *loved* holiday movies. My job was already a dream come true, but that's not what this was about. This was my chance to direct my *own* holiday movie. I'd been waiting for years for a chance to move up from an assistant director spot to a role that saw me respected as a filmmaker. *A Very Chelsea Christmas* had already gone through the tricky rounds of approvals. The budget had been tabulated and set aside. The streaming platform had okayed it to air next November. I'd already sent the calendar invites to my sister, Stella, and my closest friends, and had begun daydreaming about all of us curled up to watch it in a cozy chalet somewhere, cups of steaming hot chocolate with splashes of Baileys in our hands. And hey, maybe my parents would watch it, too—and maybe they'd even feel nostalgic.

I was getting ahead of myself. Still. I was *so* close. I couldn't let—I *wouldn't* let a small geographical mix-up ruin everything.

"*I'll* do it," I blurted out, startling myself. I looked quickly at Roberto, who raised his eyebrows.

Elijah looked up from his phone. "Hmm?"

"I'll get the permits." I swallowed and straightened my shoulders, keeping my eyes on Elijah.

"That's going to take weeks," Elijah said. "You know that."

"I'll go there." The idea came to me suddenly, and the words spilled out just as quickly. "To Chelsea. Myself. I'll get them in person."

Roberto's eyebrows shot up. I felt just as surprised at my own plan.

"You're going to *go* to Canada yourself?" Elijah studied me, his eyes glinting with curiosity. "It's six days till Christmas."

I ran a finger along the inside of my silver hoop earring. "Yes. And I'll get the permits before Christmas," I said more confidently than I felt. "My holiday plans just fell through, anyway. I've got time."

I could see my boss making the calculations, evaluating my record, my work ethic. I knew he was also considering the miracles I'd pulled off for him in the past, and I also knew that the list of impossible feats I'd executed would go on for some time. That was why I'd gone from co-op student to intern, PA to third-assistant director, then skipped straight to assistant director, all in record time at Epic—and all in record time for this industry. There was the Ferrari I'd procured for *Rudolph in Rome*. (A street bruiser on a Vespa turned out to know just the right mafioso, whose price for a one-day rental was well within our budget.) And also the anti-malaria pills that saved Belle Bilodeau when we were shooting *Noël on the Nile*. (Never leave home without them, my mom had said that year, when she'd really been trying to improve our relationship.) And, most recently, when Persephone Lane's stunt double broke her ankle, requiring me to don a blond wig, then parkour from the balcony on an apartment building to a warehouse roof for *Whiteout in Williamsburg*. (There is a reason "stunt double" is a legit, trained profession. I was still recovering from the trauma of that one.)

"Fine," Elijah decided. "But I need the film permits in my inbox by December 25. Otherwise, we're shooting *I'll Be Home for Christmas*, in Vancouver. It's a fine script. It's what people want. It's easy."

But *A Very Chelsea Christmas* was mine. "*Merci beaucoup*, Elijah," I said. "Consider it *fini*."

CHAPTER TWO

Sunday, December 21, 5:00 p.m.

Reframe the negative into a positive, that's what my therapist would say, I thought as I took a sip of wine from the tiny plastic cup, then set it down on my tray table and looked out the window at the gray sky above the clouds. But how do you reframe getting dumped into something positive when you've invested four years in a relationship you thought was actually going somewhere?

The truth was, I wasn't really heartbroken about the relationship ending. The *real* issue I had with Tomas dumping me was that I'd known things weren't going well. For months, in fact. There had been so many red flags, it was like we were in Switzerland, not LA. And that was the problem: I had chosen to *be* Switzerland in our relationship—to not rock the boat until after the holidays. We'd planned to spend this Christmas together on the beach in Tenerife, and I was really looking forward to Tenerife—once I'd gotten over my disappointment that Tomas hadn't wanted to stay home for the holidays, that is. Another Christmas without any of the Christmassy things I'd always thought I'd have at this point in my life. Like every single one of my friends had.

"Why would we stay home when we don't have to?" Tomas had argued.

"Because it's one of the most popular Christmas songs ever?" had been my rebuttal. Perry Como thought being "Home for the Holidays" had some appeal—and so did millions of other people. And I'd thought maybe if we stayed home this once, we'd do all the Christmassy things I'd always longed to do that we never did because we were never home at Christmas to enjoy them: pick out a tree, hang cute decorations and twinkly lights, fill stockings for each other to open on Christmas morning . . .

But Tomas had no interest in that. "Our friends all complain about how early their kids wake up on Christmas morning, and how much of a mess they make, and how they're exhausted by 9:00 a.m. Zoey, our friends are *jealous* of our lifestyle, and you want to *trade that in* for something more domestic? Maybe we'll get there one day, but until then, why wouldn't we sleep late and wake up on a beach somewhere far, far away?"

He was right. Our friends *were* jealous of our lives. All of our friends were married. Most had kids, and their lives were about juggling jobs with toddler sing-alongs and jockeying for exactly the right Montessori. I used to love that they were jealous of our lives. But that didn't matter to me anymore because I was jealous of *their* lives. And I knew that we'd never get there. I studied the clouds outside the window. He was right to end things.

But . . . how could things start out so great and then . . . oh, what even happened? The plane bumped and I steadied my wine. How did such intense feeling, actual electric attraction, neutralize into whatever existed at the end between Tomas and me? Or was that the thing: If you felt *such* a spark, it was bound to short-circuit eventually?

I sighed and leaned my head against the window. Even though I didn't really want to be with Tomas, it stung that he didn't want to be with me. It was the rejection that really burned.

Reframe, Zoey, reframe. I closed my eyes and took a deep breath. What Tomas had done was positive. The end of any relationship meant moving past the bonds of responsibility to someone else. I could do whatever I wanted whenever I wanted. Tomas had freed me. He'd *romantically liberated* me. Yes, that was it. I smiled and took another sip of wine. I felt better already.

Except for the part where I had no plans for Christmas and had Airbnb-ed out my apartment for the week, so I didn't even have a place to live now that Tenerife wasn't happening. Where was I going to go? Was I going to have to call Mom? The plane was emerging from the clouds, and the view outside the window briefly paused my spiraling internal monologue. Far below, I could see forests of ever-greens, all frosted in white.

🌲 🌲 🌲

Two hours later, after landing in Ottawa, and deplaning with my carry-on luggage, I made my way to the customs line. "Purpose of your trip?" asked the agent.

"Business," I said.

The official's head swiveled up from my passport photo to my face. "What sort of business?"

"Location scouting."

"For . . . ?" He raised an eyebrow. He had a bald head and a brown mustache, and friendly brown eyes. I smiled, and he smiled.

I rattled off the usual spiel: "I work for a production company that specializes in holiday movies, and we're look-ing to shoot one in Chelsea, just across the Quebec border." I found that when vagueness didn't work, it was better to be über-specific.

"I'm familiar with the location of Chelsea," he said wryly.

I smiled again. "Right. So I'm finding places where we can film."

"In Chelsea? Why wouldn't you do it in Wakefield?"

"What's so special about Wakefield?" I'd never heard of the place.

The agent shrugged. "It's bigger. More picturesque. More shops. More people. Plus, it has the covered bridge."

A covered bridge? How very *Bridges of Madison County*. Sounded nice, but no. It had to be Chelsea.

"Chelsea's beautiful this time of year," I insisted, as though snow only fell on this one town.

He shrugged again, found an empty page in the little booklet, and stamped something with a maple leaf. "Yeah, well. Enjoy your stay."

I made my way through the airport, following the signs that all included English and French. *Exit-Sortie. Arrivals-Arrivées.* I rolled my carry-on out of the terminal into the falling snow—which only confirmed my decision to not film this in Vancouver like Elijah suggested. If it was this snowy here, I couldn't wait to see the winter wonderland that awaited me across the bridge in Chelsea.

I paused at the crosswalk that led to the rental car area as a passing vehicle's headlights illuminated the big flakes, giving an illusion of falling space. The tires on wet pavement rolled by with the noise of ripping Velcro. As I trudged toward the kiosk to pick up my rental, I thought how nice it would be not to have to imagine what a scene would look like with a layer of white over it—which was often the case when scouting locations for holiday movies. Plus the snow was a good omen. The last movie we shot with actual flakes on the ground, *Ski Town Santa* with Benji Goldman, was a perennial streaming hit. Maybe my movie would become a Christmas classic, too.

My phone buzzed as I was waiting in line for the rental car. "What's the vibe in the Canary Islands?" Stella asked. "Is it like, boho chic or classic minimalist?" My younger sister worked at Anthropologie, so she described most things in life in terms of style aesthetic.

I took a deep breath. "Canceled the trip," I said, trying to sound breezy. "I'm in Quebec. Or, I'm about to be. Tomas and I are done."

"What?" she said in alarm. "When?"

"Ten days ago."

"Zoey! Why didn't you tell me?"

"Honestly, Stell, it isn't a big deal. And I didn't want to spoil your honeymoon. How was it?" Stella and her husband, Eitan, had been on safari in South Africa for the past month.

"Lots of animals. Lots of sex," Stella responded. "But don't change the subject. Did Tomas go on the trip?"

I peered toward the front of the line impatiently. There were still a few people ahead of me. "Not sure. I got a refund on my ticket. I wasn't going to chance that he'd also decide to go, and we'd end up on the plane together—and then sharing a room because the resort was fully booked for the holidays." I'd already assistant-directed a holiday film with the one-bed trope—I did not need to live the real-life version with my ex-boyfriend.

"Oof," she said. "Okay, so how *are* you?"

The line to the front counter inched forward. "Okay. Fine. Honestly, it had been over for months, I just . . . hadn't done anything about it. Because of the trip."

"Because of *Christmas*," she corrected me, then paused. "Wait, so what are your Christmas plans? Didn't you Airbnb your apartment?"

"I'm working."

"You are *not* working on Christmas Day. Nobody works on Christmas Day, Zo."

I sighed. "I'm securing a permit so we can start shooting *my* movie after Christmas."

"Oh, well, that's cool. But you'll be done when, tomorrow?"

Someone tapped me on the shoulder, and I looked up, realizing there was a large gap between me and the person in front of me. I stepped forward.

"Come here," Stella was saying. "It won't be Christmas, but it'll be a fun hang-out-with-your-now-Jewish-sister-and-brother-in-law break! Too bad Hanukkah didn't fall at the same time. You could've made challah with me."

I smiled. "You know how to make challah?"

Part of me couldn't believe Stella had converted to Judaism for Eitan, but at the same time, it made total sense. Now *she* was liberated from the pressure to re-create a magical Christmas when she, like me, had no frame of reference—aside from that one magical Chelsea Christmas years ago, that is.

I could hear Stella's keyboard keys clicking. "Look, there are direct flights to Boston out of Montreal. You're so close. Please come." She paused. "Although, I'll have to work on the 26th. But on the 25th we can hang. It's something, at least." She didn't wait for me to respond. "You're coming here. Text me when you figure out which flight you'll be on."

"Okay," I said reluctantly. I loved Stella but it seemed more depressing to visit someone who wouldn't be celebrating

Christmas than to be alone. "It'll be at least a day or two till I get there, though. After I've finished work."

This seemed to satisfy my sister, and I told her I had to go. "Love you." I hung up, the picture of Stella and me filling the screen. It was from years ago, from that perfect, snowy Christmas we'd spent in Chelsea with Mom and Dad. The two of us were young—I was eleven years old, Stella was nine—sitting in front of a sparkling Christmas tree in matching pajamas. I'd snapped a pic of the actual photo on my fridge before leaving home thinking it would be a good omen for this trip.

The idea was to create a perfect Christmas on-screen that felt as special as the one that Stella and I had experienced— once—and to exorcise the litany of disappointments all the other Christmases had been.

Like the one when I was seven.

It was still dark out when I'd been awakened by the sound of glass breaking. *Santa*, I'd thought, climbing out of bed as quietly as possible. I'd tiptoed to the stairs and peered down to the living room below. My father was draped across the couch, his leg on the coffee table, a broken wineglass on the hardwood floor. My mother asleep on a nearby chair.

I'd gone back to bed only to wake up at dawn to the same scene. No stockings. No presents. No Santa. I'd thought he hadn't come because my parents had been in the living room all night long. I'd assumed my parents would apologize and assure Stella and me that was the case. But they didn't. The best they could do was hand us each an unwrapped box of drugstore chocolates before going to bed to sleep off what I now knew to have been terrible hangovers.

The next year was no better. My father had left us (for the first time), and my mother had been too depressed to think about Christmas, so there were no stockings in the morning, no half-hearted attempts to make things right. No Christmas music, no special breakfast. No games by a fire. That was the year I really figured out the truth, not just about Santa, but about Christmas itself: that it's only a magical holiday if you have someone to make it magical for you.

"Next! *Suivante!*" a voice called, and I shook myself out of my daydream, then realized I was at the front of the line.

I slipped my phone into the pocket of my white wool coat and shuffled up to the desk, handing my rental confirmation over to a guy who looked barely old enough to drive and who took forever to type whatever it was he needed to type into the computer. "And of course you'll take the additional coverage for $14.99 a day?"

"No thank you, I have coverage on my credit card," I said, impatiently looking at the time on my phone.

"Are you sure? It's bumper to bumper. You won't have to worry about a thing."

"Yes," I said.

"Yes, you'll take it?"

I exhaled and smiled, and tried to remain calm. "Just a basic car, no frills, no extras."

"All righty," he said, then disappeared through the swinging doors behind him.

My eyes flicked to the wall-mounted flat-screen TV, which was tuned to the news channel. A red banner scrolled across the bottom just under the day's stock price listings: TEMPERATURE FLUCTUATIONS CREATE OPPORTUNITY FOR SEVERE WINTER STORM STARTING IN 24–48 HOURS, it read. RESIDENTS IN THE GATINEAU AND NATIONAL CAPITAL REGION WARNED TO PREPARE FOR POWER OUTAGES AND ICY CONDITIONS. Absently, I wondered how close Chelsea was to the Gatineau region. Wasn't Gatineau Park the spot I'd listed for the walk-in-the-snowy-woods scene—when the heroine, Ruby, finds the lost Labrador retriever that belongs to Jacques?

The clerk finally reappeared, jangling a set of car keys. "Good news!" he exclaimed. "You've been upgraded to a Land Rover!"

The extreme cheer on his face suggested I'd just won a billion-dollar lottery. Then an actual important question occurred to me. "Does it have four-wheel drive and heated seats?" I felt proud of myself for considering this, given the potential snowstorm en route.

"The Land Rover? Absolutely, for sure."

I nodded. I was especially proud of myself for thinking to ask about four-wheel drive, instead of *only* thinking about heated seats.

Five minutes later, once my suitcase was stowed in the trunk of the Land Rover and I had Google Maps guiding me on my phone, I was pulling out of the parking structure into the snowy streets, anticipation fluttering in my stomach. The windshield wipers created a hypnotic hum. I fiddled with the dial until I found Christmas music and blasted the volume, singing along to Mariah Carey's "All I Want for Christmas Is You." The route Google Maps had me on was taking me through downtown Ottawa. I passed people bustling through a market area, laden with shopping bags. Streetlamps were adorned in lights and greenery and big red bows. At a red light I slowed to a stop opposite a park with . . . a guy on cross-country skis? I squinted to get a closer look. Yep, Lycra tights, a fitted jacket, a knitted cap—what did they call that in Canada, again? I went through the list of Canadianisms in my mind, the one I'd studied while writing the screenplay, searching for the right word. Ah, right. *Toque.*

I smiled as the skier, his face covered by his balaclava, dug his poles into the snow, and swished his dagger-skinny skis through the park. It was the perfect holiday movie scene— though I'd probably lose the balaclava. It was a bit *Fargo* kidnapping, rather than swoony holiday romance.

The light turned green and the car inched forward as I scanned the area for ideal shots. It's the curse of the location scout, to be perpetually seeking possible places to film. I'd developed the habit several years ago, when that was my principal responsibility for Epic. My eyes rested on the copse of maple trees at the far end of the park, and the way the streetlights danced on the snow created some possibilities, which I mentally filed away—just in case Chelsea wasn't as *parfait* as I remembered and we needed an extra spot. But I knew it would be. A fire truck whizzed by, its siren wailing. I edged along the busy street, my head whipping back and forth to soak it all in. A car horn honked so I picked up the pace a bit.

As I drove, I worked through the list of locations we needed. Christmas tree farm. Cozy café. Boisterous pub for the climactic sing-along. Quaint residence that accommodated at least a twelve-foot tree, because anything less looked too small on TV. Every Epic production had a certain budget for locations, and Roberto had already blown some of this movie's with nonrefundable advance payments for the Manhattan spots, which meant I had less than the usual amount set aside for my Quebec targets. But I didn't think it would be a problem. I hadn't seen Chelsea in many—correction: *any*—productions. That it was unused as a film location meant its residents would hopefully be excited about the attention, which, in an ideal world, would translate to lower fees to use the spots in their town. That would help me secure more places in Chelsea, which would make the movie feel and look like it had a higher production budget.

But the truth was, it wasn't making a Hollywood movie on a shoestring budget that thrilled me—more than anything, what gave me all the feels when making these movies was that while bringing a fictitious story to the small screen, we were bringing joy to a town. When a shop owner saw the place that they had poured their heart and soul and long hours into on the screen, they felt *happy*. Their livelihood was immortalized. Not to mention the economic bump they'd get. It brought Christmas joy, sometimes year-round. I loved that.

As I made my way across the Ottawa River, the cars began to spread out, and soon I found myself rolling over an empty two-lane road leading through snow-covered forest. This was more like it. Untouched snow. Massive trees. The glint of Christmas lights on houses in the distant hills. Not a car horn honking, not a siren wailing. It was quiet except for the Christmas music on the radio. I turned off the highway onto a smaller street. Old-fashioned lampposts lined both sides of the road, their amber bulbs emitting a warm glow in the dark and around the big sign that read *Village de Chelsea*. I smiled at how quaint it all was, imagining opening the movie on a shot of this exact stretch, when suddenly a deer bounded into the middle of the road. Khaki-colored with muscular flanks and a white tail, it stopped right in front of me, staring at me with large, almond-shaped eyes. It had antlers and looked almost like one of Santa's reindeer, but of course they weren't real, and this animal, mere feet in front of me, was very real. I gasped, slamming my foot into the brake pedal. It depressed to the floor and the SUV slid forward—straight toward the deer, which was frozen in place. I gripped the steering wheel as I continued to glide across the icy surface, my heart racing. "Oh no, oh no," I muttered to myself. Hitting a deer at Christmas was the last thing I needed. Talk about a bad omen. Then, just as suddenly as the buck had run out onto the road, the SUV skidded to a stop with a foot or two to spare. I stared at him, then put the car in park to settle my rattled nerves and take in the scene. I looked out the passenger-side window to where the deer had disappeared. Just past the cemetery I could see a charcoal wrought iron gate running alongside the road, encircling a traditional, Gothic-style church nestled deep in brilliant white snow and visible only by the tiny white lights that dotted the perimeter. I smiled.

A minute later, once my heart rate had slowed, I eased the SUV along the road again. As it curved, a massive Christmas tree came into view. Multicolored lights wrapped around it all the way to its top, which disappeared into the low-slung clouds. The tree glowed in the dark sky. I remembered this tree. Back then, benches had surrounded it, and Stella and I had sat on them, sipping hot chocolate after skating on the nearby rink. Where had we gotten the hot chocolate? Had we made it at the cottage and brought it in a thermos? Or had Mom and Dad bought it for us at a little café? Some details were so clear, while others were a wistful fog. And yet, the feeling I had from being in Chelsea was already coming back to me: warmth, happiness.

The little inn where I'd booked a room was a few feet away, and I pulled the SUV into the small lot beside it.

I grabbed my white wool coat from the back seat, found the camel cashmere gloves I'd tucked into the pockets, and pulled them on. Then I pulled out my rolling suitcase. I climbed up the small snowbank, dragging my suitcase over it and onto a snowy sidewalk, looking down at my Bailey UGGs, which, come to think of it, might have been a footwear fail in this weather. My toes were already numb, and the wet snow was beginning to seep through the suede. I stopped and buttoned my coat, pulling the collar up to my earlobes. I wasn't exactly warm, but I didn't care. The sight of this picturesque town warmed me instantly. White and colored Christmas lights twinkled on houses and bushes and trees. Fluffy snowflakes fell from the sky, landing softly on every surface. I sighed contentedly. I was here—in the prettiest town, the backdrop of my happiest Christmas ever.

The houses on the main road were small and upright, like Monopoly game pieces, and sided in brightly painted wood— yellow, aquamarine, ochre. Their steeply angled metal roofs meant the snow gathered only on the eaves, like icing on a gingerbread house. The sign for each little house indicated its specialty in French: *Boulangerie. Fromagerie. Bibliothèque. Le Pub du Village.* The notes Roberto had prepared said that the reception desk for the Auberge Rouge would be closed when I arrived, so I'd have to pick up my room key from La Petite Grocerie, a few wood-sided houses down from the inn. As I approached, I admired the painted wraparound porch. Set onto the right side of the porch was a red, green, and white canoe, and standing upright in the middle of that was a fully decorated, *real* Christmas tree. I could imagine the owners having a conversation about the canoe at the end of summer, and where to store it until the next year: "Let's set it on the porch and put a tree in it! It'll be festive decor!" I lugged my suitcase up the snowy steps to the porch and reached for the doorknob. The door was locked. I then noticed a hand-written sticky note on the door: *Key in mailbox.* So much for security. I peered in the mailbox next to the door and there was the key, just sitting there, taped to a note in cursive French. I tried and failed to translate, hoping it didn't say anything important.

As I walked back to the inn, my breath fogged in the night air and the surrounding snow sparkled in the moonlight as my boots squeaked over it. The Auberge Rouge was a two-story apartment-style building set among the pines and leafless maples, each room's door opening from the exterior of the structure. I glanced at my key. Room 204. I pulled my suitcase up the metal stairs, passing both dark and illuminated windows. The drapes of one were open to reveal a couple at a kitchen bar, glasses of white wine before them. Across gangways and around the rear side of the building I found 204.

Inside, a large woven carpet in reds and golds covered the hardwood floors. The bed was low to the ground and swathed in crisp white cotton. In the corner was a real fireplace, a small stack of logs neatly piled in front. Nearby was a worn leather chair, a reading lamp forming an arch over it. A trio of books was stacked on the small table beside it. The scent of eucalyptus wafted in the air. The space felt warm and inviting. I was only here for two nights, and now I wished I'd thought to book for longer.

My phone buzzed. As I was reading the text from Misha, inviting me to her place for Christmas, another one came in from Stella. I was grateful for my best friend and for my sister, but right now, I needed to focus on my Christmas *movie*, not Christmas itself.

I looked at my watch—8:00 p.m. Despite the long day of travel, I wasn't tired. I was still on LA time, so it was only five o'clock in my mind. What should I do? I could walk around the town, or watch a movie in bed. I could also head to the pub for a drink. I decided on the last option: It wouldn't be open in the morning, and this would give me a head start on scouting.

🌲 🌲 🌲

Ten minutes later, after I'd freshened up in the bathroom, running a brush through my straight hair and swiping my lips with some light pink lip gloss, I was back outside. I walked down the steps to the road, snow dancing all around me. Across the street, at the green-and-white pizzeria, people gathered around a bonfire. I could hear the rumble of music and boisterous laughter and scanned my eyes over the colorful buildings, searching for the correct Monopoly piece. Finally, I saw the small brown house, brightly lit from within, with the sign out front that read: *Le Pub du Village*. I began making my way toward it.

The steps were wide and led to a wraparound porch, the eaves covered in twisted birch branches glimmering with tiny golden lights—a nice effect. I snapped a photo with my phone to add to the shot list before climbing the stairs, making my way around a cluster of people leaving the pub. The heavy door opened to the smell of beer and roasting chestnuts. Mason jars hung as lanterns from the dark paneled ceiling, and Edison bulbs looped around the circumference of the room. To the left was a long oak bar, wineglasses hanging by their stems from a wire rack. High-top tables and backless stools filled the rest of the space at left. The right side of the bar had a lower ceiling, and featured low tables littered with glasses both empty and full. There wasn't an empty table in the place, but it seemed like there was just enough space for me to stand with a row of others at the bar.

I squeezed through the crowd—Excuse me, *excusez-moi*, sorry, *pardon*, who knew I'd retained so many French words while writing the screenplay?—until I reached a small break near the corner of the bar and waved to the bartender, a guy in his forties with a full black beard, red toque, and matching red waffle shirt. Each finger had a thick ring, and on the left side of his neck was a large cursive tattoo—a word I didn't recognize, partially hidden by his beard. He caught my eye and waved back, then let out a hearty laugh and shouted something French in a deep voice. I decided to assume he wanted to know my drink order and while what I really wanted was a gin and tonic, I had absolutely zero idea how to say that in French.

The barnwood wall behind the bar featured a spattering of signs, and I focused on one with a wineglass and the word *vin* underneath.

"*Vin*," I shouted.

He laughed. "All right, a glass of wine. White or red?"

So much for my convincing French.

"Red," I said, wondering if there was any chance of getting more specific, but the bartender was already nodding and pulling a bottle from the counter behind him and popping the cork. A moment later he held out the glass by the bowl, and I took it by the stem just as someone beside me drew his attention. The bartender gave a thumbs-up.

"You should've had the gin," a voice to my right said. I turned. The guy was large—round head, round belly, his shirt tight and bulging at the buttons. The area around his mouth was speckled with stubble—not short enough to be five o'clock shadow, but not long enough to be a beard. Just regular unkemptness. His hair was greasy and his glasses were spotted with fingerprints. He gave me a smug look and I winced. There weren't supposed to be smarmy men in my picture-perfect holiday town.

"*Deux gin tonics*," he shouted to the bartender, then looked at me and stuck out a hand.

"Stéphane. And you are? Aside from gorgeous, that is."

Eww. I grimaced. "Zoey," I said reluctantly.

He pointed at the wall of bottles. "They distill their own gin in-house. You've gotta try it." The bartender pulled a large clear bottle off the shelf behind him—the label reading GIN in block letters.

Maybe Stéphane wasn't so bad. "I actually wanted a gin and tonic," I admitted, taking a sip of the wine, which was surprisingly delicious, especially for a pub. "But I didn't know how to say it in French."

First rule of thumb when location scouting: Even if the person seems smarmy, be friendly, because you never know who they are. For all I knew, this guy could own the place. Even though scouting was all about judging a place by its appearance, the same rule shouldn't apply to people—even if the person in question smelled like corn chips.

"I just did." Stéphane chuckled. "Gin and tonic. *Gin tonic.* I got you one."

I shook my head. "Oh, no thanks, I've got the wine now." I held up my glass. "And an early morning tomorrow."

"There's no such thing as an early morning. Tonight's the winter solstice," he said loudly. "Longest night of the year. Gotta drink to get through it!" He looked around. "All night long, amiright?" He reached for the two glasses the bartender held out and downed one before slamming it back on the counter.

"Go on, try it." He shoved the other glass at me, slurring his words as he leaned close, his breath thick with gin and—was that chicken wings? Empty as it was, I felt my stomach turn.

"No, really, you go ahead," I said, already sensing I needed to get a move on. I just hoped this guy wasn't actually the owner.

"I bought it for you," Stéphane said, his tone suddenly laced with aggression.

Here's the thing: I never let guys pay for my drinks—especially not in a strange place, when they are clearly drunk. I braced myself, then took a step back, looking around. "Ah, there's my friend." I pointed vaguely across the room. But Stéphane also stepped back, closing the sliver of space where I'd planned to make my escape.

I forced a wide grin. "Anyway, enjoy your night." I turned to squeeze past him, but it meant brushing up against his large frame. I squeezed my eyes shut and held my breath as I pushed past. But then, suddenly, there it was: his hand on my ass.

"Seriously, dude?" I spat at him. My skin crawled. Stéphane grinned, as though I was paying him a compliment. "Don't touch me."

"Pourquoi pas?" He leaned so close that I could *feel* the words on my ear. I lifted my hand, prepared to slap him across the face, but a loud voice to my right gave me pause. The asshole's head whipped to the left, toward the voice. I turned to catch the profile of a man, about my age, maybe a bit older, tall and broad-shouldered beneath a chestnut plaid flannel shirt that had just enough structure to hug his body. Chiseled jaw, nicely groomed beard. Dark brown hair that was smartly swept to the side. Now *he* I could happily judge by appearances. Why couldn't *that* guy have wanted to buy me a drink?

I watched, stunned, as the shacket-wearing guy said something else to Stéphane in even more terse French. I fixated on his full lips.

He turned to me. *"Ça va?"* he asked, his voice lower, softer. His hazel eyes bore into me. His lashes were so long. I stared blankly at him, trying to figure out how to respond to his question. I felt light-headed.

"Are you okay?" he asked me in English. His accent was faint, his tone smooth.

But before I could answer, Stéphane interjected: *"I* was talking to her."

"Talking *at* her is more like it," the guy beside me said. "She didn't seem interested in talking to you." He looked at me. "Were you interested in talking to him?"

"It's none of your business, dude," Stéphane jumped in again, before I could respond. I raised my eyebrows and watched as he came toward my knight in plaid, pushing him and forcing him to take a step back. The handsome man steadied himself, then said something in French. Stéphane shook his head, then took a swing. I yelped and moved out of the way just before my plaid knight caught Stéphane's arm in the air mid-swing. A crowd had formed around us, oohs and aahs and gasps filling the air. Stéphane swayed. They stayed like that for a moment, then he ripped his arm away and threw his glass down on the bar, sloshing liquid in all directions as he brushed past my knight. I watched Stéphane push through the crowd as they jeered at him. Eventually, he made it out the front door.

I turned around. "You must have a way with words," I said, barely able to hear my own voice over the pounding of my heart in my ears.

The stranger's jaw was hard. "Something like that. Are you okay?" He turned to meet my eyes, and I felt flutters all the way to my toes. I'd never seen lashes so long and thick— real ones, that was. I forced myself to look away, but only made it as far as his chest. It was so broad his shirt lay perfectly smooth and flat. Then I remembered he was waiting for an answer. I blinked. "Yes, I'm fine," I said to his pec muscles. "Thank you."

"*Bon*," he said. I met his eyes again. He shook his head. "He isn't from Chelsea. He's not one of us." There was an arrogance to his tone that was surprisingly sexy. As though he owned the town and felt responsible for the people in it.

I felt sheepish. "Oh, well, neither am I," I said with a small smile. "But at least I didn't grab someone's ass or try to knock you out. Maybe that counts for something?" I laughed.

He raised an eyebrow. "Well, then, on behalf of the town, I'm sorry you had to experience that."

"You don't have to take personal responsibility for that guy," I said quickly. "It's not your fault." Then it dawned on me. *This* guy probably owned the pub and didn't want assholes giving his place a bad rap. "Can I buy you a drink?" I asked. "As a thank-you?" I realized that my offer was, in theory, mildly hypocritical—but I didn't smell like corn chips. And I wasn't drunk. And this kind man had done a nice thing. *And* if he did own the bar, it was a surefire way to find out.

For a moment he looked like he was considering it, but his expression quickly clouded. "No, but thank you. Enjoy your stay." His gaze held mine for a split second longer than necessary and I enjoyed every millisecond of it. Then, suddenly, he turned and weaved through the crowd and out a side door.

I exhaled a breath I didn't know I'd been holding. Who *was* that guy? Based on his few words, probably a Chelsea resident who just wanted to make sure his perfect town kept the good in and the bad out. I walked back to the bar. He was probably married to his high school sweetheart. He was probably going home to a beautifully decorated place with a real Christmas tree and a few presents already wrapped underneath the tree, just to get his kids, who were tucked into bed, excited for the big day.

He was the kind of guy Jacques, the hero of *A Very Chelsea Christmas,* would become—hot, kind, responsible. I made a note to find an actor who looked like my shacket-wearing good Samaritan.

I downed my wine and headed out the same door, back into the snowy night.

♣ ♣ ♣

A short walk home later, I was back in my room, in my cozy pajamas and tucked into bed. While writing the screenplay I'd used my memories from nearly two decades ago for the locations in Chelsea, and the feelings it evoked. Somewhere in the back of my mind I hadn't been sure that my recollections would match reality. On the plane, I had worried about the place not being a suitable film location. What if the buildings had been neglected over the years, left to deteriorate or fall victim to vandalism? Or the opposite, and the town had been taken over by commercialism and development? Or, what if it hadn't changed at all, but my memory had glorified a place that was simply bland?

But actually, the reality was better—asshole encounter aside. The little I'd seen when driving into town and walking to and from the pub confirmed the description I'd set out in my screenplay, but amplified it by about a million: A quaint main street filled with shops in tiny, colorful houses wrapped in tiny colorful lights. A fresh wreath with a red bow on every door. Frosted evergreens. People walking hand in hand on sidewalks. Toques and plaid and fires and French accents. I flipped open my laptop, hit play on a Christmassy playlist, and, until my eyelids were heavy, made notes that would make the movie even more magical.

CHAPTER THREE

Monday, December 22, 8:00 a.m.

My eyes opened to the pine-paneled ceiling. Sunlight was streaming through the windows. I stretched, remembering where I was and smiling, feeling excited about the day. I reached over to grab my phone, turning off airplane mode, but surprisingly, it didn't come alive with texts. Then I remembered that I was now three hours ahead. It was 8:00 a.m. in Chelsea, but in LA everyone was still asleep. It made me feel as though I was finding bonus time.

After a long, hot shower, I pulled on a pair of black Lululemon leggings and an oversize black-and-white-striped sweater with red heart patches on the elbows. I swiped mascara on my lashes, dabbed gloss on my lips, and then slipped into my white coat and UGGs. I dug through my suitcase and found the pink beanie with the faux-fur pom-pom that I had tucked away and put it on.

Outside, it felt like I was stepping into a live reenactment of Bing Crosby's "White Christmas." Snowflakes fell charmingly from the sky, and untouched snow glistened in the sun that peeked through the clouds. It looked so much like the cotton-wool blended "snow" blankets we used on set when we needed "Christmas" but there wasn't any snow. As I passed a bench on the sidewalk, I ran my gloved hand through the snow, just to make sure it was real. In front of the inn, two little boys were rolling the final snowball to create the head for their snowman while an older gentleman, maybe their grandfather, looked on, sipping from a paper cup with an orange lid. He looked up, noticed me, and gave a wave and smile. I couldn't have written a more wholesome, perfect scene in my movie. I smiled and waved back. Then I followed the path down the steps to the road. Along the main street, baskets of poinsettias and evergreens hung from Victorian lampposts. At the end of the street stood the Christmas tree I had seen the night before, and while last night it had looked stunning, all lit up against the night sky, it was just as impressive in the daylight—it had to be at least twenty feet tall and half as wide. The colored lights still shone bright and the large gold star on top glinted in the sunlight. It reminded me of the tree the Whos down in Whoville danced around in Dr. Seuss's *How the Grinch Stole Christmas!* Dolly Parton's "Christmas on the Square" pumped through the air from small speakers affixed to the lampposts. I smiled and breathed in the honey-and-pine-scented air. This town was holiday movie gold.

🌲🌲🌲

I kept walking, the snow crunching under my boots creating its own musical accompaniment, until I reached a brown barn with a red door that I had noticed on my walk home from the pub last night. The porch had a fresh garland wrapped around its posts and railings, and the barnwood sign above the door read *Rendez-Vous Café*.

Inside, the toasty air felt like a soft blanket, warming my cheeks from the cold air outside. The smell of freshly roasted coffee and banana bread made my stomach grumble.

As I waited in line behind a woman and a small child, I took in the space. Faded rugs lined the scuffed hardwood floors and Tiffany-style lamps created a soft glow. Framed newspaper clippings reporting local events decorated the walls: the centennial anniversary of the town; a 2018 photo featuring the Chelsea-born members of a Quebec team that had won its first Canadian field hockey championship; and multiple photos of a 1998 ice storm that turned the town into a crystal wonderland and shut it down for nearly a week.

In the corner of the square room was a sideboard decked with handmade candles and a small Christmas tree adorned with knitted ornaments. Clusters of people sat on worn sofas by the real wood-burning fireplace, and at small tables in mismatched chairs. It all felt vaguely familiar, like watching a remake of a holiday classic. This was definitely the café where Stella and I had gotten hot chocolate and then sat by the big tree on the main street.

"*Bonjour,*" said the woman behind the counter. Her curly salt-and-pepper hair was pulled back in a low bun, wire-rimmed glasses were nestled on top of her head, and a black pen was tucked behind her ear. A red apron was cinched at her waist, and a black-and-white name tag pinned on her shirt read *Lise*.

"*Bonjour*," I said, scanning the chalkboard above Lise's head. Each of the dozen beverages was written in a different color of chalk.

"Are you visiting?" Lise asked with a smile. I nodded. "Then welcome to our *petit village*."

"Thanks," I said. "I think I might have actually visited your café before. Would you have been open around twenty years ago?"

"*Bien sûr*," she said. "Henri and I opened in 2004, the year we were married. And we'll celebrate our china anniversary in the spring. Won't we, Henri," she called to a short, rotund man at the other end of the bar. His bald head was shiny, but what hair he lacked up top he made up for with a white beard that touched his chest. He didn't look up at his wife, but grumbled something. She responded in French and he swiveled the frother away from the espresso machine, wiping it down with a rag, then turned toward us.

"*Bien sûr, ma chérie.*" He smiled.

Lise turned back to me. "Well, then, welcome back, after all these years!" she said, tugging at a tuft of frizzy hair above her ear. "*Heureuse de te revoir!* Now what can I get our loyal customer?"

"A café mocha and a croissant, please," I said, smiling back at her.

Lise rang in my order, then got to work, bustling around the counter, pulling out a metal jug, pouring milk, steaming it. "So how long will you be with us?"

I considered her question. It all depended on how long it would take to get enough of the town on board to film. For exterior shots, I'd need permission from the mayor's office. And then I needed at least a half dozen other locations.

"A day or two," I said, exhaling. The thought of settling into a few days here, away from LA and my usual routine, felt *nice*. In fact, it felt nice to location scout—I'd forgotten what it was like to be out on my own, exploring a new place, getting familiar with it. Over the last few years, I often just bustled into a town for the shoot, never really getting a sense of the geography. And there was so much in Chelsea for me to take in.

"Well, then, you must make the most of your time here. We have so many things going on over the holidays." Lise plucked a scroll tied with a red ribbon from a small wicker basket next to the register and handed it to me. "This will help."

I slipped off the ribbon and unrolled the slip of paper, smiling at the charm of it all, and scanned the handwritten list of events: a crafternoon of wine and wreaths. Paint your own ornament at the elementary school. A book swap at the church.

"We'll be having an acoustic holiday sing-along tomorrow night by the fire," Lise added.

"Oh, that sounds lovely," I said, craning my neck to see the fireplace, which had a golden fire crackling away in it.

"So what brings you back to these parts?" she asked.

"I'm actually looking to film a holiday movie here in town," I explained, watching her eyebrows rise and the corners of her mouth follow. She turned excitedly to her husband. "Really? You hear that, Henri?"

Henri grunted.

"Is the movie romantic?" she asked, her hands clasped together.

I nodded. "Very romantic."

She practically swooned. "Ooh, I love a romantic holiday movie. I watch them every year. So, it would be set here? In Chelsea?"

I nodded again with a big grin, delighting in her joy. Her enthusiasm meant that she'd be open to her café being in the film, which was ideal. The coffee shop was small, but it was the perfect spot for the meet-cute, when the main character, Ruby, spills coffee on herself and Jacques, the love interest, offers his toque to clean it up. The best thing about the spot was that it didn't have a lot of windows—it was always better to illuminate the location the way you wanted with professional lighting, rather than worry about the changeable weather outside.

Lise handed me a brown paper bag and a white paper cup with a blue snowflake stamp on its front. In the foam of my coffee she'd made a tree, sprinkling it with crushed peppermint candies.

"Looks beautiful," I said. This was just one reason why scouting holiday movies during the holiday season was so special—these little touches added to the magic. If we filmed in the café, I'd definitely request that Lise and Henri create the coffees for the scene. I took a sip of the mocha, closing my eyes and savoring the chocolate, coffee, and hint of peppermint. "Wow, this is quite possibly the best mocha I've ever had."

Lise smiled and blushed. "Well, anything you need from me, just let me know."

"Actually, there is something," I said, leaning on the counter. "Would you mind if I take a few photos? I won't get any of your customers in the shots." I never promised to use a location until I'd seen at least a half dozen sites—I hated to get someone's hopes up and then dash them later because we'd found a better spot, or encountered some budget constraints.

"*Bien sûr, bien sûr.* Whatever you need." Lise clapped her hands. "Imagine, our little shop in a holiday movie." She shrugged her shoulders, like she was giving herself a hug.

"Our little shop—and what are you promising away?" Henri grumbled but he was smiling as he shimmied over beside Lise and slung an arm over her shoulder.

"Don't you worry about a thing," she said, ruffling his beard.

I walked around the café and snapped a few photos of the fireplace, the stairs that led to the second floor, and the little corner nook filled with puzzles. I walked back to the counter and picked up my coffee cup. Sometimes I had to pinch myself to remember that I was *so* close to having my own movie come to screen. I always cared about the films I directed, but this one—my very first screenplay—was going to be even more magical.

"So, what's next on your list?" Lise asked, wiping her hands on her apron.

"Well, maybe you can help me. Is there a farm perhaps where everyone cuts down their own Christmas tree? Or even a lot that brings trees in?" I asked, taking a sip of the hot coffee and feeling it run through my body.

"Ah yes, of course, the Beaux Bois farm. Only place to get a tree in Chelsea," she said. "Not that anyone would ever think of competing with Beaux Bois. The farm's been in the Deschamps family for fifty years, at least." She paused and sighed, her expression clouded for a moment, before she blinked it away. "If you head out this door"—she pointed to the front door of the café—"and drive thataway on the main street, you take a right at the corner, then you follow the *chemin* Kingsmere up that way, toward the Mackenzie King estate. It'll be on your right. You can't miss it. There's a sign, of course, but look for the interesting roof that goes up for two stories of gabled windows."

"Thanks," I said, pulling out my phone to get a sense of the route. I typed in the address of the cottage where we'd stayed years ago. An involuntary grin spread across my face when I saw that it was very close to the farm. Even though Dad thought his old boss had torn down the cottage, looking at the image on Google Maps had confirmed it was still there. I couldn't wait to see it again in person. And, if luck was on my side, chat with the new owners about the possibility of setting the movie in their home. I hadn't given Roberto the details when he'd been sourcing because it had seemed a bit *too* random, but now that I was here . . .

I looked around once more, pulled on my hat and gloves, said goodbye to Lise and Henri, grabbed my coffee cup and croissant, and headed out into the cold.

I trudged along the snowy sidewalk, cutting between two identical houses, one blue, one yellow, to the parking lot, where my rented SUV was covered in a thick blanket of snow. I opened the back of the SUV, hoping to find a brush, but it was empty. I looked in the back seat, but was out of luck. Was I supposed to *ask* for a snow brush at the car rental agency? I groaned in frustration. With no other options, I pulled down the cuff of my pristine white coat, grasping it with my palm, and then swiped across the back windshield to create a small passageway in the snow. Then I did the same on the other windows. Sleeves now fully soaked and horrifically gray, I slid into the driver's seat, and started the Land Rover. One rendition of "Silver Bells" later, the car had warmed up enough that I could clear the remaining frost with my windshield wipers before making my way out of the parking lot, following Lise's directions.

As I headed out of the town, the little shops lining the street gave way to a thick forest, the evergreens frosted in fluffy snow that glimmered in the sunlight. I followed Lise's directions, up the winding road, imagining the tree farm I'd written into the script: A large expanse of land filled with trees, obviously; a nice modest but well-kept house; a barn off to the side with a few animals for kids to pet; a tractor to take everyone out to find their perfect Christmas tree; and a fire to sit and sip hot apple cider or hot chocolate by afterward.

A few minutes later, a long row of tall, thin evergreen trees bordered the road on my right, standing like soldiers in the snow. Up ahead, a metal pole held up a wooden sign that read *Beaux Bois*. I slowed at a break in the trees, where a plowed driveway met the road. I made my way up the long drive toward the colonial-style home with the sloped roof and two stories of gabled windows, just like Lise had said. I parked the SUV in the large, open, shoveled area to the left of the barn and took in the big house. Smoke billowed from the chimney, and my heart felt warmed. It was almost exactly as I'd imagined it looking in the movie.

```
EXT. Tree farm, daylight, snowing.
Ruby gets out of the car and looks
around.
                RUBY
          (talking to herself)
   You just need three things to have
   a really good Christmas: Christmas
        spirit, yourself, and a tree.


              JACQUES
   You always liked to talk to yourself,
              didn't you?

Ruby startles.
```

                    RUBY
                (surprised)
    Jacques? What are you doing here?

                  JACQUES
              That's my line.

I bit my lip. I loved this movie so much. And having this farm be the setting where Jacques and Ruby see each other again for the first time would make it feel so magical.

As I stepped out of the car, a large husky bounded toward me, tail swishing, its thick gray-and-white fur ruffling side to side. "Oh, hello, there," I said, holding out a hand. The friendly dog sniffed it, its icy blue eyes fixed on me, before flopping over on his side in the snow. I leaned down and rubbed his belly, then stood and took a deep breath.

In an ideal world, the owner of the house and tree farm would say yes to filming and it wouldn't be a big deal at all because they could happily take a weeklong vacation in January when tree-selling season was over, with the compensation we provided for the use of their property. Fingers crossed.

I made my way up a recently shoveled path, dog by my side. On the covered porch was a wooden swing with cushions and a black-and-red-plaid blanket slung over the back, a weathered wicker couch and matching chairs, and a small table. There was also a Christmas tree, fully decorated in silver balls and lit with multicolored lights. On the forest-green door hung a fresh wreath with red holly berries and a matching red velvet bow.

Before I could ring the doorbell, the husky scratched at the door, then lay down and rolled onto his back. "Again?" I said, laughing, but bent down to scratch his belly a second time. His back leg twitched in delight.

A moment later the door opened. "Some guard dog," a voice said. I looked up and nearly lost my balance.

Those hazel eyes. Those lashes. The neatly groomed beard hugging his chiseled jaw. It was him. I couldn't look away. He wore a blue waffle shirt and gently faded jeans, brown leather hiking boots with the laces undone. A gray-and-blue toque with an orange pom-pom covered his head, coming down just above his thick eyebrows, which, for a moment, disappeared under his hat. He looked just as surprised to see me.

"You again," he said, sounding amused, before bending down to ruffle the fur on the dog's head. The husky instantly righted himself and rubbed against his master's leg.

"Cute dog," I said, standing up, trying to ignore my heart loudly pounding in my chest.

"That's Simon." The guy stood up, too. He seemed puzzled. "He's supposed to bark when someone shows up."

Now I was puzzled. "He's supposed to bark every time someone comes to buy a tree?"

"Yes."

"Well, I'll take that as a good sign. Hi," I said. "I didn't actually get to introduce myself last night. I'm Zoey." I extended my hand.

"Ben," he said, grasping my hand. His grip was firm, and my entire body warmed at the touch. His hand was soft except for the calluses where his fingers met his palm.

A vision of him chopping down a Christmas tree appeared in my mind. The handshake was brief, much to my disappointment, and when he pulled his hand away it jolted me out of my split-second fantasy. *Pull yourself together, Zoey.* I blinked but when my eyes opened they were on his biceps instead. My knees wobbled.

It was a surprise—I'd envisioned a graying man owning the farm. That's what I'd written into the script. But this— *this guy*—was *so* much better. The son of the Christmas tree farm owner. Maybe Jacques, my main character, needs to work at the tree farm, not just *visit* the tree farm.

Ben whipped off his hat, revealing the mass of dark brown hair that I remembered from the previous night. "You didn't need to trek out here to introduce yourself."

"Oh, that's not why I'm here," I said quickly. I could feel my cheeks reddening.

Ben rubbed the stubble on his jaw. "Great. So then you're here because . . . ?"

"I wanted to see the tree farm," I explained, gesturing to the crowd of trees behind me. "Do you think you could show me around?"

"*Absolument*," he said. As he leaned out past the door, I caught a whiff of pine and soap. My breath caught in my throat. He pointed to the right. "Trees are over there. All balsam fir. Cut your own—but if you want help, Gérard can do so. He is in the barn?" He craned his head, then turned back to me. "*Oui, il est là.*" He pulled back into the house and shoved his hands in his pockets. I tried not to notice how tightly his biceps flexed at that action.

Ben watched me, his eyebrows raised. I blinked, reminding myself I was here to look at trees, not his biceps. "The barn, over there." And he jutted his chin toward the distressed wood.

I swallowed and then smiled sunnily. As dreamy as he was, I had a job to do. "Perhaps *you* could show me?"

Ben looked amused. I had a feeling he'd be the person I would have to negotiate with about using the tree farm in the movie, and I had to play this right. Based on the night before, at the pub, Ben seemed like a tough sell. I hoped that the fact the movie would be filming after Christmas, when business at the tree farm would be slow—plus the fee we'd pay him—would make this an easy deal to come to.

"Allons-y." His broad shoulders brushed past me and a moment later I was hurrying to keep up. Simon trotted alongside Ben. "Barn," he said, pointing to what was clearly a barn, then kept going. "Six-foot balsam firs," he said, pointing again, this time at needled trees bundled up in netting. "Seven-foot balsam firs," with a point to a similar scene. "Eight-foot." Then, to a bundle of tiny trees, perfect for an apartment or bedroom, *"Petits."* And finally: "Cut your own." He gestured toward a gravel road that headed up the hillside.

"Um, thanks," I said, sticking my hands in the pockets of my coat. "So . . . you must be busy this time of year. But what happens the rest of the year? What are you doing in, say, early January?"

Ben looked over at me, confused. "Why do you ask?" His jaw clicked. "I thought you came for a tree?"

"Oh, I don't want a Christmas tree." My stomach was a bundle of nerves. This was the pivotal moment.

He frowned. "You just asked me for a tour and you don't want a tree? It's December 22. What is it that you want then?"

There was just the touch of an accent to his speech. Wa-ant. His tongue rolling over the word, turning it into two syllables, as though teasing me.

"I—actually—I'm here because I'm scouting locations for a movie here in Chelsea," I said. I felt weirdly anxious. "We want to start filming the second week of January. Do you mind if I poke around in the barn, take some photos?" I held up my phone and smiled expectantly at him, waiting for a reaction like Lise's: excitement, delight. Almost everyone I had ever approached when location scouting was flattered and thrilled at the prospect of their home or business being in an actual movie.

"You can take all the photos you want," Ben said agreeably.

That was easy. "Okay, great," I said with a smile. My tensed shoulders relaxed.

Simon hurtled toward us, a stick in his mouth. Ben reached down to take it, and tossed it in the air. The dog chased after it, his legs disappearing in the snow. Ben turned back to me, his eyes narrowed, his mouth a firm line. "Not a chance you can shoot a movie here, though."

What?

The dog returned with the stick. "*Très bien,*" Ben said kindly, taking the stick and patting the dog on the head. How could he be *so nice* to his dog and *so rude* to me?

I raised my eyebrows in surprise, then narrowed my eyes back at him. Few things irked me as much as someone standing in the way of my objectives—and all I cared about right now was getting my movie made here in Chelsea. "Is that up to you, though?" Maybe it was Gérard I needed to speak with. I looked toward the barn, but couldn't see anyone.

"Yes, it's up to me." Ben's voice had an edge. "*My* farm, *my* decisions."

"Really? You own this place?" I was surprised. "You look really young." I knew it was a jerky thing to say—I *hated* it when people at work commented on my age—and I felt a *bit* bad saying it, but it was a genuine question. The house was so big, and he had so much land . . . And he probably only worked a few months of the year—there was just no way Beaux Bois was *only* his, was there? And Lise had said the place had been around for fifty years. So while *Ben* might not want to bother with dealing with a film crew, I was willing to bet his father—or mother or uncle or older brother—would feel differently.

"I own this place, yes," Ben said tersely, setting his jaw and his gaze on me. For a moment I nearly got lost in those thick lashes again. Wow, he was *really* doing a number on me. *He is standing in your way, Zoey*, I reminded myself.

Maybe he didn't realize that he'd be compensated. "Surely January is quiet around here. A film is good for the local economy, and the per diem can be significant for the businesses where we actually shoot." Still, he gave me nothing. "Is there anyone else I can talk to?" I tried to sound diplomatic, though I knew I still sounded like I was challenging him.

"No. It's just me now," Ben said, clearing his throat. "I can see that this project is important to someone, but I'm not interested in being a part of it." His tone had a finality to it, as though he expected me to nod, turn, and leave dejectedly. But he didn't know *how* important this film was to *me*. Sorry, hot stuff, but I wasn't going to lose now, not when I was this close to the perfect location for my film.

"Can I tell you a bit more about the film?" Before he could refuse, I rambled on. "It's actually a holiday movie. Crowd-pleaser!" I gave him a big grin. "And you know, what's a holiday movie without a tree farm?"

"What *is* a holiday movie without a tree farm?" Ben parroted, his voice oozing with sarcasm. I scowled at him. Was he *mocking* me? "Listen, I stand corrected. It's *clear* your movie is important to *you*," he said, his voice softening. "But I still have no interest in my farm being part of it."

"But this place is *perfect*." I threw my arms out and waved them around. "Have you heard that Taylor Swift song 'Christmas Tree Farm'? That's basically Beaux Bois! We could get the rights to play the music when we first see the farm—"

"Stop."

"You don't like Christmas movies?" I asked in disbelief. "And you don't like Christmas music either?"

"No, but I'm in the business of Christmas *trees*, not Christmas movies *or* Christmas music." Ben then turned and motioned toward his house and the driveway. He was asking me to leave. I reluctantly started to walk back along the path, Simon trotting beside me.

I wasn't about to give up, but I *was* starting to feel desperate. "Isn't there *anything* I can do to convince you? What if I guarantee your adorable dog is in the film?"

Ben rolled his eyes at me. "Simon's not a show dog. He's a farm dog."

We reached the front steps of his house. Ben walked up to the porch, and Simon followed him, showing his loyalty. "What if I just take the photos and—" I began.

Ben turned. "You're welcome to walk around and take as many photos as you like," he said, interrupting me. "Buy a tree. Don't buy a tree. But there's not going to be any movie. *Non, merci.*"

And the next thing I knew, Ben and Simon had gone back into the house, the hanging wreath swaying as the door latch clicked closed. A period at the end of the sentence.

I blinked. Okay. Not exactly the most auspicious of beginnings. I probably should've gotten in my car and moved on, but the farm was just *so* perfect. And on principle, I didn't want Ben to think that I was the kind of woman who gave up so easily.

I started down the steps and instead of going straight to the Land Rover, decided to take a walk around the lot. I wondered if Ben was watching me from one of those wide windows on the second story of his gorgeous house. Would he be impressed at my determination, or paranoid that if he turned his back I'd call in the film crew and we'd start rolling the cameras, stat?

This farm would work even better than I'd imagined. It was on so much land that we would be able to really spread out, to see the actors front and center with the incredible snowy, gorgeous, *real* scenery behind them. The tall snowy trees, the barn, which would look magical once we got the lighting crew to add a few thousand tiny white lights to it— inside and out. The large open space in front could easily accommodate a sleigh and maybe even horses. And once people saw how beautiful this place was on TV, they'd be flocking to see the real deal next Christmas. I bet his sales would double, triple, even.

Eventually, when my toes were numb and I had at least a hundred pics, I headed back to the Land Rover. Maybe Ben could put his foot down when it came to whether Beaux Bois was in my *Very Chelsea Christmas*, I thought as I climbed into the driver's seat, but he couldn't keep a tree farm out of my film, or keep me from using his farm to re-create my own version of Beaux Bois somewhere else.

I started the SUV and pulled down the road, farther and farther away from Beaux Bois. No tree farm, no problem. This was all the Act 1 setup. And there was no time to dwell on one "no," because I had to focus on getting things done. I'd find an empty space—a school football field could do nicely—and stage the tree farm exactly how I wanted. No curmudgeonly guy, regardless of how handsome he was, could keep me down. On to the next.

CHAPTER FOUR

Monday, December 22, 10:00 a.m.

"How's it going?" Roberto asked when I answered his call a few minutes later.

"You're up early." It was only seven in LA.

"Couldn't sleep. Kept envisioning my head on a chopping block."

"It's all going to work out," I reassured him overenthusiastically—not because I felt the need to put on a show for Roberto, but because I knew he would report back to Elijah, and I didn't need Elijah thinking, for even a second, that we wouldn't be filming my movie come January.

"Oh, that's awesome," he said, sounding relieved.

"Everyone's great. It's all going so great. Totally great." That was three *greats*. Maybe I was overselling the situation, just a bit. I turned down a side street with grand Tudor-style homes, any of which would be incredible as the central house in the film, though my first choice was going to be the cottage we stayed in when I was a kid. "Listen, I gotta go."

"Okay. Let me know if you need anything," he said.

"Uh-huh. All right. Thanks, Roberto." I hung up.

The perfect house—the one I wanted to use as the one Ruby stays in with her kids—would be tucked into the forest, overlooking the Gatineau River, and would provide stellar establishing shots without neighboring houses being disturbed. In a word, it would be perfect.

I turned onto a narrow road, snowbanks as high as the SUV's windows on either side, and then I saw it: The gray Tudor-style house, with two cars parked in front of a double garage, the driveway coated in a few feet of untouched snow. I stopped the car and looked out the window at the house. I could almost see Stella and me building the fort in the front yard. The steeply pitched roof was dusted with snow and icicles hung down over the leaded-glass windows on the second floor. Stella and I had shared a room, and I remembered how excited we were on Christmas morning, waking up before the sun and rushing down the spiral staircase to the front room where the owners had left a beautiful tree, fully decorated. How Mom and Dad had hung stockings filled to the brim from the mantel over the fireplace. It had been the perfect Christmas. And all these years later, it would make the perfect house for Ruby. I could imagine Jacques walking Ruby to the door and kissing her softly under the mistletoe . . .

I got out of the car, slinging my black leather handbag over my shoulder and trudging through the blanket of snow to the front door, leaning over the snowdrift to knock. The brass lion head echoed in the still air. Minutes passed. I knocked again, but there didn't seem to be any movement inside the house.

I pulled the Epic Productions letterhead out of my purse, rummaged for a pen and scrawled a note to the owners, including my phone number. I tucked it into the mailbox, crossed my fingers, and said a silent prayer that they would soon return home, be thrilled at my offer, and call me.

Next on my list was an adorable home decor boutique back on the main street, just a few doors down from the café and across from a cheese shop. Ten minutes later I parked before the greenery-filled shop called La Jardinière. I pushed through the front door, my entrance provoking a carillon from the sleigh bells hung from the doorjamb. The scent of holly and cinnamon filled the air. I looked around in awe. An entire wall of shelves was piled with plush folded blankets in soft shades, while ceramic trees and shimmering ornaments adorned another. A velvet couch in the corner was layered with gorgeous throw cushions.

"Come in, come in," a friendly voice called. I craned my neck to see a woman in a cherry-red sweater standing behind a hardwood butcher block, arranging evergreen leaves in an hourglass vase. Her hair was styled in a smooth gray pixie cut, and glasses were perched halfway down her nose. "*Comment allez-vous?*" she called in a singsong tone, waving a sprig of holly above her head. A berry went flying through the air and she covered her mouth with her free hand. "*Oh mon dieu,* Mireille," she muttered to herself before scurrying around the edge of the table into a space between two potted evergreen trees, out of sight. She called out something else in French, and I cycled through the three French phrases I knew but came up blank. "Uh, *bonjour,*" I called back.

Her head finally appeared from behind a candy cane poinsettia plant. "Welcome, welcome," she said, switching to English. "I'll just help Xavier, here, and then be right with you."

A man at the counter held hands with two little girls who barely reached his waist.

"Has the rain started yet?" she asked the man.

"Rain? Are you kidding, Mireille? It's a winter wonderland out there."

"And shouldn't you two be in school?" she asked the little girls.

"No school!" one of them cheered.

"Closed early for the holidays," the man explained with a smile. "Because of the storm. I'm not complaining—gives me more time to spend with these little ones."

"Xavier, you are truly one of a kind. You know most parents hate the idea of school being canceled, right?" Mireille said, shaking her head.

"Ah, snow closures are one of the great joys of being a kid," he said. "More time on Daddy's rink, right?" he said to the two girls. They cheered again and I beamed at them. They were adorable. Then I looked back to the guy. There was something about him that seemed *familiar*. He resembled Ben from the tree farm, in a way. Maybe it was the beard or the chiseled cheekbones or the deep-set eyes. I couldn't put my finger on it. And yet, looking at him did not give me all the feels the way looking at Ben had this morning. He lacked that *je ne sais quoi* of Ben. I found it both fascinating and infuriating.

"Could be 1998 all over again," he said to the florist.

"The TV says it could be *worse* than 1998," Mireille said. "You should stop grinning," she added, giving Xavier a stern look.

"Can't help it. Been prepping for something like this for years." She passed him the arrangement and he thanked her. *"Allons-y, mes filles."* He smiled at me. *"Au revoir."*

I smiled politely at him, but peeked out the window. It didn't seem like there was a storm brewing—and I sure hoped the weather station was wrong. A snowstorm would totally affect my day. If schools closed, there was a good chance businesses would, too. I glanced at my watch. Every stop needed to count.

"All right, now, it's your turn. Is it your first time here?"

I nodded and spun around, taking in her makeshift workspace: pots in gold and silver piled high with evergreen branches, and on the wall behind her counter hung a dozen different wreaths, all adorned with bows in festive shades.

The shop was cluttered and cozy, so we'd have to move out much of the beautiful decor to fit the cameras, lights, a wind machine near the door that would help with that "coming inside from the blustery weather" effect. I looked up. The ceilings were high. And the walls were already white, which would make the actors pop on-screen.

"I'm Mireille," she said, her entire face lighting up when she smiled.

"Zoey," I said, trying to remember the last time a shop-keeper in LA introduced herself to me. I loved LA and I loved my life there, but there was something so special about small towns. Or rather, this small town. "You have a beauti-ful store."

"*Alors*, what can I help you with, Zoey? Hostess arrange-ment?" She held up the holly berry she'd been looking for, then tossed it into a small waste bin. "Who are you staying with—let me guess: *la famille* Richelieu?" She shook her head, and popped a sprig of holly into the vase. "*Non,* it must be *la famille* LeBoeuf. *Ou* Marchand?"

I held up my hands as she continued to rattle off very French-sounding surnames. "I'm not visiting anyone. I'm staying at the Auberge Rouge. It's *so* nice. And I just *love* being here." I smiled sunnily at her. "I'm actually in town because I'm scouting the location for a holiday movie." I paused and waited for the reaction. Even though holiday movies were most popular with women in their forties and fifties, like Mireille, there was no guarantee she was a fan. And if she wasn't, I knew I'd have my work cut out for me to get that yes. I crossed my fingers, hoping Mireille wouldn't be like Ben.

"Scouting . . . ," Mireille repeated. "You mean the movie would be *filmed* here?" Her eyes were wide, tiny lines dis-sipating out toward her graying temples.

I nodded and smiled. "Yes. In town, but I'm also looking for shops and thought maybe . . . " I trailed off and looked around. "This shop is so adorable. It could really work."

She placed the eucalyptus in her hand back down and then rubbed her hands together like she was warming them, and beamed. "That's *so* exciting." She leaned over the counter and said, in a lowered tone, "Do you think maybe there'd be an opportunity for *extras*? Not to ring my own sleigh bells, but some say I look a little like Mrs. Claus." She laughed, throwing her head back. "And I *do* supply the wreaths for every door in town."

"Ooh maybe," I said. "The casting is handled by another part of the company, but I'd be happy to put in a good word." I bumped up the wattage of my smile. "How busy will you be in January?"

"Winter is one of our busiest periods. So many people stop by on their way up to Camp Fortune or *le parc de la Gatineau*. Even people just looking to get out of their house pop in for a blanket or candle. *Hygge,* it's a real thing."

I nodded. "Of course. I get it. Are you open every day of the week? Or is there maybe a day you're closed early or open late that we could film here?"

"We're closed Wednesdays, actually."

"Could we shoot in here on a Wednesday, then? We wouldn't need more than a day."

"*Bonne idée,*" she said excitedly. "*Bien*, tell me what you need to make this happen."

I shrugged happily. "Not much else. I do have to get final sign-off from my production team, so if you don't mind, I'll just grab a few photos for the files, and then once I have approval I can let you know compensation. I don't have a *huge* budget but I can offer you a little something for the trouble."

"Of course." She waved a hand. "I'm not worried. And you do whatever you need. I'll just get back to my evergreen branches."

A few minutes later, after taking photos of the store and getting Mireille's contact information, I had everything I needed.

"Where are you off to now?" she asked curiously.

"Town hall," I said, slipping my phone into my purse. "To get a permit." Even though I still needed at least another three locations, I didn't want to put off the town permit—just in case I needed an appointment, or it took a day to complete.

"Ah, yes, of course. But not today. It's not open."

"But it's Monday," I said, confused. What town hall isn't open on a Monday?

"Town hall's not open Mondays," she explained with a shrug. "But it *is* open Tuesdays. You'll still be here tomorrow?"

"Yes, but . . ." I trailed off. Why hadn't I thought to make an appointment as soon as I'd booked my flight? I sighed. No sense dwelling on that now. I'd spend the rest of today securing the other spots, which I hoped would be easy. Maybe Mireille's and Lise's enthusiasm would help convince other business owners and the mayor anyway. I just hoped that Ben from the tree farm's *lack* of enthusiasm wouldn't cause me more trouble.

"Good thing, too, that it's closed," Mireille was saying. "The storm looks like it's heading here earlier than it was supposed to." Mireille sounded worried.

I turned to look back outside. There were already multiple feet of snow butting up against the doorways of the shops across the street, and pathways were covered. Had it been snowing that much? I hadn't noticed. Truthfully, I wasn't worried. If anything, more snow now would mean there'd be plenty come January, when filming was to begin.

"The temperatures are expected to warm up, just a little, just enough to make rain, then freeze. My boys are in Kanata for a tournament."

"Hockey?" I guessed.

"What else? I told them they might have to stay there if the storm starts as soon as we think."

"I hope they make it back," I said. This storm sounded confusing. Was it rain? Snow? Warm? Cold? Regardless, it was a hot topic.

"*Moi aussi!*" She chuckled. "*Donc*, Zoey, if you don't have an appointment with Mayor Deschamps then surely you have time for lunch?" She stretched out her arm and pulled back the cuff of her red sweater to look at her watch. "Yes, it's perfect timing for lunch. We'll go to the pub. You'll love it. Put *that* spot in your movie, too."

"The Village Pub?" I asked, making a face.

"What other pub would there be?" Mireille looked amused by my expression.

"I went there last night," I said. "It didn't go well."

"Nonsense. You can't mean le Pub du Village." Then she tilted her head back and forth. "Ah, it was the winter solstice last night. So maybe things got a bit rowdy? Anyway, it's nothing like that during the day." She headed down the middle aisle and toward the exit, motioning for me to follow her.

"But what about your shop?" I asked, looking around.

She flipped the sign to *Closed*, then held the door open to me. When I was out on the sidewalk, she firmly shut the door. Keys jangled as she slid them into the lock, then turned. "It's closed. People understand. Everyone must eat a good lunch. And le Pub du Village is the heart of the town. You can't film a movie without le Pub du Village. Come on, you'll see."

CHAPTER FIVE

Monday, December 22, 11:30 a.m.

Mireille was right: The pub was completely different in the daytime—and absent of the boisterous debauchery from the previous night. Empty beer bottles on the tables were replaced with tiny bud vases, a single daisy here, a single daffodil there. The floor was no longer sticky, and instead of pulsing rock music, instrumental Christmas carols played softly over the speakers, just barely audible over the laughter that emanated from nearly every table. And the air smelled like gravy—thick, rich, meaty gravy. My mouth watered.

Beside me, Mireille waved to a woman in a corner booth. "Ooh, there's Renee," she said as she took my hand. "She's one of my best friends. You're going to love her."

"Lucky coincidence, seeing your friend here," I said brightly.

"Not really," she said. "It's a small town. If we didn't sit with Renee, we'd join them—" She nodded to a pair of pretty young women at another table, their heads close together over a phone. "That's my son's girlfriend and her sister. Or them"—Mireille waved to the couple on our right—"that's my, well, that's my mail carrier and his wife. But we're very friendly, though *maybe* it would be a bit weird to have lunch with them. Anyway, you get my point."

I grinned. I had definitely found another ally in my moviemaking mission. Surely *one* of these people would love to see their home in next Christmas's biggest holiday movie. I'd make sure Mireille introduced me to everyone she knew in the pub.

As we approached, Renee slid out of the booth to greet us. She had dark skin, wide-set eyes, full lips and her shiny, shoulder-length black hair hung in box braids, with gold and silver charms scattered throughout. She looked to be about my age, which surprised me. This was Mireille's best friend? There had to be at least twenty years separating them.

Renee wrapped Mireille in a hug I'd give a friend I hadn't seen in a year. Mireille introduced me and Renee beamed at me and leaned in to kiss me on one cheek, then the other.

"So . . . where are you staying?" Renee asked once I'd sat down.

"The Auberge Rouge?" I said.

"You say it as though we might not have heard of it." Renee laughed and I realized she was right—there were only two places to stay in town, at least, as far as I could tell when I'd booked my room. "And what do you think?" She leaned forward, her elbows on the table.

"Oh, it's great. I love it. So much space. The bed's a dream. The rain shower, too."

"It really is wonderful, isn't it?" Renee said eagerly.

"Renee." Mireille's tone was warning. She looked at me and rolled her eyes. "Renee *owns* the Auberge Rouge." She turned back to Renee. "That was too tricky—what if Zoey'd said she hated it?"

"I wasn't trying to *trick* her," Renee protested. "How can I get a straight review out of anyone if everyone knows I own the place? If she didn't like it, I'd like to know. Then I can make it better." She took a sip from her mug. "Except, there really is no way to make it better, because it's simply perfect. Isn't it, Zoey? You must come back for *cinq à sept* in the *salon*."

"*Cinq à sept?*"

"Yes, it's cocktail hour. A tradition. You have an aperitif, maybe some cocktail *saucisse*. Ooh, we may even do it outside today, if the weather stays this warm. Have a bonfire."

A waitress approached the table. A thick lock of her blond hair was braided into a headband from one ear to the other. She was wearing a black apron over a waffle-knit shirt and leggings. "*Bonjour* Mireille," she singsonged, then smiled at me and placed two leather-covered booklets in front of us. "*De l'eau?*"

"Yes," Mireille said. "Noémie, this is Zoey. Zoey's visiting from Los Angeles, and she's looking to see if Chelsea might be the perfect spot to film her movie. Isn't that exciting?"

"What kind of movie?" Noémie squealed.

"A *holiday* movie," Mireille confirmed, then turned to me. "Noémie's parents own the pub. I'm sure she could introduce you to them if you like."

Noémie gasped and I grinned at her. "For sure! They would love that. Ooh, I can't wait to tell Delphine when she gets home."

"You must need a pub in the movie, no?" Mireille asked me.

"Maybe," I said. I was trying to play it cool, but I already knew that this spot was perfect. We could remove half the tables and set up along the far wall, and it would still look like a full pub. And last night's shenanigans were proof we could make it boisterous—though a controlled boisterous, with no ass-grabbing or drunk jerks. The budget was going to be the trickiest part, I knew, because if last night was a typical night in this town, I was facing a massive bar bill.

"Zoey, what would you like?" Mireille was looking at me.

The film permits, Mireille. But she probably meant more like, burger or salad.

"She must have the poutine *évidemment,*" Noémie said, looking to Mireille and Renee for confirmation, then turning to me. "You must have the poutine."

"Of course," I said excitedly. "I love poutine."

"You've had poutine?" Noémie raised an eyebrow. "I thought you were from LA."

"We have poutine in LA," I said. Normally, it was the other way around—often I came upon small-town people defending their town, trying to convince others that they had everything big cities had.

Mireille looked to Noémie, who was shaking her pen at me. "Oh no no no no no. You haven't had poutine until you've had poutine in Quebec."

"We use St-Albert cheese curds," Renee jumped in, as though she were part of the menu team. "There's nothing better than St-Albert cheese curds. You'll see."

"*Parfait*," I said, and the women all laughed. Based on their enthusiasm, I was excited to try the real thing. I ordered a Diet Coke and watched as Noémie flitted away, but then the pub's front door swung open and something—or more appropriately, some*one*, caught my eye. My heart jumped.

Ben.

He pulled off his tan leather gloves and shoved them in the pockets of his brown plaid shacket, then shrugged out of the coat and slung it over his arm. His light blue shirt hugged his broad shoulders and firm chest. If there was any breath lodged in my chest, it was completely inaccessible at the moment. I watched as he removed his toque and mussed his thick brown hair. Heat crept up the back of my neck. It was as though I were watching some sort of lumberjack striptease. I knew I was staring, but I was *just* far enough away and partly obscured by a table of four that I knew there was no way he could see me.

He surveyed the room, then started walking in our direction. As he passed a handful of tables, he nodded, shook hands, fist-bumped, and backslapped, and I couldn't take my eyes off his face: those hazel eyes, those full lips. He was a jerk, that was for sure, but why did he have to be *so* good-looking? He would make an excellent extra in the film. Scratch that, he'd steal the show. And the last thing I wanted was him getting in the way. He'd stood in my way with his tree farm denial, but I wanted him out of sight, out of mind when I got back here to film.

"Has anyone ever told you it's not polite to stare?" Mireille whispered in my ear. I jumped, startled, and my chair made a loud screech. Renee laughed loudly and Ben looked our way.

Dammit. I slunk down in my seat, hoping he'd get distracted en route. I didn't want to *talk* to him. I just wanted to drink him in for a moment or two. But now I was mortified. I made a silent vow never to look at him again.

As I stared at the floor, a pair of rugged boots appeared inches from my UGGs. I looked up.

Ben looked down at me. So much for not looking at him again. His golden-brown eyes locked on mine and he smiled a part-friendly, part-amused, part-very-very-sexy smile, then shook his head slowly like, *Whatareyoudoinghere?*

I shrugged as if to say, *Surprise!*

"Zoey, this is Benoît," Mireille said.

Benoît, not Benjamin. His sexiness factor rose at least ten points at this information.

"Benoît, this is Zoey, our new friend." She winked across the table at Renee.

"We've met," he said. "Twice. I didn't realize she was joining us for lunch."

Joining them *for lunch?*

I wasn't going to let Ben get the upper hand here. "I didn't realize *you* were joining *us* actually," I retorted, then looked to Mireille for confirmation that this was not planned, but she was suddenly very interested in the flowers in the bud vase on the table.

Ben didn't respond and instead sat down, slinging his jacket over the back of his chair, before sticking out his hand. "Nice to see you again," he said politely. An odd formality, given our history, but I swiped my palm, which was, for some reason, suddenly damp, on my leggings before I gave his hand a quick shake, mouthing *Liar* so only he could see. His jaw dropped and he blinked a bunch of times at me.

"You've met already? Where?" Renee said, leaning forward on the table, as Noémie arrived with our drinks. A flash of Ben grabbing the drunk guy's arm last night, right here in the pub, came to mind, but I decided against sharing that little tidbit. It put Ben in the spotlight as some sort of plaid-clad hero, and that was absolutely not the side of him I needed to highlight.

"I popped by his farm this morning," I said simply, taking a sip from my glass.

"For the movie?" Renee asked, curious.

I nodded reluctantly. "Yes, just to check it out. But it was really not the right vibe for the film." I looked at Ben out of the corner of my eye. He was smirking at me.

"Really?" Mireille's voice rose an octave. "But a tree farm in a Christmas movie? Seems so perfect."

"Yes, so perfect—*if* it's the right tree farm. But Beaux Bois just *wasn't* a good fit." I shrugged, trying to appear regretful.

"Too bad, really, because there's a fantastic scene at a tree farm in the script. But you put the wrong place in a movie and it can throw off the entire vibe. Make it feel *cheesy*." Then I turned and looked at Ben directly. *Take that.*

"Well, I for one cannot wait for this movie. A movie set in Chelsea will be *très magnifique. Très romantique. Très . . .*" Renee trailed off, starry-eyed.

I wanted to hug Renee. I hadn't told her a single thing about the movie and yet here she was, singing—or rather, *sighing*—my praises.

"Disruptive?" Ben finished her thought. I scowled at him. Why did he have to be so cynical about the whole thing? All I was trying to do was bring joy to the small screen—and to a small town at the same time. He could refuse to let us film at his farm, fine, but why did he have to be so negative about my movie?

A moment later, Noémie deposited a pint of Stella Artois before Ben, even though I hadn't seen him ask for it. "Hey, Ben," Noémie said. "Did you hear? Zoey's going to film a movie here."

Ben met my gaze. "We'll see," he said, clucking his tongue, as though he had any say in whether or not I filmed in the town. Before I could respond, he turned his attention back to Noémie. "*Poutine, s'il te plaît, Noémie*," Ben said.

Noémie frowned. "*Désolée*, Ben," she said, then followed it up with something else in French.

"What?" he said in disbelief. "How can you be out of cheese curds?"

"Delivery's delayed. They're worried about getting caught in the *tempête de verglas*," Noémie said.

"Fine," he said. "I'll get the crêpes."

She disappeared, then returned a moment later with Mireille's tourtière, Renee's salad, and my plate of very cheesy poutine.

"*You* took the last of the cheese curds?" Ben looked at me, his eyebrow raised.

I bit my lip and shrugged, but secretly cheered on the inside. "Yep," I said before digging in.

"*La tempête de verglas* is supposed to start on Christmas Eve," Mireille said.

"You should probably be on your way to . . . wherever it is you're headed, before you get trapped in town," Ben said to me.

I wiped my mouth with a napkin. "Oh, don't worry about me, I'll be long gone before Christmas Eve." I pointed to the poutine with my fork. "This is *really* good." I smiled at Ben, who rolled his eyes.

"Back to LA?" Mireille asked.

"Mm," I said noncommittally. These three strangers didn't need to know that, at present, I didn't really have any plans for Christmas.

"I can't imagine a warm Christmas," Mireille said. "Does it even feel like Christmas in Los Angeles?"

Before I could respond, Noémie returned with Ben's crêpes. I passed him the glass bottle of maple syrup. He shook his head.

"You don't want maple syrup on your crêpes?" I'd definitely written a scene where Jacques made crêpes for Ruby—and served them with maple syrup. Was that wrong?

Ben shook his head. He cut into his plain crêpes and took a bite.

"I thought everyone in Quebec loved maple syrup on everything," I challenged him.

"That's *Elf*," he said.

"Everyone loves maple syrup." Renee leaned over and swatted Ben on the shoulder with her napkin. "But Ben supplies the maple syrup to the pub," she said as though that explained everything.

I shook my head. "What do you mean, *supplies* it?"

"Supplies it, makes it," Ben said between bites.

"You made that maple syrup," I repeated, pointing at the bottle. "I suppose you're going to tell me that it came from the very same balsam firs you also sell as Christmas trees?"

He looked at me like I had a hole in my head—and syrup was dripping out of it. "Not from balsam firs. I make the maple syrup by tapping the *maple* trees, which are beyond the *balsam firs*. And then I sell it, mostly to individuals, but also to a few places, like the pub. The quicker they run out, the more I need to supply and I'm fully tapped—no pun intended—for the year. *So*"—his gaze was steady, his tone infuriating, as though he were educating a child—"it has nothing to do with quality and everything to do with the quantity." He paused, raising a well-groomed eyebrow. "I'm selfless, really."

Mireille cackled and Ben gave her a look, but his eyes crinkled at the sides. I stared at his cheekbones a split second too long.

I watched as he took another bite of crêpe. Who *was* this guy? What next? He knits booties for reindeer?

"So," Ben said a moment later, looking at Mireille and Renee. "I assume Zoey's trapped you all here, talking your ears off about this *movie*?"

"Hey," I said crossly. "I'm not trapping anyone!"

"I invited *her* to lunch," Mireille said. She patted my hand.

What was Ben's problem? I wasn't going to get into it with him again, but now that I had some support in Mireille and Renee, I decided to take my chance. "Ben, I don't get it. You *own* a Christmas tree farm. You *make* maple syrup. I don't see why you don't want to be part of the movie. Did I mention that everyone will be compensated?"

"I would expect so," Ben said with a scoff. "And did I mention that there are dozens, *hundreds* of other snowy towns? You don't *need* to film in Chelsea."

I shook my head. "Oh, but I do. This would be our first movie actually *set* in Canada," I explained, trying to stay calm. "We've filmed in Vancouver before, but it's usually a stand-in for some made up town—Anywhere, USA. And we rarely get the chance to shoot in real snow."

"You've *never* made a holiday movie set against actual snow?" Ben's expression suggested I'd just told him that I advocated for the ritual slaughter of puppies, just for fun.

I took a deep breath. I could feel Renee and Mireille watching me. "We're often filming in summer—or somewhere quaint but too far south to actually *get* snow. So we're usually using fake snow."

"Fake snow?" Renee asked.

"They used to use asbestos. Can you imagine? How much cancer did *that* cause?" I looked from the two women, whose eyes were wide. "Now it's a mixture of recycled wood products. Cellulose. You can spray it and it sits there, exactly the same, for days. But it's nothing like the real thing—when it's this beautiful." I waved a hand toward the window behind me.

"Let me get this straight," Ben said. "You film snowy movies in places that don't actually get snow." His eyes met mine. In this light they were so dark—like 70 percent chocolate fondue. "How do you expect your movie to capture the magic of Christmas? Whatever happened to authenticity?"

"You know what's authentic? Using an *actual* real, working Christmas tree farm in Chelsea, Quebec, for a Christmas movie that's set on a working Christmas tree farm in Chelsea, Quebec," I shot back. I had an overwhelming urge to smack him on the side of the head with the maple syrup bottle. He was so *contrary*.

Ben put a hand to his head. "You're giving me a headache. Can we talk about something else?"

Mireille dismissed him with a wave of her hand. "Shush." She turned to me. "The suspense is killing me," she said. "Can you just tell us what the movie is about?"

I clasped my hands together. "I thought you'd never ask." I ignored the face Ben made and cleared my throat as though I were making a pitch to the studios. "The movie starts with a montage—it's a family with two girls, about nine and twelve, and they're driving with their parents from Virginia to Chelsea, Quebec. The dad's boss has lent them his cottage for a week—like a holiday bonus. And it's the best week for the older of the two girls, Ruby, who's our main character. It's her first truly snowy Christmas, so she does all the things she's only read about or seen in movies: skating and building a snowman and making snow angels. And there's also a boy, Jacques, who lives next door. They're just friends but you can see there's a bit of puppy love happening there."

Mireille leaned forward.

I spread my fingers in the air and continued. "Flash forward and it's fifteen years later. It's Ruby's first Christmas as a single mom and she wants to make it special for her kids. They're younger—three and five. She remembers this quaint town of Chelsea where she went as a kid. She had such great memories of it, so she says, what the heck, let's just go there."

"She rents the same cottage? And the guy is next door?" Mireille threw a hand to her forehead. I laughed, and Ben muttered something under his breath, but I ignored him. If he didn't want to listen to my incredibly romantic movie plot, he could leave and go back to *not* selling maple syrup or whatever else he needed to *not* do today.

"Not quite," I said. "The cottage has been torn down, so she gets an Airbnb, and her kids convince her to get a tree— and who does she run into at the tree farm? Jacques, of course." I watched with satisfaction as Mireille and Renee swooned. Just talking about this movie filled me with so much joy, like helium in a balloon. I *knew* everyone would love it when it was finally out next year.

"Jacques is just as Ruby remembered," I went on, "but he's older now, too, of course. He's also *very* good-looking." I winked at Renee and Mireille.

"At first things are just as they were fifteen years ago—they're the best of friends, as though no time at all has passed. But now there's real chemistry between them, too. His tree farm offers sleigh rides and hot chocolate by a bonfire"—I glanced at Ben—"and he takes Ruby's daughters on a sleigh ride, and then he invites the three of them over for dinner, to make pizza in his stone oven. And once the girls have fallen asleep, he and Ruby sit by the fire, drinking wine and catching up."

Mireille fluttered a hand near her face. "Oh, so *romantique*," she said softly.

"*So romantique*," I agreed. "It's a night to remember forever," I added pointedly.

"And they make sweet love . . . ?" Renee jumped in.

"Maybe." I shrugged coyly.

"Oh, come on," Renee said, exasperated.

I laughed. "All right, all right. Yes, it's a really good night by the fire, okay? But then, the next day things are weird between them. Jacques pulls away. This is what he wanted—he never forgot Ruby, and he always loved her—but at the same time, she's just visiting, she and her kids have a home to return to. And he's afraid of getting too attached, and losing it all." I paused and picked up my fork. "Anyway, I can't tell you anything else. All I can say is that something happened to him and Ruby doesn't know what because he won't tell her. And how can she fix it if she doesn't know what the problem is?"

"Maybe it's not her problem to fix," Ben interjected.

My head spun toward him. I'd forgotten he was there. "I didn't know you were interested in the plot of my movie, Ben. You don't *like* Christmas movies, remember? You don't *want* my perfect characters to meet on your farm."

"Well, *I* certainly love Christmas movies, and I'm very interested in the plot," Renee announced. "Just hearing about it is already making me want to cozy up in front of the screen with one of Mireille's alpaca blankets."

"I have to agree," Mireille said.

I shot Ben a look as I polished off the rest of my poutine, which had gone cold from neglect but was miraculously just as good as it was hot.

Noémie suddenly returned. "Ben," she said, touching his shoulder.

"Hmm?" Ben said, looking up.

She looked nervous. "My mom and dad are worried about driving to Montreal tomorrow—you know, with the storm and all—and everyone wants the day off so I've got to be here. I hate to ask, but do you think you could go pick Delphine up from the airport?"

I watched as Ben seemed to consider this for a moment. *Delphine?* My stomach felt like it was twisting into a knot. *Who's Delphine?*

He finally nodded. "Sure, Noémie. I'll text her to get her flight info and let her know." He pulled out his phone.

The single knot turned into a double, and I tried to shake myself out of whatever was happening to me. Why did I care who Delphine was, or whether Ben picked her up from the airport? Frankly, if I was being honest, my time in this town would be a whole lot happier without him around, naysaying my movie to anyone who'd listen.

Noémie grinned. "Oh, that's great. She's going to be thrilled."

CHAPTER SIX

Tuesday, December 23, 8:00 a.m.

The next morning I was up before my alarm, prepared to be at Mayor Emile Deschamps's office before it opened at 8:30. I couldn't believe how successful I'd been yesterday—I'd even gotten the school principal to agree to let me use the football field as a tree farm, just as I'd planned. I still didn't have the main house, but I had a good feeling that meeting the mayor was going to solve that issue, too. In a small town like this the mayor was *sure* to know everyone—and pull exactly the strings I needed to secure a house. Ideally, the cottage where I'd spent that blissful Christmas, but at this point I was willing to use any of the river-facing homes I'd seen yesterday. I couldn't wait to be in touch with Elijah with the good news that I'd pulled off a miracle just days before Christmas.

As I got ready in front of the mirror, I thought about what would come next, once I'd wrapped my work in Chelsea. What if I stayed here? The notion was absurd. Yet being here had ignited my Christmas spirit. For a while, between hustling and trying to find different locations, I'd forgotten that I had nothing to look forward to once the permits were secured. I was grateful for Stella's offer to spend the holidays with her and her new in-laws, but I couldn't help feeling it would just make me look pitiful. If not Stella's though, what? And was there anything more alone than becoming single *right* before Christmas? I shook my head. *Stop wallowing, Zo.* Focus on the task at hand: getting the town permit. Although this was just one more permit, it was *the* permit, the one that everything else hinged on. A Christmas tree farm, a coffee shop—really, we could find these things anywhere. Any set designer worth her salt could take a vacant building from anywhere from Michigan to Minnesota, erect a few signs with French Canadian notices, *et voilà*—a Christmassy shop in Chelsea, Quebec. What would be much more difficult was if we couldn't shoot exteriors here, or use any public thoroughfares. The charm of *actually* being in Chelsea was what would make my movie really shine. If my meeting with the mayor went poorly, then Elijah would have every reason to cancel my production and take on *I'll Be Home for Christmas* instead.

I hurried out to the Land Rover in the snow, which was falling in big, heavy flakes. Inside the SUV, I flicked on all the buttons—defroster, heat, seat warmer, and waited for the car to warm up. It was *cold*. I wondered if the storm was still on its way, but then dashed the thought from my mind as I pulled the Land Rover onto the road, past Rendez-Vous Café and onto the main road. There wasn't a single car in sight, just trees lining the road and snow gently falling around me. A few moments later, Google Maps instructed me to pull into a nearly empty parking lot. I was at town hall. The modern building was covered in red siding, a tall metal pole proudly flying the red-and-white Canadian flag to greet visitors. As I climbed the steps to the entrance, I mentally rehearsed what I was going to say. I'd explain Epic's track record with holiday movies, how we've had the number one movie for three years running—and how whenever our films featured real places, the economy benefited for years afterward. It would be the same for Chelsea. Especially given the overwhelmingly positive response I'd gotten from everyone so far. Everyone except Ben, of course, but there was no need to mention that solo naysayer. The truth was, getting a town on board was usually the *easiest* aspect—easier than shop owners. And yet my knees were jittering. I was nervous because this movie was different. It meant so much to me, and the movie was riding on the mayor's buy-in.

I smiled as I approached the front desk. "*Bonjour,*" I said to the kindly looking woman behind it. She had short auburn hair, and wore a creamy white turtleneck sweater. "May I speak with the mayor, please?"

"About the filming of the movie, eh?"

I startled. People *really* talked here, didn't they? I shrugged, then grinned. "That's right. I'm sorry, I would've made an appointment, but I only got into town Sunday night and didn't realize the office wasn't open yesterday, so I thought—" I was rambling, talking fast and barely breathing. I could feel my hands shaking. *Rein it in, Zoey.* If the mayor's heard about the film it's probably a *good* thing. The only person who'd have said anything negative about the movie would've been Ben, and why would he bother? I took a deep breath before continuing. "I thought I'd just show up this morning. I hope that's okay?"

"*Bien sûr*," she said before directing me to take a seat in the waiting area. I sat on a threadbare, comfortable couch and flipped through the local paper—*The Low Down*—which was written in English, surprisingly.

A moment later I heard the click of a door latch, and stood.

"You? *Again?*" a voice said. A *very* familiar, *very* smooth voice that simultaneously annoyed me and sent shivers up and down my spine.

I spun around and saw Ben walking toward me. Today, instead of his lumberjack coat, he was wearing a big black Canada Goose parka, a red toque, and black leather gloves, which he removed and tucked under his arm before blowing into his hands and rubbing them together. His cheeks were flushed from the cold.

"You're like a senior waiting to get into the drugstore," he said dryly, his tone teasing. But I wasn't in the mood for another encounter with him, teasing or not. I exhaled slowly. *Be cool, Zoey, be cool.* I refused to let him get under my skin.

"What are you doing here?" I said, my tone as icy as the weather outside.

"I have an appointment."

"Well, so do I. And don't try to say you were here first. You have a red nose, and I don't."

He nodded. "I didn't realize there was a prize for the first person here."

"The early bird gets to talk to the mayor first. And I'm the early bird," I said before sitting back down. I wasn't about to get into an argument with Ben right before my important meeting with Emile Deschamps.

"Ahh," he said mock-seriously, which both infuriated me and made my heart race. He turned to the woman at the desk.

"Marie, is there coffee?" Without waiting for a response, he turned my way.

"Want a coffee?"

I was *dying* for a coffee. "No thanks."

He shrugged, then disappeared down a hallway. Time passed. Enough time that I picked up the newspaper again. I checked my phone. Replied to Stella's second text about my flight info. And now with each passing moment I became more convinced that Ben had just used the coffee as an excuse to steal the first slot—my slot—to meet with the mayor. Finally, I looked at Marie. "Do you know when the mayor will be free to see me?"

She glanced at her computer, frowned, and then looked back to me. "He's free now. Just down the hall." She pointed in the direction that Ben had gone. "Second door on the left."

So Ben *hadn't* taken my spot? I grabbed my things and headed down the hall to the door, which, reassuringly, read EMILE DESCHAMPS.

I knocked.

After a moment the door opened, and standing in front of me was Ben.

My mouth fell open. "You *did* steal my spot," I said under my breath.

He gave me a bemused look, but I brushed past him into the empty room. I turned back around. "Where's the mayor?" I whispered.

Ben paused and then smiled ruefully. "*I'm* Emile Deschamps."

My heart stopped. "But . . ." I faltered, trying to puzzle this out. "You told me your name was Ben."

He sipped from the mug in his hand. "It is. I go by my middle name."

"You go by your *middle* name?" I shook my head. "So . . . Emile Benoît Deschamps?"

"Winner, *gagnant*!"

I sighed.

The corners of his mouth were turned up and his eyes were twinkling, like he was thoroughly enjoying every second of this.

I felt light-headed. I reached out to the wall to steady myself. "*You're* the mayor. *You're* the *mayor* of Chelsea." I wasn't sure how many ways I planned to confirm this information, but I still couldn't process it. At this point my lips were just moving, words floating out into the air.

Ben nodded, now grinning widely, which infuriated me because this was nothing to be happy about—unless you were Ben and you didn't want a movie filmed in your town and you knew exactly why I was standing there.

"Yes, I'm the new mayor. Just a few months now. I've taken over for my father, who was the mayor before me.

Same name so they didn't have to change the nameplate. Handy, economical *and* environmentally friendly." He took a sip of coffee and I drank him in. He was no longer wearing his puffy coat. Instead a thin navy sweater hugged his chest and biceps. His jeans were dark and fitted, and as he turned to walk toward the large mahogany desk my eyes went straight to his ass—and how the jeans hugged his butt perfectly. Behind his desk he gestured for me to sit in the leather wingback chair. "So, what's on your mind, Zoey?" he said, one perfectly groomed eyebrow raised.

Good thing he couldn't read my thoughts. *Get your head out of his pants, Zoey. This guy is standing in your way—again.*

"You know why I'm here," I said, trying not to let my frustration show. Sure, maybe Ben-the-tree-farm-owner didn't want a movie filmed on his property. But maybe Ben-the-mayor would have a different perspective. Maybe he'd be supportive and excited about it. It was time to go for it.

I tucked my hair behind my ear, then threw an arm in his direction to shake hands, as though we'd never met. "I'm Zoey Andrews. I'm directing a movie—"

"Whoa, whoa, whoa." He held up his hands rather than accepting mine. "You're a director? I thought you were a location scout."

"No, not really. I'm just scouting because we had a mix-up, and this is *my* movie. It's my script and it's really important to me." Maybe if he knew how important this film was to me, he'd concede? I paused to sit in the chair, then looked him directly in the eyes. "Listen, Ben, let's cut to the chase. Maybe you didn't want me to film at your farm, and your home, and I can completely respect that, even if I think you're making a mistake. But I can tell you that you, as the mayor, should seriously consider my offer. I have a ton of experience with this stuff, and filming the movie here would be great for Chelsea's economy."

"Oh yeah?" he asked sarcastically. "Is it always great for the economy?"

I nodded, ignoring his tone.

He grimaced. "You have absolutely *no* idea what's good for the economy."

"Yes, I do," I insisted, sitting up straighter. "It'll be good for the economy when we shoot. We'll take over every room at every inn and bed-and-breakfast; we'll use the restaurants. That's a lot of money into the wallets of your residents. Then, once the movie comes out, and it's a hit—and it *will* be a hit—people will start looking up Chelsea, trying to determine if it's a real place. And when they realize that it is, they'll visit. You're Canadian, you must have watched *Schitt's Creek*? It'll be like that, only better because those locations were spread around Ontario, and there's no actual town called Schitt's Creek. But with this, I'd be featuring the town itself, and the businesses, too. People will come, they'll stay at the Auberge, they'll eat at the pub—"

"You're trying to tell me the future of my town," Ben interrupted, "but this isn't *A Christmas Carol*. You don't *know* that's how things will go."

"This has nothing to do with *A Christmas Carol*—which, by the way, Ben, is not the kind of movie we're making," I said pointedly. "Surely you've seen the style I'm talking about—the kind Mireille and Renee both love?" I pull out my phone. "Like *The Twelve Dates of Christmas*? *A Smoky Mountain Christmas*? What about *The Christmas Setup*?"

"I'm not watching a Christmas movie right now."

"I'm not asking you to pop popcorn and pull up a chaise lounge. I'm—"

"Chaise longue," he corrected me. I ignored him.

—"just showing you that holiday movies are huge." I held out the Netflix app, glad it was days until Christmas, which really hammered home the point. Half the top trending movies were holiday romances.

"Most of these films are by Epic Productions. I worked on them. They're so popular. And could make your town famous like that—" I snapped my fingers. "And that kind of popularity doesn't fade after a year."

Ben snorted. "Zoey, our town functions perfectly well. We have zero unemployment, zero buildings for lease. We don't need a sudden surge that the town won't be able to manage, and then have it drop off again in April."

"That won't happen!"

"Listen, Zoey." Ben's voice was calm. "I can tell you care about your work. I care about my work, too. And for me it goes far beyond my work as mayor, or my work on the farm. I care about the *people*, and the town itself. And there's no way that you can say the same." He stared at me, his jaw jutting out stubbornly.

He was so arrogant. "You don't know anything about me or what I care about. And that's all beside the point. Let's get rid of emotion, shall we?"

"That doesn't seem particularly easy for you to do," Ben said, picking up a stack of papers from his desk and shuffling them, as though talking to me was just too boring to bear.

I narrowed my eyes. "Ben, *I'm* in charge of this movie. *You're* in charge of this town. Let's make a deal. If it's number of shoot dates, lay it on the line. If it's money, give me a number." I crossed my arms. "Tell me what it's going to take."

Ben just shook his head. "My father never allowed film permits. It messes with parking. It causes shops to close. It brings in people who care nothing about the town, like the guy who pursued you so aggressively at the pub." I felt my cheeks go pink at the memory of my first meeting with Ben. How I'd felt light-headed when his eyes met mine in the pub. "But more importantly," he continued, "my father was mayor so he could make sure that this town didn't change. Chelsea doesn't have a Tim Hortons on our main strip. There's no chain pharmacy, no big box stores. And now that I'm here, now that I'm mayor, that's my job. It's *easy* to say yes. It's *easy* to be swayed by offers that sound enticing. But it is much harder to say no. I'm sorry." For the first time since we'd met, he actually looked sorry. "I realize that this is important to you, Zoey. But you're never going to get me to say yes to Chelsea. So we can both sit here debating this all morning, or you can be on your way to the next town while there's still time. Like Wakefield."

"What?" My eyes widened. Was he seriously passing me off to some other town, as if which town I shot in made absolutely no difference? As though he had any idea what it took to make a movie, or what I put into that script?

"Wakefield," he repeated, and I remembered the customs agent at the airport had mentioned it, too. "It's very close, just twenty minutes up the road, yet it's in a totally different district. Different mayor. She loves this kind of"—Ben fluttered his fingers as though he was trying to get cotton candy off them—"stuff. Bigger town, more shops, more restaurants, the covered bridge, the icy waterfall. You'll love it."

Wakefield sounded good. Great even. And if I hadn't come to Chelsea with my family, if my sister and I hadn't spent the best afternoon sledding down a hill we'd discovered behind the cottage, if we hadn't watched the carolers sing outside the church, if we hadn't woken up to presents in our stockings— if we hadn't *had* stockings—and our parents getting along, if I hadn't seen the magic of Chelsea then, and now, maybe, just maybe I would've considered Wakefield. But surely Wakefield wouldn't have those two adorable little girls with their father in the florist's shop. Or the couple who'd owned the café for more than twenty years. I felt a connection to Chelsea now. And when it was *Ben* suggesting the other place? Not a chance. *Especially* when he was trying to pretend like he had any idea what *I'd* love.

I watched him closely, searching for a shift in his demeanor, praying he was kidding. Could this all be a joke? Was there any possibility that any second now Mireille and Renee would burst through the door, letting me know they'd convinced him to let me film here? They'd all signed contracts with me—if they'd known Ben was going to stand in my way, why'd they bother?

It was time to beg. "Ben, please, I know—"

Ben's mouth formed a straight line. And those eyes with the long lashes that now infuriated me were fixed on mine. "My final answer is no. *D'accord?*"

"What?" I said, confused.

"D'accord." He enunciated every syllable. "It means okay."

But it wasn't okay. He wasn't giving in.

Ben strode across his office to the door, then grasped the handle and pulled it open.

I could feel the pressure building behind my eyes but there was no way I was going to let him see me cry, so I just nodded. "Fine," I said, then grabbed my coat off the back of the chair, turned, and rushed out of his office, down the hall and past reception, not letting myself slow down even to pull on my coat. I pushed through the glass doors and out into the heavy, wet, falling snow.

Only then did I stop moving. And only then did I let the tears flow.

CHAPTER SEVEN

Tuesday, December 23, 9:30 a.m.

On my way back to the hotel, I kept replaying the scene at the pub my first night in Chelsea, when Ben had almost gotten into a fight with that guy for not leaving me alone. If we hadn't met under those circumstances, would it have made a difference? No, that was ridiculous. It wasn't like *I* invited the drunk asshole to the pub and forced him to grab my ass.

I didn't want to give up on Chelsea, but I didn't see any other option—except Wakefield, despite it being Ben's suggestion. And I *really* didn't want to take his advice. But I *had* to get a permit to shoot somewhere or Elijah would be forced to greenlight *I'll Be Home for Christmas* instead of my movie. I had not come this far, figuratively *and* geographically, to wait another year. Anything could happen in the space of twelve months. Elijah could leave Epic and his replacement could cancel any plans for *A Very Chelsea Christmas*. Another script could come in featuring a similar story line and trump mine. I could leave Epic for another gig and someone else could wind up directing my movie.

So as devastated as I was not to shoot in Chelsea, Wakefield was my only option to keep my movie alive—my plan B. That's what I told Renee before climbing into the Land Rover.

"What are you going to do? Go home for Christmas, then?" Renee had asked as she helped me pack up my car.

Hardly. That's what Stella would want—she'd texted again to see if I'd booked a flight yet. But how could I think about Christmas when I didn't have a plan for my Christmas movie?

A quick search on my phone revealed the number for the Wakefield town hall, and when I called, a cheery voice transferred me to another equally cheery voice, Agathe Garnier, mayor of Wakefield. Just as Ben had predicted, she was thrilled at the prospect of her town being in a Christmas movie. She informed me that she had planned to close town hall early because of the impending storm. She said she was headed to her cottage for the holidays, but would wait until eleven if I could make it there by then. I was grateful for the time crunch anyway, since it seemed like the weather *was* getting worse. The heavy snow had turned to sleet.

The windshield wipers swished back and forth but couldn't seem to keep up with the sleet. I flipped the knob to make them go faster, and then flicked on the radio, turning up the dial to hear George Michael croon through "Last Christmas."

"*I gave you my heart, but the very next day, you gave it away,*" I sang along.

Sounds about right, I thought. I gave Chelsea my heart. And Ben had ripped it out, goddammit.

For the hundredth time that morning, I replayed the moment in his office where he'd said no and then practically kicked me out. Not that I'd wanted to linger, but still. It was humiliating.

As I pulled onto the main street, the Land Rover's tires slid and I fishtailed into the opposite lane. I gripped the steering wheel and righted the car. Good thing no one was on the road. The sleet was turning into freezing rain by the minute, which in turn made the pavement slick. Thank god for the four-wheel drive.

I sighed sadly as I passed the adorable houses I'd seen when I first came into the town, admiring the different colors: red, blue, pastel green, which reminded me of the little village the owners of the cottage we'd rented when I was younger had set on the fireplace mantel. The tiny ceramic houses had been nestled in fluffy white cotton, a string of multicolored lights turning each house a different hue. My heart hurt. Leaving Chelsea was hitting me hard.

And just as quickly as vibrant and sweet Chelsea had appeared, it disappeared, and the landscape changed. The quaint houses were replaced by evergreens that stood tall and proud, their branches still heavy with snow despite the rain. The road ahead disappeared into a winter wonderland and, suddenly, for the first time in days, a sense of isolation struck me.

I wanted to celebrate Christmas. I wanted to cut down a tree and decorate it, to make cookies and host an open house.

I wanted to hang stockings by the fire, and create my own traditions. Oh, how I longed for it all. When was I ever going to get my Christmas wish?

On the radio, Bing Crosby sang "I'll Be Home for Christmas," as if taunting me.

Never mind, Zo. It'll happen one day. And for now I still had my work. And then, sure, I'd go see Stella, and then the holidays would be over and it would be back to work for another year.

The SUV chugged along up and into the hills, and the road narrowed, barely wide enough for two cars. Snow and slush covered the yellow line, and so I used the ditches on either side of the road for guidance, staying in the middle between the two depressions.

Soon the rain eased. I gripped the steering wheel tighter, trying to keep my focus on the road ahead. Even though it was still morning the entire world on the other side of the blurry windshield was gray, as though a flick of the windshield wipers had turned everything from full color to black and white.

My phone rang and I looked over, seeing Elijah's name. Nope. I couldn't deal with him right now. Not until I got to Wakefield and had something positive to report. I hit the *X* on my phone, sending him through to my voice mail.

Heading into a gentle curve, I fishtailed again on an icy patch. I eased off the gas and slowed to a crawl. The temperature gauge on the Land Rover said 1°C, whatever that meant. It was taking me longer to get to Wakefield than I'd anticipated. How long would the mayor wait for me? Toward the end of the curve I spied a car in the ditch. No one was inside. I shuddered. Moments later I accelerated into a straightaway, then thought of the car in the ditch, and lifted my toes off the gas.

The hill began to incline, but my tires spun, skidding. I gasped and hit the brakes, then tried climbing the hill again. This time, the tires thankfully grabbed hold of the road and churned through the slush.

I tried to muster enthusiasm for Wakefield. What would I say to Mayor Garnier? I considered the truth: After years in the male-dominated industry of holiday movies, I finally had a chance to direct my first feature, and the only thing that stood in my way was a municipal permit to shoot in a quaint town in the Gatineau Hills. The idea was to bond, woman to woman.

I bit my lip. But what would I do if she said no? I considered the utility of an ugly cry. But Mayor Garnier wouldn't say no. She couldn't. They never did! Except . . . Red-hot irritation toward Ben flared in my gut.

Some time later, I finally passed the first driveway I'd seen in ages. Then another. The rural road slowly gave way to a wider street, with houses on both sides. Then came a *quincaillerie*, a *fromagerie*, a *resto-bar*, a poutine stand. A sign warned of a ski hill ahead just as my phone told me to turn right onto what appeared to be the main street. A gust of wind salted my windshield with sleet. I felt despair at the idea of traipsing around this town in my waterlogged UGGs. But, I resolved, it would be worth it. What a Christmas present to myself it would be, I told myself, to resolve this crisis, to head into the holidays with this stage of planning sewn up.

As I passed a sign that pointed to Wakefield's covered bridge, I turned off the main road to see this highlight of the town that everyone seemed to talk about when they mentioned Wakefield. Mayor Garnier had promised to be in her chambers for another half hour, and I wanted a quick peek of the bridge before I met with her. I rounded a turn and came upon a gap in the trees, and my eyebrows raised in surprise. It was a genuinely impressive view—snowy hills giving way to ice-covered banks, with the river below open and flowing fast. Upstream from my vantage point was the scarlet covered bridge, the length of a New York subway train car, standing out against the white snow and the gray sky. It was even more impressive than the famous structure in *The Bridges of Madison County*. The entire structure was wood, from the siding to the support beams to the roof. Rain was beating against the side of the bridge, but I imagined how beautiful it would look with the snow falling onto it on a crisp night.

A little farther on a sign told me the bridge was pedestrian only. I longed to walk the bridge, to experience it for myself, but there wasn't time—and the rain was so heavy I'd be soaked through in seconds. And I couldn't afford to be late to the mayor's office.

Twenty minutes to eleven. Now I felt the pressure of time. I needed to keep moving.

The road ahead climbed another hill. Then something weird happened: Halfway up, the Land Rover slowed . . .

and then began sliding backward. Frantically, I pressed hard on the brake, pumping it, but nothing stopped my backward motion. My rearview mirror showed a clear road behind me, no cars. Thank god. It was terrifying, sliding backward in a car with no control. I tried to calm my racing heart. Everything was fine. I was a great driver. I'd had my license since I was sixteen, which meant that I'd had my license almost as long as I *hadn't* had my license. I'd driven through sandstorms and a low-grade tornado. This was nothing.

The Land Rover finally stopped sliding near the bottom of the hill and, relieved, I glanced at the clock. Seventeen minutes to eleven.

I pressed down on the gas pedal. The wheels spun. And the Land Rover stayed still.

Fine. Be that way, my teenage self retorted at the car. I reversed along a flat section, passing a figure (who might as well have been a spacewalking astronaut, he was so covered up) as he threw salt on his driveway.

Back now, a good way from the hill, I assessed my situation. The road ahead climbed at a slope. It was a gentle ascent. Not even enough to justify a set of stairs. Home in LA, there were driveways much steeper than this. I just needed a little speed. So I shifted the transmission into drive and floored it. The wheels spun again and, again, the car stayed put. I decreased my foot's pressure on the gas. The car eased forward, gained momentum, and suddenly the SUV and I were climbing again. *Yes!* A quarter, then halfway up the hill. I pressed harder on the accelerator. The tires spun. I eased off, and they gained purchase again.

Then, as three-quarters of the hill was behind me, just as I was feeling hope that I would make it, the Land Rover came to a stop. I floored it and rubber hissed over ice.

Please?

Oh god, please get me out of this mess.

I was just ten feet from the crest of the hill. Ignoring my spinning wheels, obstinately declining to acknowledge my foot pressed all the way down to the floor on the gas, the car slid backward.

Noooo.

I was shaking. Everything felt blurry. I tried to breathe, to stay calm, but all I wanted to do was squeeze my eyes tight and make this entire situation go away.

I pressed on the gas, but the SUV slid backward—again. This time, it slid at an angle, toward the passenger side, so that the SUV was now perpendicular to the road. Then I hit something. Suddenly, the world was spinning. The words *Joyeux Noël* on a yard sign spun past me once, twice, three times.

"*Joyeux Noël*," I repeated like a prayer.

I spun the steering wheel, pumped the brake, pressed the gas, and none of it did anything. I shut my eyes and screamed. The car continued to spin, and then, finally, came to a halt with a loud crunch.

As much as I wanted to keep my eyes firmly shut, to block everything out, time was ticking. I pried open one lid, then the other. At first, it wasn't clear what had happened. The road was in front of me. Then I twisted in my seat and saw the answer: a mailbox, pressed deep into the back end of the

Land Rover. But okay, I was fine. And the mailbox hadn't actually broken the rear windshield. Maybe the car would still work?

I looked at the time. Ten minutes to eleven.

Surely I could twenty-seven-point turn myself out of this situation. I put the car in gear and tapped the gas with my boot. The tires produced their by-now clichéd response: They spun. I put the car in reverse. Why? Not sure. The mailbox was still *right there*. Anyway, the same thing happened. The transmission was already set to 4WD. I tried 4WD low. I tried 2WD. Nothing moved the Land Rover. Each action provoked the same response. In a word: nothing.

I put the car in park, leaned my head against the steering wheel, and shouted a bunch of F-bombs into the dash, each one punctuated with a fist to the wheel. And then, for variety, the classic Quebecois curse word: *tabernac.*

Swearing didn't help.

Think, Zoey!

I grabbed my phone from the center console. A few taps on the map app told me that it would take just five minutes to walk to the municipal building. *These boots were made for walking, Zoey. Let's do this.* I shoved my phone in my pocket, pulled on my cashmere gloves and stepped out of the Land Rover. My UGGs promptly slid out from under me. I grabbed the door handle, and hung on, which prevented me from submarining under the vehicle.

Conditions seemed to have changed in just ten minutes. All of a sudden, it was cold, and it seemed as though the surface of every single thing around me was covered in a thick layer of shellac. If I had ice skates, I could have glided down the road, the picture of grace. (Or at least, the picture of someone who'd skated a few times in her life.) Had I more time I would have snapped some pics, the setting was that beautiful. Wasn't there a level on one of the *Super Mario Bros.* games that featured a world made entirely of ice? Stella and I used to be obsessed with the game when we were kids. Actually, hadn't we gotten that game under the tree that snowy Chelsea Christmas? It must have been a sign that the game had come to mind. And if the video game was accurate, the best strategy to beat the level was to stay off the ice.

That gave me an idea.

Still holding on to the door handle, I put one foot against the front tire and then pushed forward toward the shoulder of the road where the mounds of snow had melted enough in the rain to reveal bits of gravel encased in a layer of glass. I held my arms out, hoping it would help me glide farther. Just as I was slowing down, my toe touched the pebbled ice. Luckily, the surface wasn't as slick as the road. I stepped gingerly onto the bumpy surface. Things got even easier when I reached a snowbank. Ice covered that, too, but not enough to support me, and so I had good purchase with each step that broke through the surface crust. Step, break, sink. Step, break, sink. It was exhausting, but it had been three days since my last HIIT class. I could use the workout.

By the time I reached the top of the hill, my hair was stiff with ice, my coat had hardened to something like GORE-TEX armor, and it was now five to eleven. But now I confronted my greatest obstacle yet. My route required me to cross the road at a four-way stop, across smooth asphalt that was as slick as ice . . . because it was *covered* in ice. And gently tilted back toward the Land Rover, a good forty yards down the hill.

I stepped from the snow to the gravel, no problem, then gingerly set the sole of one of my UGGs onto the slick surface. Shifting my weight onto my front foot, I tested the— what had my senior physics teacher called it? Coefficient of friction? My UGG stayed steady. Great. Slowly, gently, cautiously, I moved my back foot from the gravel onto the road past my front foot. That, too, stayed stuck in place. Huh. The old laws of physics still seemed to apply. Feeling as though I was stepping from a space shuttle out into emptiness, I stepped forward, and again, and again. Halfway across the road now. Once to the other side I would be able to step back onto gravel. To snowbank. To municipal building. To meeting with mayor. To permit. To movie. To directing. To happiness. All of it, the path that led from this. Next. Step.

My front foot slid an inch on the ice. Whoops. *Easy, Zoey.* But when I adjusted my balance to stop from sliding, my back foot slid more. And that was all it took. "No," I cried. "Not now!" And before I knew it, I was sliding on both feet down the icy pavement. Knees bent, hands spread, shifting weight from leg to leg like I was powering down a wave on a surfboard, past the snowbanks and driveways I'd just so painstakingly climbed past, gaining speed with every moment I stayed aloft.

🌲 🌲 🌲

Elijah lived in a single-story mid-century modern place sprawled high atop Topanga Canyon, the artists' and film-makers' enclave between Santa Monica and Malibu. It had a pool and a view of the Pacific Ocean miles below, and felt as remote as the moon from the city's bustle. Holiday movies had been good for his bank account, and in the early days he used the place to host Epic Productions' wrap parties, complete with fire-eaters, aerialists, and exotic animal trainers.

On the night of one of these legendary parties (I couldn't remember the occasion or the specific attraction Elijah had hired), I had been working to iron out some production problem or other, one that needed resolution to keep us on schedule, and so I was late to get up to his house in Topanga. I drove myself in my college-girl ride, a yellow Ford Fiesta, and in my haste to make it up the mountain I was on the last of the hairpin switchbacks that led to Elijah's pad—when I slid straight off the road into an arroyo. I was miraculously not hurt, but the impact had blown the airbags and the paint on my car was scratched up by sagebrush. When the dust had settled, I looked out the driver's-side window, and by a cruel quirk of geography, I could see Elijah's place from the spot where I'd ended up. It was just a hillside away, in all its glory: the illuminated pool, the caterer's spread, the tuxedoed bartender and the live band and the guests, my friends and colleagues, dancing to the beat of the live band. All of it was so close, and yet, so distant. It felt so unjust. So unfair.

I felt a similar sense of inequality as I slid my way down the hill in Wakefield. *Noooo!* was the chorus, the hook, and the bridge of the song that played on a loop in my mind. I suddenly hit a rough patch, lurched forward, and stepped onto unfrozen asphalt, but the two paces it took to check my speed put me back onto frozen ground. And then my feet slid out from under me. Now I was on my bum, the ice cold under my cheeks, flying down the hill. My right hand caught something—a rock or twig—but only for a split second. But it was enough to twist my body so that I was now headed down the road backward. I craned my neck to see where I was going while simultaneously flailing, trying to grab on to anything possible, but there was nothing. And quickly approaching was a blue pickup truck. It passed my SUV and was moving slowly toward me. *Would the driver see me? What if they ran me over?* Zara's white wool be damned, I thought before leaning back, pressing my head against the ice, and stretching my hands out to increase the amount of friction between my body and the road. Sure enough, the starfish pose slowed my progress, and the pickup truck slowed, too, pulling over onto the shoulder and stopping exactly where the road curved, exactly in the spot intersecting with the road's fall line, so that first my legs, then my waist, and, finally, even my chest slid under the raised truck bed. I came to a stop at the bottom of the hill with my chin directly underneath the truck's driver's-side door.

As I lay on the ground, contemplating how my day had devolved to this, I heard a whirring sound as the window of the truck was rolled down. I watched a head emerge from above and look at me.

"Well, that's certainly one way to get down the hill," said Ben laconically.

Of course it *had* to be him.

The emotions within me collided. Aggravation that this guy, in competition to win the Most Frustrating Person on the Planet Award, had to be the one to see me like this. Relief that a capable man and also, just possibly, an ally, at least in my quest to get up this godforsaken hill, had materialized. Outright puzzlement that I, my body, my sympathetic nervous system, in this fight-or-flight moment, had reacted not with anger or fear or indignation at the sight of Ben but with *attraction*, so that the first thought that popped into my brain when I recognized his face above me was, *Damn, those light brown eyes that fit so well with his cheekbones and strong brows are the kind of eyes I could stare at forever*—if *they didn't belong to the worst person in the world.*

I burst into tears.

"Zoey Andrews, *non*!" Ben exclaimed before hurriedly opening the door. He was careful, delicately stepping over me as he got out of his truck. Through my sobs, I had time to notice that he was wearing tall, matte-black boots. Bogs, I thought. How does he always seem to be a poster child for weather-appropriate attire? But before I could take in the rest of his look, Ben's feet slid out from under him, and in the next second *he* was flat on *his* back on the black ice, right alongside me.

"*Tabernac*," he said.

"Now you know what it feels like," I said with a sniffle.

He took off his toque and handed it to me. "To dry your tears."

I wiped off my cheeks and, without thinking, used the hat to wipe my nose. "Oh," I said, realizing what I'd done. "Sorry."

Ben shrugged, produced another toque from somewhere in his parka, and said, "Keep it." I pushed it into my purse, which was still slung around me. Then Ben set his head at an angle.

"I don't know that I've ever seen my truck from this vantage," he said.

"How's it look?"

"Like it needs a good wash." With both hands he gripped the footrail and used that to pull himself back up. When he was standing, he extended a hand my way, and I used that to get myself up, too. "We can't stand here," Ben said, nodding up the hill. "Others may be sliding into us at any moment."

"What about my car?" I looked forlornly at the Land Rover, which sat sadly on the side of the road, the mailbox still poking into it.

Ben shook his head. "Without snow tires, you'll be in another ditch around the next bend."

"But I got the kind with four-wheel drive."

He raised an eyebrow. "Doesn't matter much," he said, "if your tires can't grip on the ice. Most of the people who live in the bush have the kind with metal studs."

I groaned, then pulled out my phone. It was 11:03. "I'm already late to get to town hall. I need my car."

"Or a ride with snow tires," Ben said with a grin. "Come on. Hop in."

Seconds later we were both buckled into Ben's elevated truck cab. A flash of movement in the back seat made me turn and squeal in surprise. Simon leaned forward, sniffing, tail wagging. "Hey, buddy," I said, reaching out to scratch his head. He tried to lick my hand.

Ben did something with a lever somewhere and from below us there was a grinding of gears, then, once the truck was in drive, it began creeping forward, slowly at first, then with more speed.

I stared out the window as we passed the Land Rover, then I faced forward and held my breath as Ben climbed the truck to the top of the hill, toward the spot where my slip-sliding had started, but then we were past it. I could see the Wakefield town hall. *I had been so close!*

As we pulled into the parking lot in front of the building, I looked around. The lot was empty. Not a good sign. "I'll wait for you," he said.

I hastily unbuckled myself, then rushed from the truck cab across the lot, slipping and falling on my butt. *Ouch.* But no time to stop. I got up and kept running toward the front door, where a sign said *Your Gateway to La Pêche, Quebec!* I reached out a gloved hand to pull open the door that would lead me to my appointment with the woman who was going to save my movie. But nothing happened. The door wouldn't open. Even when I wrenched it with both hands.

Tabernac, I thought without irony.

I ran around the side of the building, my feet sloshing through the sleet, and found another door. Also locked. Same with an entrance off the back by a loading dock. The three doors were the only entrances to the building.

I looked at my phone. It was 11:07. Even if Agathe Garnier had waited until eleven like she'd promised, I was late. I leaned forward and pressed my head against the wall. How close had I come to seeing her?

I began making my way back to Ben's truck. My eyes were dry this time—all I felt was a deep, dark depression. I opened the passenger door.

"No luck?" Ben said, not looking up from his phone. Simon's snout was on the console between us.

I let out a frustrated groan as I climbed into my seat. "No." I slammed the door.

"Don't take it out on the truck," Ben said.

I glared at him while I tried to figure out what to do next, what this meant for my movie.

He shrugged. "Well, then, it wasn't meant to be, huh?"

Something about his indifference rubbed me the wrong way. Maybe for him it was no big deal, but for me? No permit meant no movie. No movie meant the year I'd spent writing this screenplay, working long hours, not being a very good friend, bailing on plans, not realizing that Tomas was *not* the one sooner—it was all for nothing. Maybe he'd throw in the towel, but not me. I wasn't giving up this easily.

"This is partly your fault, you know that, right?" I didn't mean to say it, it just sort of came out. I bit my lip.

Ben's eyebrows knitted. "My fault? I just saved you *and* gave you a ride here."

"Yes." I sighed. "But I wouldn't have been in such a rush to get here if you had just told me you were never going to give me the permit in the first place," I said slowly, as it dawned on me. "Like, say, *yesterday*, when I came to your farm. You must have known I'd need a town permit for the movie. But you made me wait until today, and even then, you made me wait to see you." It wasn't totally Ben's fault I didn't get to Agathe in time, but these were the facts. And he sure had contributed to the situation. I hung my head and tried to take a deep breath. *Think, Zoey.*

"I know where the mayor's cottage is," Ben finally said.

"Good for you," I said, my eyes closed. I did *not* want Benoît Deschamps's help. It wasn't just him, I didn't want help, period. When you rely on someone else, you're at their mercy. I needed to figure this out on my own. And I didn't even *really* want the Wakefield permit. But what I wanted—the Chelsea permit, to be back in my own car, to not have a wet butt—these were all crushed dreams.

"Actually, I should call her." I looked at Ben. "Would you happen to have Mayor Garnier's number?" I asked, my tone softened.

"No," Ben said.

I looked at him skeptically. "You know where her cottage is but you don't know her phone number?"

"*Oui.* I was at her cottage for an Outaouais event last summer. But it's not like she gave out her cell phone number."

I weighed my options, which weren't many.

"Fine," I conceded.

"Fine?" Ben said, sounding amused, which only irritated me further.

"Fine, you can drive me to her cottage. As long as it's not hours away. It's *not* hours away, is it?"

He cleared his throat. "You're something else, you know that?" He started the truck. "It's about *an* hour away, and the only reason I'm offering, to be clear, is that it's on my way"— he maneuvered out of the parking lot and onto the main road, retracing our steps—"to drop off the stuff in back."

I turned, craning my neck. Simon had curled up on the seat, head tucked into his legs. On the floor in front of him was a large crate of bottles, full of brown liquid. "Root beer?" I could go for a root beer. Would it be rude to ask for one, when I wasn't exactly being that nice to him?

"Maple syrup," he said with a smirk. "Remember, I make the best in the area."

"Of course. Who could live without Chelsea's finest?" Despite my terribly bad luck, I was secretly grateful he decided to brave the storm to deliver maple syrup. Otherwise, who knows what would've happened to me out here, alone.

"Tease all you like, but my customers demand it."

"And here I thought you were chasing me out of Chelsea."

"You hadn't crossed my mind, once I got you out of my office," he retorted.

"You know what? I'll just follow you in my own car." Ben was rubbing me the wrong way, and it was clear I was rubbing him the wrong way, too.

"Oh yeah?" he asked as he eased to a stop in front of the Land Rover. In the last half hour, the freezing rain had managed to ice over the entire surface of the SUV. My eye went to the mailbox denting the back of it, and then to the house a good ways down the driveway, the trees and their branches, the snowbank my SUV was sunk into. Everything around us was quickly accumulating a thick layer of ice.

"Zoey," Ben said lightly. *He's a jerk, Zoey. A jerk with a great voice, and, okay, really great hair. And eyes. Broad shoulders. But a jerk nonetheless.* "Allow me to get you to Agathe's."

"I don't want your help, *Ben*," I said, my tone angrier than I meant it to be—but I needed to stick to the plan, which at this point was not to let Ben get involved with this film permit.

"Maybe not, but I don't think you have any other choice," he said.

CHAPTER EIGHT

Tuesday, December 23, 11:30 a.m.

The mafioso don in *Christmas in Sicily* had bulletproof windows in his Palermo villa. It was a plot point, and it had been on me to find glass that was appropriately thick. After searching high and low for this glass on the island of Sicily, I'd eventually had it shipped over from the Italian mainland, on the yacht of the Russian oligarch who'd been financing the production. And *that* stuff hadn't been as thick as the layer of clearcoat that currently covered the Land Rover's rear cargo door.

But never fear: Emile Benoît Deschamps came prepared. He disappeared into his pickup truck and rummaged around before returning bearing a lighter and a flathead screwdriver. He lit the lighter and heated up the tip of the screwdriver until it was red hot before plunging it into the ice at the edge of the rear hatch. He cleared a seam that was a good foot long.

"Impressed?" He looked over at me.

"Your lighter's going to run out of fluid before you get through it all."

I pulled from my purse the travel-size can of aerosol hair spray that I took everywhere with me. "You have your tools for emergencies," I said as I handed it over, "and I have mine."

Ben looked down at the little can like I'd just handed him an alien foot. "What's this for?"

I took the can back from him and sprayed the hairspray toward the bottom of the rear hatch. "Quick, give me the lighter," I said. Seconds later I set the lighter flame into the spray.

Whoosh.

Suddenly a torch was melting the layer of ice. I'd exposed a good half of the seam between the hatch and the car when my hairspray gave out. "So much for travel sizes," I said. Luckily, it was enough. I set my hand into the latch, and pulled, and the door opened an inch. I closed it and opened it again, and with a great cracking the door opened all the way out and up, revealing my suitcase.

I climbed through the back seat to the front, grabbed the lip balm and keys from the cupholders, writhed again through the back seat, and then finally yanked my suitcase out of the back. With my purse in one hand, suitcase in the other, I looked at Ben. "That's it," I said.

He looked me over, and it was only then that I realized what a sight I must have been. My UGGs were sunk into the roadside slush, completely soaked, and freezing rain had created its coat of ice over my white wool Zara coat. I shook the crunchy, ice-covered hair out of my face. "I wish I'd thought to wear a coat with a hood," I moaned.

"*That's* what you wish for?" Ben said, amusement in his voice. He stepped forward, toward me, as if to relieve me of the suitcase but I shook my head. "I've got it," I said.

"Suit yourself," Ben said, and headed to his truck. He opened the passenger-side door and pushed the seat forward. Then, before I could stop him, he turned back toward me, took my suitcase from my hand, and heaved it easily into the seat alongside his husky.

I scowled but climbed into the passenger seat. Once buckled in, I looked around. Now that I no longer had the stress associated with getting to the municipal building on time, I had the wherewithal to notice my surroundings. The truck's cab was impeccable. No dog hair anywhere, almost as though Ben had spent the morning cleaning it, not working in the mayor's office. The dash was shiny, and the little spot under the radio held only his phone.

"Why is your suitcase so heavy?" he said once he'd climbed into the driver's seat. He adjusted his rearview mirror. "I thought you were only here for two days."

"You never know what you'll need."

"Certainly not a winter coat or proper boots," he said, then turned the key in the ignition. The truck roared to life and he put it in drive, and it started rolling forward as though this road, this weather, were no big deal at all.

As Ben merged onto the highway and out of town, I crossed my arms over my chest, but immediately regretted it. The pressure from my folded arms squeezed water from the sleeves of my coat, dripping onto my pants. I uncrossed my arms and instead shrugged out of my coat, maneuvering it around the seat belt. "Do you mind if I toss this in the back?"

"Why would I mind?"

"I don't know. This truck looks like you stole it from the Ford Museum, it's so clean," I teased, biting my lip. "I don't want to mess it up. My coat is soaked."

"You think my truck is clean?" he asked proudly.

I scrunched my nose and looked around. "If there was an award for cleanest car, which there's not because that would be the most boring awards ceremony ever, you would win. Did you just buy it this morning or something?"

"No, but that is the highest compliment you could pay me, truly. I take weird satisfaction in having a superclean car. Outer order, inner calm."

"Wooooooow," I said. "You mind if I put the radio on?" I needed something to distract me until we got to the mayor's cottage.

"Go right ahead."

I leaned forward to turn the dial. "Wow, I don't even have to go *searching* for the Christmas station," I said as Andy Williams sang "It's the Most Wonderful Time of the Year."

Ben gave me a defensive look. "So what? I like Christmas music."

"I'm not complaining." I shrugged happily. "I love Christmas music."

"You do *not* love Christmas music, Zoey," Ben said skeptically. "Just like you don't like Christmas."

"*What?!*" I twisted in my seat so I had a clear view of him—or at least, his straight nose and prominent chin. I shook my head. "I just pitched you on filming my *Christmas movie* in your town. I *love* Christmas. Just like I *love* Christmas music. Give me a line of *any* Christmas song and I'll give you the next line."

I pointed at the radio as the opening chimes of "Let It Snow!" crackled through the speakers.

I waited for Dean Martin to sing: "*Oh the weather outside is frightful,*" and then I joined in: "*But the fire is so delightful.*"

"That was easy," Ben said. "Everyone knows the words to 'Let It Snow!'"

"Fine, next song."

"You're on. I happen to be a carol aficionado myself." He turned up the volume.

"We'll see about that."

As we waited out the song, I rubbed my hands together, trying to get warm. A moment later, "O Christmas Tree" started and I smiled to myself. I had this one in the bag. Tony Bennett repeated the opening line twice, then I pointed to Ben.

"*Such pleasure do you bring me*"— I sang along.

"*How lovely are thy branches,*" Ben said at the same time. He looked at me, his brow furrowed.

"Tony Bennett," I said smugly. "*Not* the original. You gotta know your renditions, Ben. One point for me."

I could tell he was fighting a smile. "I'll get you on the next one."

"We'll see about that."

I blew on my hands. Ben fiddled with a dial for the heater. "You warm enough?"

"I'm not sure the seat warmer is working," I said innocently.

Ben gave me a sidelong glance. "Heated seats were not an option on this vintage F-150," he said with disdain.

"Actually, they were definitely an option," I informed him. "The technology's been around forever—or at least since the '66 Cadillac de Ville convertible, but whoever first owned this . . . '96 F-150 must not have opted for them."

Ben's jaw dropped, and I laughed. I loved surprising people with my party trick: a weirdly deep knowledge of cars. I was basically Julia Roberts in *Pretty Woman*—save for the stripper-with-a-heart-of-gold part.

"You know this much about cars but not enough to know you need snow tires in this weather?" He glanced at me in disbelief.

I rolled my eyes. "I'm going to choose to focus on the compliment," I said. "My dad loved cars. Taught me everything he knew."

"Loved?" Ben cocked his head.

"Yeah." I felt my stomach tighten.

Ben's forehead wrinkled. "Sorry. Did he—?"

"No." I shook my head. "He's not dead. Very much alive, in fact. In addition to loving cars, he also loved cigars, and women, too—just not enough to stick with one. He divorced my mom when I was thirteen and remarried a few times. Last I heard, he was on wife number four. I haven't seen him since a very awkward run-in on the beaches of Curaçao, when he was marrying wife number three."

Ben flicked on his turn signal and made a right onto another very snowy, very steep road before responding. "Wow. Your dad was getting married and didn't invite you?" His voice was filled with incredulity, which bugged me. My impulse was to put him in his place for being judgmental, and yet I was so often hiding the truth about my parents (because who wants to showcase their not-so-perfect family life?) that it was kind of nice to unload on a stranger. I didn't care what Ben thought of me.

"Didn't even tell us it was happening," I said. "I didn't even know he'd divorced wife number two!" Rain pelted the window, now coming at us from the right side of the car. "Safe to say our relationship hasn't recovered."

"Ouch," he said. "I can't imagine my parents being with anyone else. Or being divorced, period. Must make holidays difficult, huh?"

"Something like that," I said. The holidays were difficult, but not how Ben likely imagined. No shuffling back and forth between parents who overcompensated out of guilt like typical kids of divorced parents. The opposite for most of Stella's and my life: no one wanted us. "Imagine if we were forced to see our parents over the holidays rather than go where *we* wanted?" Tomas had said on more than one occasion. "Your parents have given you a gift, Zo." *Some gift.*

Ben cleared his throat. "Well, I can't fix your family life or offer heated seats, but I *can* direct both vents at you." He fiddled with the plastic slats. I leaned forward and held my hands in front of them.

"You know what the real problem is?" I said after a moment, to change the subject.

"Nuclear war, global pandemics, climate change—"

"My feet are soaked."

"Of course, they are," he said. "You're barely wearing boots."

"What do you mean? I'm wearing boots!" I protested.

"Ish."

I made a face. "They're *Australian* winter boots."

"They're Australian boots. I don't think they consider them winter boots even in Australia. And they're definitely not waterproof."

"I sprayed them with a very expensive waterproof spray before coming here."

"Uh-huh. How'd that work for you?" Ben asked dryly. "Also, it barely rains in Australia, so spray or not, they're likely not going to do anything for moisture."

"Wow, and here I thought you were an expert at all things Chelsea, and at pawning people off on Wakefield," I said. "I didn't realize you were also an expert at all things Australian. How'd that happen?"

"Long story," he said pleasantly, ignoring my tone.

"Well, Ben, at the speed you're driving, I'm pretty sure we've got time for a long story."

"Delphine went to Australia. And I went to visit." His tone was even.

"Ah, Delphine." At the mention of her name, my stomach lurched. Why did this woman, whom I didn't even know, whom I knew very little about, have this effect on me?

"So who's Delphine?"

"Ex," he said.

I ignored the little voice that said, *Change the subject.* "Ahhh. So that's why you're picking her up from the airport?"

"Right. Any other personal questions?" He raised an eyebrow.

"Yes, actually." I swiveled in my seat to face him. "So did you go to visit her while you were still together, or after you'd broken up? Or, did you break up while you were there?" The barrage of inappropriate questions was out before I could stop myself. But I worked in holiday romances. I loved the ins and outs of relationships—real or imagined.

"While we were sort of in limbo."

"Ahh. Guess that trip was a bust, huh?"

He snorted. "Thanks, Dr. Ruth."

"Uh, *not* trying to be your sex therapist, for the record." I was taking my stress out on him. I knew it, and I couldn't stop.

"Good to know." Ben crept to a stop at a T in the road and then slowly turned right. "This road is always a little precarious," he mumbled. I looked ahead and noticed that the "road" he was referring to narrowed to a single lane before disappearing into a thick forest.

"This road?" I gestured in front of us. "Are you sure that's what this is?"

"It's the most direct route to Val-des-Bois. We'll just be off the main highway for a bit." Ben gripped the wheel.

Despite the heat blowing on me, my hands were still shaking. I tucked them under my butt, then cleared my throat. "Well, for the record, I'm no longer a fan of the Aussies' stupid boots."

"I guess we've finally found one thing to agree on." The hint of a smile pulled at Ben's lips. "Hey, why don't I pull over so you can get your *poupons* out of your bag?" Ben glanced in his rearview mirror, then over at me. His hazel eyes showed flecks of gold.

"My *poop-whats*?" My knees were jittering now. Damn these UGGs.

"Your slippers." He laughed. "My grandmother always called them *poupons*. I forget not everyone does. Anyway. Your *slippers*. Do you want me to pull over so you can get them? They'll be warmer than those." He jutted his chin toward my feet. Even though my UGGs *were* a poor footwear choice—clearly—I didn't like that Ben was picking on them.

"What slippers? I didn't pack *slippers*."

"What do you mean you didn't pack slippers? You forgot your slippers?" Ben looked amazed and shook his head. "Honestly, for someone so set on spending time in Quebec, you're incredibly ill-prepared."

"Who *packs* slippers? Aren't they just something you leave at home by the front door or next to the bed?"

He shook his head. "It really *is* your lucky day, Zoey Andrews. I've got an emergency pair of *poupons* in the back."

"An emergency pair of *poupons*? And isn't Grey Poupon a mustard?"

"It's not Grey Poupon, it's just *poupon*," he said, exasperated. "Listen, you'll thank me when your feet are warm. Hang on, I'll pull over."

"Don't pull over. I'll just climb over your pristine seats. You're going like five miles an hour anyway."

"I'm going five miles an hour," he said, his voice tight with frustration, "so that we actually make it to the mayor's cottage, rather than into that ditch." He pointed across my chest as I unbuckled my seat belt, and my fingers brushed his. They instantly warmed, which irritated me.

I turned and pulled myself over, flopping onto the back seat. Not exactly the picture of grace. Simon looked up, startled from his nap, and I scratched him under the chin. He gave my hand a lick, then curled up again. "Where did you say the magical mustard was hiding?"

"In a box behind those seats."

I shoved my suitcase aside to make room in the middle of the bench, and leaned over the seats to feel around. Simon licked my hand again.

"Should be a large black case."

"There's no gun inside, right?" I joked, but seriously— who knew what people thought was normal in these parts.

"A gun? No. But I think there are gummy bears."

"Gummy bears?"

"Yes, you know, those little squishy candies shaped like—"

"I know what gummy bears are."

"Oh, because you seemed confused." His voice was teasing.

I managed to ease the case out from behind the seats, shocked at the size. I was expecting it to be the size of a cross-body bag, maybe, but it was huge. Inside was a treasure trove of goodies: jumper cables, first-aid kit, flashlight, batteries, puffy sleeping bag, box of matches, bottle of water, tire repair kit, one of those all-in-one tools that has seventeen screwdrivers, and a Ziploc bag of snacks: granola bars, trail mix, and gummy bears. But what I was more interested in was the pair of jeans, gray hoodie, T-shirt, and socks. "You have a full outfit in here?"

"Of course. It's an emergency kit. You need a change of clothes in case of an emergency."

I shook my head and continued to sort through the stash until my fingers grazed something soft and I pulled them out. "Aha! The *pièce de résistance!*" The slippers were knitted, two shades of tan wool intertwined with white.

"I thought you didn't know any French," Ben said wryly, looking over at me as I crawled back into my seat, slippers in hand.

"I've got a few words. I watched *Emily in Paris.*" I was only half kidding. Obviously, I'd done my research while writing the script, to make it feel authentic.

"Of course you watched *Emily in Paris,*" he said sarcastically.

I bit back a snide comment because the dude *had* just said I could wear his slippers. "These look handmade." I turned the slippers over in my hands. "And brand-new. You really are a clean freak, huh?"

Without saying a word, he held out his hand.

"What?" I said, eyeing his open palm.

"Give them back."

I clasped the slippers to my chest. "No. You're driving anyway. You can't wear them."

"I'm not going to wear them, but if you're going to be ungrateful then neither will you." Ben scowled.

"I'm not ungrateful. In fact, I'm very grateful. They look so cozy." I couldn't wait to get my feet out of my soggy UGGs.

"My *mémère*—my grandmother—knits all of the grandkids a pair every year."

"Wow, that's so nice," I said, admiring the slippers. I couldn't think of a more special gift to receive.

I pulled off a waterlogged UGG and sock, and felt instant relief. "So how many grandkids?"

"Fourteen. You met Xavier, I think. At Mireille's?"

"Hm, maybe?" I'd met so many people in the last day, I couldn't remember everyone.

"He has two little girls," Ben said. "He said he met you, anyway."

"Oh right!" I remembered the man and his daughters.

"He's my closest cousin—also my best friend."

Everyone really did know everyone in this town—and everyone really did talk about everyone else.

A blast of wind shook the truck. Ben looked over. "You okay?"

I gritted my teeth. "Let's just get there." I yanked off the second UGG and sock and let them drop on the mat.

"Here's a trick question," Ben said. "For how many years did my *mémère* knit each one of us a pair of slippers?"

I considered the math and quickly gave up. "All right, I give. How many years?"

"*Every* year. *All* the years. She's eighty-six and she's still knitting. And she's been doing it since we were all babies. I'm thirty-two. And my feet stopped growing when I was sixteen."

"Wow," I said. "That's a lot of size-eleven poupons."

Ben laughed. "Yes. That's why that pair you're holding is unworn. Haven't needed them yet."

"So . . . you don't mind if I put my bare feet in these slippers, right? My socks are soaked, too."

"Go right ahead. I'll be getting another pair tomorrow at *Réveillon*."

My feet were cold and clammy, and I pulled them together, knees wide, so I could wrap my hands around them to warm them up a bit. In the process, my knee brushed against his arm and sent a warm shot straight down to my toes. I pulled the first slipper on, then the other, instantly feeling about 200 percent happier. "It's a Christmas miracle," I said to Ben. "Thank you—these are so cozy."

He glanced at me and smiled. "A Christmas miracle with two days to spare," he said.

I groaned inwardly. Just *two* days to secure this permit. Normally, permits are secured weeks in advance. How was I going to pull this off?

His phone rang. He answered the call on speaker.

"*Salut*, Paul," Ben said.

"Are you driving? Did I catch you at a bad time?" Paul asked. I tried to recall if I'd met a Paul during my stay in Chelsea.

"No, no, it's great. Just doing a few errands."

"Ahh, *d'accord*. So I suppose our lunch meeting is off then?"

"Was that today?" Ben's voice suddenly sounded strained and I looked over at him. I may have only known Ben for a little more than twenty-four hours, but I could already tell he did not seem like the kind of guy who forgot about a lunch meeting.

"Yes." There was a pause. "Well, no matter, weather's terrible anyway. Let's just chat now, shall we?"

"Sure. I've got a few minutes."

"Busy man. Following in your father's footsteps," Paul commented, though his tone didn't really make it sound like it was a compliment. "Right, well, I wanted to talk about Marcel. He said he tried calling you yesterday and again today?"

"Did he? Things have been a bit hectic, Paul. It *is* the holidays, you know. Busiest time of the year at the farm." I leaned my head against the window and turned it slightly to watch Ben from the corner of my eye as he carried on this conversation. First, he'd forgotten a lunch, then he'd missed calls? This plot was getting interesting.

"Ah well, I said I'd give you a call. You know, they're still talking about the development project over at Roche-Bourgoyne."

Ben paused, and when he spoke again his voice sounded stiff. "I thought they were interested in moving it to Wakefield."

"Turns out they couldn't get the land they were hoping for. So they've turned their attention back to Chelsea."

Outside the window, the road wound this way and that, like a string of Christmas lights on a tree. To the right of the pickup truck was a large pond that looked like it should be on a Christmas card, perhaps with kids in brightly colored snow-suits and hats joyfully skating on it. But there was no way any kids would be playing outside in this weather. I glanced at the clock on the dashboard. Twelve-fifteen. How much longer was it going to take to get to the mayor's cottage? I wondered. And why hadn't we caught up to her at this point?

Suddenly, my phone pinged and I turned it over to look at the screen.

How did it go with the mayor of Wakefield? Mireille asked.

Not sure, I texted back. *Still trying to track her down. With Ben.*

Bonne chance, she texted. A second later she added a hot pepper emoji. I laughed though I didn't know why she was sending that emoji in particular. I turned my attention back to Ben, whose voice had just risen an octave.

"Paul, you know how I feel," he was saying. "And I know you feel the same way. Please don't be swayed because Marcel is a friend."

"It isn't about that, son," Paul said gently. "You know I've always thought about the town first, and what's best for it. But we can't deny that people are moving away. There are no jobs. This development would help."

My eyes widened, and I tried to focus on my phone so Ben didn't think I was eavesdropping—which I totally was. I wondered how well Paul knew Ben. If the mayor wouldn't let a movie crew come in for a couple of days, he certainly wasn't going to be excited about a new development. Even *I* could see that, and I didn't even really know Ben. The reason why he'd "missed" lunch with Paul and the phone calls from Marcel was becoming clear.

"If there are no jobs, people are going to buy units to flip them as investments," Ben countered. "It's not going to generate jobs."

"But there's a plan. Now it includes a hotel."

Ben sighed. "Great, so bring in tourists that the town can't support? Paul, I don't mean for this to sound harsh, but you're not thinking straight."

"Ben, I've given it so much thought. It's all I've thought about. For months. I haven't wanted to bring it up with you because I knew you needed time to heal, and that you wouldn't want to think about this right away."

Heal from what? I glanced over at Ben. His jaw was tight. Past him, out the window, I could see a cabin nestled in the trees.

"But this isn't the short term, Ben," Paul was saying. "The hotel brings visitors. The spa is already a draw, the main street a bonus. The hotel will bring *jobs*. Those people will move to the area."

"The last thing Chelsea needs is more density, Paul." Ben's voice was harder now and his knuckles were white gripping the wheel. Was it the wind or the conversation?

"Hear me out. They're offering a competitive plan to bring them to the area, a discount for living in the building."

"That's just to get the buy-in the developer needs to break ground." Ben lifted a hand off the wheel to rub his forehead. "I guarantee it. And whoever these people are, looking for work, they're not thinking. What if their hours get cut? What if the hotel doesn't get the traffic, and then they raise the rent? What if Chelsea can't keep up?"

But Paul was not giving up and I raised my eyebrows at his persistence. "It can. But, Ben, if the population continues to decrease at the rate it has been and you don't find a way to bring more tourism to the area, with or without this development, then the shops that are in Chelsea right now won't survive. So you start with a project like this. It increases revenue for everyone in the town. The shops get more stock, hire more staff to help more customers. It's a cycle, and I just don't see how it can't work. And I also don't see how it can hurt to try. Particularly when there are no other options coming our way."

The sleet was heavier and more intense now, as though mimicking the conversation I was listening to. I thought about my parents' marriage and all the years they avoided any sort of conflict. They'd run away from each other, distracting themselves from the problems in their relationship. They certainly never had an honest conversation like the one Ben and Paul were having. Their avoidance of conflict was the main reason I never ran away from a tough conversation, or an argument. Even at work, I almost ran into the conflict. Conflict meant you *cared*. So I found myself rooting for Ben in this situation, because at least they were *talking* about the problem.

"Okay, Paul. I've heard enough," Ben said, cutting off Paul in mid-sentence. He said something else in French.

"Ben, just think about it," Paul said. "Think about it over the next few weeks. In the new year, we should talk."

"My father would never allow this," Ben said quietly.

Paul paused for a moment before responding. "Your father is dead, Ben."

CHAPTER NINE

Tuesday, December 23, 12:30 p.m.

Silence filled the air after Ben angrily ended the call, and for the last few minutes I fixated on the swooshing of the windshield wipers and wasn't sure whether I should look at Ben, say something, or just stay quiet. I listened intently to the sleet, which was banging a staticky rhythm on the roof and sides of the truck. I knew I should probably stay quiet, but staying quiet wasn't really my style, and maybe he wanted to talk about it?

"So *that* sounded like a fun conversation . . . ," I said tentatively.

"I don't want to talk about it," Ben muttered.

I ignored him. "Who is this Paul guy anyway?"

Ben finally looked over at me, his jaw hard. "Zoey, I said that I don't want to talk about it, and certainly not with you. You have no idea what's going on in Chelsea."

I had enough of an idea that Ben didn't want Chelsea to change—not by development and not from a movie. But why—that much I didn't know, but now wanted to. "So enlighten me. Maybe an outsider's ear is exactly what you need."

"I didn't ask for someone to talk to." He sighed.

"I think someone needs a gummy bear," I said, and he looked at me again.

"What?" He paused. "You think this is because I'm hangry?"

I shrugged. "If the snack fits."

Ben slowed the truck as we approached an intersection where the traffic lights were off. No green, no red, no flashing amber. Nothing. "Is that weird?" I turned to him, hoping to be reassured. My hot irritation with Ben was quickly cooled by worry and I wanted him to tell me that these lights had never worked, not that something was amiss.

"Power must be out," Ben said. He cautiously brought the truck to a complete stop and we sat there for longer than seemed necessary, given there was no traffic. Truth be told, we hadn't passed another car for miles. I looked around. The intersection was surrounded by dense forest, the trees tall, white, and imposing, the tops disappearing into the gray sky. There were no buildings or other signs of civilization. I peered through the sleet-streaked glass, holding my breath. The rain competed with the rhythmic sound of the windshield wipers and an unfamiliar French Christmas song on the radio.

After what felt like an eternity, he tentatively began to inch forward, and I breathed a sigh of relief as we cleared to the other side.

"So what time *is* your flight out?" Ben asked as he picked up speed.

"Well, uh . . . I didn't want to book a flight, since, until this morning, I hadn't been sure what time I'd actually be leaving Chelsea," I said, fibbing. "You know, because I didn't know what time I'd get to the airport."

"What?" Ben turned to me, his eyes wide. "That's stupid."

"Tell me how you really feel."

"It's two days till Christmas and we're on the cusp of a serious storm, Zoey. If you have any hope of making it to your family by Christmas you *need* to be on a flight today. Hell, you needed to be on a flight yesterday. If the power's starting to go out, it's not good. I'm surprised we still have cell service."

"I get that it's bad, but it's not *that* bad, is it? Like, people must be used to this weather around here?"

"Says the woman who lives in sunny California. The *tempête de verglas*?"

There was that phrase again, the one I'd heard so many times.

"What *is* the *tempête de verglas*? Isn't it just a bad snowstorm?"

"It means 'the ice storm.'"

"Like that movie that came out when we were kids? The one with Christina Ricci where the parents go to the key party?" I gave a small laugh, trying to calm my nerves, which were rattling in my body like ice in a glass.

"Hardly. Ever heard of the ice storm of 1998?"

I shake my head, staring blankly at him.

"It was one of the worst storms in history," he said. "And it sort of came out of nowhere. First there's snow, then sleet, then rain—"As Ben rattled off the weather we'd experienced so far today, I shivered. "But then the temperature dropped suddenly, freezing everything in sight. Most of Eastern Canada and the Northeastern U.S. was covered in a thick layer of ice. The weight of the ice brought down power lines and trees. No one was prepared for it. Power went out. No heat or water either. People were stranded. There was this feeling of isolation, like it was the end of the world." A wave of nostalgia clouded Ben's face.

"Whoa," I said, my body going numb. "And you were what, just a kid?"

He nodded. "I remember it so clearly even though I had to have been only about five or six. It was a Monday—the storm had started on the Sunday but we all still went to school the next day." He looked at me and explained, "It's Quebec, things don't really stop for weather. But school ended up letting out early and the buses drove us home. My cousin Xavier got out at my house. His parents left work early and came over, neighbors, too. People were worried but also just sort of excited and interested, like we weren't sure what to make of it all. We all hung out in the basement, but once it was time for everyone to go home for dinner, there was just no way anyone was leaving. We made up beds so everyone could stay over. And we lost power before we even went to bed that night. Thankfully we have a wood-burning stove so we were at least able to heat our house. A lot of people weren't so lucky."

"That must have been really scary," I said.

"It was crazy." Ben nodded. "But as a kid you don't really realize how bad it is. I just thought it was fun to have so many people in the house. But now, as an adult . . . you realize how serious it can be. People died in that ice storm."

"Okay, but what are the odds that happens again?" I challenged. "And it's nothing like earthquakes. Now that's something to be worried about. And yet people don't leave LA."

"I'm not trying to compare the ice storm to an earthquake, but this one's going to be serious. We shouldn't even be out here. We should turn back." Ben's phone pinged, interrupting our debate. He unlocked it before passing it to me. "Can you see who that is?"

The phone was cold in my hand. "Xavier," I said. "He says: *U still picking up Delphine?*"

Delphine. I'd forgotten about Noémie asking Ben to pick Delphine up at the Montreal airport today.

"You're still going to the airport?"

"That was the plan." His jaw clicked.

"But you just said you wanted to head back. Were you planning to leave Delphine stranded at the airport?" I looked at him in disgust. "God, you're a terrible boyfriend."

"Ex, not that it's any of your business. And I was not planning to leave her stranded. Her flight has already been delayed once. There's a chance it'll be canceled altogether. I actually thought that"—he nodded at the phone—"was her texting to let me know what's going on with her flight. Can you make sure she hasn't texted?"

"So you're just gonna leave Xavier hanging?"

"Tell him I'm not sure about the airport. But that I'll be over early tomorrow, regardless, to help set up and make the caribou."

"Caribou?" My fingers hovered over the letters, debating how much of that message I actually needed to type.

"It's a warm drink. Quebec specialty. I make it over the fire in Xavier's backyard every Christmas Eve, for *Réveillon*. Oh, actually, can you let him know I've got a ton of red wine and maple syrup but ask him if he has an extra bottle of rye? Just in case we need a second batch."

"Anything else? Maybe I can type out the last three chapters of the book you're reading for you?" I teased. He clucked his tongue and shook his head. "You *asked*."

I typed *Text u later*, then exited out of that chat and clicked on Delphine's name. My heart pounded as I read the last text from her: *Can't wait to see you.* Above that, a message from Ben confirmed he'd be at the airport by five. I wasn't on Team Delphine, but I was intrigued with the useful tidbit of information that Ben was going to the airport.

"So you *are* going to the airport."

He gave me a sidelong glance. "No."

"No, what?" I said innocently.

"I'm not driving you to the airport," he said. "That's where you're going with this, *oui*?"

"I'm not sure whether to be offended or impressed."

"I know your type."

"I'm not a *type*." What would that type *be*, anyway? Ambitious, single women with no plans for Christmas?

"Why *not*?" I challenged him. "If you're going there anyway . . ."

"Because you're driving me crazy," he grumbled.

A loud crack echoed around us. Startled, I dropped the phone. I reached down to pick it up, and as I was sitting back in my seat, a thick branch whipped into view, landing on the windshield and getting trapped by the wipers. I grabbed Ben's arm. He didn't slam on the brakes, but rather pumped them, which slowed the truck, even on the ice-covered road. The branch flew off, and he let out a low whistle, then patted my hand with his free hand. I exhaled.

"Are you okay?"

"Uh-huh," I lied. "I can't believe that didn't break the windshield." My heart felt like it was taking up my entire chest.

"Seriously," he agreed, craning his neck forward. There was no way to avoid more branches, if that's what he was thinking. Trees lined both sides of the road, their branches swaying.

Another gust of wind rocked the truck. Ben gripped the wheel tighter, struggling to keep control as the tires seemed to slip every few seconds. I could feel tension emanating from him.

"This doesn't seem good," I said, my voice tight with fear. "Should you slow down?" I said, even though I knew we were only going about ten miles an hour. I also knew that no one likes a back seat driver, but I didn't care. I was worried.

In the actual back seat, Simon was alert. He was sitting in the middle, his nose resting on the center console between us again. I rubbed his long snout, mostly to comfort myself.

"That's why I said we should turn back," Ben replied, his face grim. He seemed to be ping-ponging back and forth, trying to decide what to do. "I've got to be home for *Réveillon*. I can't miss it, not this year of all years . . ."

"The *Réve-what*? What is that?"

He furrowed his brow. "*Réveillon.* The ultimate Christmas tradition. Surely you have that in your film?"

I shook my head. Not yet, anyway. But there was no time like the present to pump him for authentic Quebecois traditions for my film.

"Thank god I didn't give you that permit then," he said.

"God, you're awful—" I blurted out, but got cut off by a loud crack as the truck veered off to the right. I gasped and reached for Ben's arm again. I wanted to hold tight to him, with both arms, but it was also probably a terrible idea to be holding on to him at all. I released my grip, instead grasping the sides of my seat, my fingernails digging into the soft leather.

A large tree loomed in front of us. Beyond that, the headlights from the truck illuminated the dark expanse of a pond, its surface partially frozen and treacherous.

"Watch out!" I pointed. Simon barked, clearly sensing danger.

Ben steered back onto the road, narrowly avoiding the tree.

"I thought you had studs," I said tightly.

"I do, but it's no match—the roads are icing over as soon as the freezing rain hits the ground. It's the *tempête*. It's getting worse by the minute—and a lot earlier than it was supposed to, that's for sure." Despite this, it felt as though the truck had its grip on the road—at least for a moment.

"How far are we from . . . the main road or . . . anything?"

"I'm not sure," Ben said, which didn't quell my anxiety.

"Shouldn't you know where we are?" It sounded more critical than I meant. "Didn't you grow up here?"

"I never take this route," he said tersely, then glared at me. "We're only on this road for you. To get you to the mayor's house. I'm the one who wanted to turn back, remember?"

We went silent. Ben kept his hands at ten and two on the steering wheel, slowly inching the truck forward. I focused on rubbing Simon's nose and scratching his ears. The wipers continued their superspeed dance across the windshield. Every so often, the truck would jerk to one side or the other and I'd grab at my seat in panic until Ben righted us. I wavered between keeping my eyes wide, not to miss anything, and shutting them tight, bracing myself for the worst. Each second felt like an hour, like we were moving in slo-mo.

Up ahead, an abandoned farmhouse, close to the road, came into view, its roof partially collapsed, its windows smashed in. It had given up. I couldn't give up. At this point I couldn't think past the mayor's house. We had to get there.

Then, suddenly, everything shifted into time-lapse mode. As we drove over a bump, the truck's back end swung out. Ben eased his foot off the gas and twisted the steering wheel to correct it, but the truck kept sliding to the right, impossible to stop.

"Dammit," Ben said, and I screamed as we sailed toward a cluster of trees, just to the right of the farmhouse. I could see a lake right beyond the farmhouse, mere feet away, and I froze in horror, praying that we weren't headed for it. With a sickening *thunk* the truck smashed into the thick trunk of an old maple, the force of the collision pushing me against my seat belt, knocking the breath out of me. I tried to scream again but nothing came out. Then everything went black.

CHAPTER TEN

Tuesday, December 23, 1:00 p.m.

Everything was blurry. I blinked a few times, and the world in front of me came into focus. The sleet was still pounding on the windows, relentless. That's what was making everything blurry—the windshield was covered in a thick layer of snow and rain. I rubbed my neck. It was sore. I twisted it to the left and let out a wail. Amid the curtains of deflated airbags, Ben was slumped forward on the steering wheel, lifeless.

"Ben?"

He didn't stir.

"Ben?!" My stomach clenched. I reached over to touch his shoulder, then pulled him back from the steering wheel. His head rolled back against the headrest. Simon suddenly jumped up from the back seat and began licking Ben's face as though it were coated in gravy.

A frightened, stilted scream escaped my lips and I clamped my mouth shut. *Breathe.* What did I learn in first-aid training?

My hand shook as I reached over to put two fingers on his neck. It was warm. His skin was soft, with just a bit of stubble where his beard was trimmed short. I quickly found his pulse. It felt normal, steady. *Okay, he's alive. He's alive.* I examined his face and his body. He didn't look like he had any injuries.

Okay, so he was unconscious. I pulled my phone out of my pocket and flipped it over. Who could I call? Who was going to come and rescue us? The picture of Stella and me as kids, in matching striped pajamas, sitting in front of a Christmas tree, stared back at me. So did the words in the top right corner that read: *No Service.*

I groaned in frustration. I'd probably have better luck with Ben's phone—maybe he was on a different, local provider and still had service? I could call Paul. Or Ben's mother. Or Mireille or Lise or Renee. Surely he had their numbers in his phone. Surely he had the whole town's numbers in his phone. I rummaged around for the phone in the console between us, but couldn't find it. I leaned over to look down at Ben's feet and spotted it on the floor next to the brake pedal. I unbuckled my seat belt, pressing my right hand to the dashboard to prevent myself from sliding forward. The truck was at a steep angle and I was worried that too much movement could send us straight for the pond. I leaned across the console and over his legs, picking up the phone. The plastic case felt cold in my hand. I tapped the screen to bring it to life. The phone was locked, but it didn't matter: Ben didn't have service anyway.

We shouldn't even be out here, Ben had said. *We should turn back.* This was what he'd been worried about. And I'd forced us to keep going.

I took a few deep breaths, trying to slow my heart, which felt like it was running away, trying to escape my body, to get out of this situation. Could I blame it? Simon nuzzled against my face and I gave him a hug. I was glad he was safe, and grateful for the company.

I looked outside. The tree we had crashed into was a foot away from the windshield. The truck was angled precipitously toward the icy pond, less than ten feet from the farmhouse, and I was suddenly grateful for the giant maple tree that had stopped us in our tracks. The tree was preventing us from sliding farther toward the ice. But what if the weight of the truck pushing against the tree was too much for the tree to bear? Would the pond's ice support a truck? Somewhere, something hissed. I squinted through the freezing rain. Was that smoke coming out of the hood of the truck? We had to get out of here. *I* had to get us out of here.

Simon looked to me, his eyes wide as if to say *What now?*

"I know, boy, I'm trying to figure that out." Even though the farmhouse was close, Ben probably weighed at least 80 pounds more than me. How would I get him to the farmhouse, let alone out of the truck?

But what other option did I have?

I put my soggy UGGs back on, then looked around the truck, then climbed between the seats into the back beside Simon. I rummaged around for essentials: my coat, and hats and gloves for both of us. Then I tentatively maneuvered myself back into the front, praying again that the shift of my weight wouldn't make a difference to the precarious teetering of the truck. I pushed Ben's hat and gloves into my pocket, slung my bag across my body, and braced myself. The freezing rain was coming down in ribbons. I pulled on the metal handle to push open the door. It didn't budge. I tried again. Nope, it wasn't opening. My throat felt tight, like I was about to start bawling. I tried one more time, pushing my entire body weight hard against the door. This time it opened just enough to let me squeeze out. I cautiously set the toe of my UGG on the frozen ground and immediately slipped. Thankfully, my foot caught on a raised branch poking through the cloudy surface. Simon whimpered and I turned back to look at him. "It's okay, Simon. Zoey's gonna get you out the other side. Don't you worry."

The wind whipped the pom-pom on the top of my hat. I wrapped my thin wool coat tighter, doing up the measly two buttons and pulling the collar up, but it wasn't going to do anything against the heavy rain and snow. Holding on to the slick surface of the truck, I stepped gingerly around the back of the cab to Ben's side of the truck. Ben's door handle was frozen in place, and I couldn't move it. And because of the way the truck had wedged itself against the tree, the handle was at shoulder height, making it hard for me to get any leverage. I needed something to pry it open. There was probably something in the emergency kit, but I was worried about shifting any major weight around. My fingers dug into my bag until they finally wrapped around my house keys. I flipped one key forward and dug it into the door handle to chisel away at the ice. Freezing rain beat against the side of my face and I tilted my head to try to deflect the stinging pellets. My hair was slick on my face and I swiped at it, but I didn't stop hacking away at the door handle. I had to get Ben out.

Slowly, the ice started to chip off, and then the metal door handle lifted. The door swung open and Simon leaped out onto the ice. Holding on tightly to the side of the door, I leaned over Ben. "Ben," I said. He didn't move. "Ben," I said again, louder, and shaking his arm. "Ben!" This time I shouted. Simon barked at my feet. I removed my glove and touched Ben's cheek with the flat of my palm. It was warm, soft, alive. I pressed the button on his seat belt buckle to release the belt, gently pulling it across his body with one hand and holding him in place with the other. How was I going to get him out of here?

One step at a time, Zoey.

I just had to make a decision and act on it. I was Ben's only hope. I had to put everything I had into getting Ben and me out of this situation and to safety.

For years, in my late teens and early twenties, I'd been a lifeguard. That training was ten years ago now, but once you learn how to move a body that's much bigger than yours, you never forget. That, combined with three HIIT workouts a week this past year, paid off.

I maneuvered Ben to the left, his back toward me, so I could slip my arms under his armpits. I clasped my gloved hands together over his broad, firm chest, and slowly leaned him back, letting his head fall to the crook between my neck and shoulder. I took one step back, preparing myself for the weight of his body. Breathing deeply, my nose filling with his scent of cedar and soap, I took another step back. Ben's upper body fell onto my chest and I braced my legs, contracting my quad muscles.

Step, pull. Step, pull. Slowly, inch by inch, Ben slid out of the truck as I put one foot behind the next. I was already breathing heavily, and we were only a few feet from the truck. I buried my face beside his to protect us both from the sleet and wind, which was whipping, swirling, coming at us from all directions. One step, then the next. I had to just keep moving.

Simon raced toward the farmhouse as though knowing that's where we were headed.

My hands were numb through my soaked, impractical gloves. My feet were frozen. But my body was on fire, the back of my neck drenched in sweat.

I didn't let myself think about what would happen if the farmhouse was filled with snow, if the roof was completely collapsed. If it was infested by rats. Or worse, by other people who wouldn't let us in.

The wind whipped my hat away, but I couldn't let go of Ben to go after it. I tried to convince myself that his pine smell was wafting from a warm bath. Maybe the farmhouse wouldn't be so terrible on the inside. Maybe there'd be an old claw-foot tub. I imagined myself soaking in it—that's why I was wet, not because we were stranded in the middle of an ice storm.

I was less than five steps from the farmhouse, but it felt like five miles.

The ground was thick with slush, and my feet sank through, straight up to my knee, far past the tops of my UGGs and soaking my pants. I stopped to look at Ben. The lower half of his body was soaked from me dragging him through the snow and sludge, and his upper half was wet, too, but from the freezing rain pounding on us.

A flash of something moving caught my eye. My heart thudded. I craned my neck to see past the trio of trees to my right. Was it just a branch? And then I saw two beady eyes looking at me. A deer. Neither of us broke gaze.

The deer looked like the one I saw when I first got into Chelsea, but, of course, it couldn't be the same one. We were so far from there, and this place was probably full of deer.

A moment later, it finally blinked, then seemingly nodded at me before turning and disappearing from sight.

I exhaled and took another breath. I could do this.

I readjusted my arms under Ben's arms and gave him one final pull toward the farmhouse. The steps were covered in ice, and I laid him down, then gripped the railing to pull myself up, praying it wouldn't give way. I twisted the rusty door handle, clicking it back and forth, but it wouldn't budge. Simon inspected the open window to the right of the door, looking from me back to Ben, as though deciding what to do next.

I moved to stand next to him and peered inside. It was mostly empty, but seemed safe. I carefully, gently, began climbing through the window, making sure not to catch my clothes on the broken glass. A moment later I was standing in a square room. I closed my eyes for a moment and took a deep breath. Tears pooled in my eyes, threatening to spill over at any moment. I'd made it. I swiped at my eyes with the backs of my hands and the farmhouse came into clearer view.

The floor was damp, puddles in places. Sleet streamed into one corner where the roof had caved in, a pile of snow and slush accumulating on the floor. The place smelled dank and musty. I looked around. The room was empty save for a lone rocking chair, missing its seat, in another corner. I walked into the middle of the room, the floorboards creaking. The kitchen to the right had old wooden countertops that were sagging and cracked. A broken table—only two legs still intact—was overturned. In the sink, a few pots and pans were caked with dirt. Cobwebs hung in the corners of the room, and the cream-colored walls were stained and peeling.

Despite the neglect, little details of the home remained— the far wall featured a crooked photo, a clock. On the open shelves, an old board game, a lamp, a stack of records. It was clear the place had once been loved and cared for, though whoever had called this place home had long ago abandoned it.

Satisfied it was safe, I turned around and hurried back to the door, opening it.

Ben was still on the steps where I'd left him, but Simon was now at his side, nuzzling him. The husky looked up at me and then made a noise, like a door creaking open, as though he was trying to talk. "We're going to get him inside, aren't we?" I said to Simon. "I'll need your help."

I knew nothing about what it meant to be unconscious, only that Ben would need time to recover. And he definitely needed to be warm. He must be freezing in his wet clothes.

I reached down to get Ben into the now-familiar position, looping my arms under his armpits once again, then maneuvered him toward the door, over the threshold, and inside. My arms shook. My fingers had lost all feeling, but I gave everything I had to pull Ben as far away from any windows and the cold wind as I could, to the middle of the room. Should he be on his back, on his side? Should I curl him into the fetal position so he could keep himself warm? I looked around, searching for something, anything, to bundle him up in, but then felt silly. *Don't be ridiculous, Zoey. It's not as though there would be a blanket lying around in this place, just neatly folded on a shelf, waiting for you.*

I turned my attention back to Ben, and began working his wet coat off. Underneath, I found that his thin navy sweater was also wet. My heart felt heavy with worry. I had created this situation—I had insisted we keep driving into the storm to the mayor's cottage. If Ben had had his way he'd be home by now. Instead he was here, in this dilapidated place in the middle of nowhere, unconscious. I looked at his face. He was still, his breathing shallow and labored. Getting to this farmhouse had been the goal, but now that we were here, it wasn't enough. I pulled out my phone and stared at the screen: it was black. I pulled out his: still no service. In a panic I spun around, searching the walls for a landline. No such luck.

I turned my attention back to Ben. I needed to get him warm, quickly. I looked down at my clothes. Both my pants and top were soaked from the storm and sweat, from getting us here. Despair washed over me. What was I going to do? I pulled off my gloves and blew on my hands. What would happen to Ben if I didn't get him out of his wet clothes?

Wait—the truck. My suitcase. Ben's emergency kit. Dry clothes. The sleeping bag, the candles, the matches. If I could get them and bring them back to the farmhouse, we would have something to help us warm up.

I looked toward the broken window. Outside, the wind was howling, the freezing rain still pounding down as heavily as ever. Was I really going to go back out there? Just the thought filled me with doubt, but I tried to ignore it. If I'd learned anything from working in the entertainment industry, it was that self-doubt was not an action plan. It was a helpless move that showed weakness. I was tougher than that.

If Simon were a Saint Bernard, he could go out to the truck and retrieve our things, and I could stay with Ben, but he wasn't. No, I'd have to go alone. I squared my shoulders and pulled open the door, which made Simon jump to his feet and look at me curiously. I shook my head and pointed to Ben. "Stay," I said firmly. If Ben woke up he could be scared or confused. Having Simon by his side would at least reassure him.

The husky walked over to Ben and sat down, his eyes on me.

"Good dog."

I stepped out onto the porch and closed the door. In the few minutes that I'd been inside the farmhouse, the temperature outside seemed to have taken a steep nosedive. One tentative step at a time. Just as I was taking my third step, I heard a loud crunch and the ground collapsed under my foot, sending it through the ice, down into the two feet of snow and slush below. I put all my weight on my right foot to pull my left foot out but the added weight caused the ice to give way under my right foot, sending it down just as my left foot broke free.

I swiped at a tear, and pulled myself onto the ice again just as the limb of a large maple broke off and fell to the ground in front of me. I gasped, then jumped aside, slipped on the ice, and fell on my hip. I screamed in frustration, pulled myself up again and took a few more steps toward the truck. But in the time we'd been gone the truck had slid past the tree, and the front end of it was submerged in the pond. I gasped. Water covered the driver's side up to the seat, and I knew there was a good chance that by the time this storm was over, the truck would entirely be in the water. We'd been right to leave. Bracing myself on another tree trunk, the rain stinging my face, I pulled open the halfdoor that gave access to the back seat.

The emergency kit was on the floor, behind the front seats, and I gently pulled it out, paranoid that any movement might jostle the truck enough to send it completely into the pond. I placed the kit on the frozen ground and then reached for my suitcase. Once both were out of the truck, I shut the door and began walking back toward the farmhouse. Both cases were heavy and unwieldy, the wheels of mine catching on the ice and snow with nearly every step. Tears—some from the sleet and some from sheer exhaustion—hovered on my eyelids, but I gritted my teeth and dug my feet into the ice, squeezing my thighs to steady myself.

A few minutes later, I had made it back into the farmhouse. Simon, who'd been at Ben's side, ran over to me, wagging his tail and nuzzling his snout against my leg. I'd hoped that Ben would wake up in the few minutes I was gone, but he was exactly as I'd left him. Still breathing. Still warm. Still unconscious. I quickly stood up. I had to get him out of his wet clothes otherwise he would freeze. With numb fingers I started with his boots, fumbling as I untied the double-knotted laces. I worked his sweater up his body, sliding his arms out and then the rest of the sweater over his head. Underneath, his navy T-shirt rode up, revealing his taut stomach. The T-shirt was cold and damp, and I paused, then lifted that off, too. My breath caught in my throat. His chest was broad, his skin smooth, with little hair. On his left arm a tattoo of a tall, thin evergreen tree wrapped around his bicep. So the Christmas tree farm guy had a Christmas tree tattoo. My eyes wandered over his torso, taking in his smooth skin. It was difficult not to stare. But I shook myself out of it and took a breath. I had to get his pants off. I focused on his belt buckle, then pulled the square metal back, and it released the prong from the wet brown leather of his belt. What if Ben were to wake up at this very moment, just as I was undoing his pants? What would he think? *He would think you were trying to save his life.*

And I was—while also admiring the scenery. And what scenery it was. Undoing the single button at the top of Ben's jeans revealed a whorl of fine brown hair that led from his navel to . . .

Don't get distracted, Zo.

But it was legit distracting. I gulped. Although I was wet and freezing, a rush of heat coursed through my body.

I pulled down the zipper. My fingers shook as I began shimmying his jeans over his hips. I paused. Was he going to be one of those big-boxers-with-dogs-on-them kind of underwear-wearing guy? Or would he . . .

He was the smooth, tight, boxer-brief kind of guy. I let out an involuntary satisfied sigh, then pulled the jeans down and off his legs and into a heap on the floor. Now I had to get Ben warmed up. I opened the emergency kit and pulled out the sleeping bag, quickly unzipping it and wrapping it around him, tucking it in at the sides. Would that be warm enough? I should get him dressed, but one look at the dry jeans was too much. As I considered what to do, I noticed that my own hands were trembling. My soaked clothes were making me colder by the second. I had to get them off.

I took a deep breath and stripped off my jeans, then my sweater. Quelling all doubts, as well as any thoughts at all, because if I did think about it I would perhaps realize how crazy this was, I got under the sleeping bag beside Ben. I retucked the sleeping bag around us, then ran a palm over his back, his arms, his chest, to create friction. I wrapped my arm around him, and closed my eyes. Skin to skin, our body heat intermingled, and I listened to his breathing, slow and steady. Then the thought occurred: What if he didn't wake up?

I couldn't think like that. I squeezed him tight against me. Ben *had* to wake up.

This—taking care of someone in an abandoned farmhouse while they were unconscious—was probably the closest I'd come to a domestic life in a house in the past five years. Even with Tomas, there was nothing like this. Sure, we had a nice couch and an Eames chair that I found on Facebook Marketplace, and Tomas had hung some bright original paintings on the walls—but there was no *caring* for each other. There were parties. There was hot sex. There was the planned vacation to Tenerife. But there was very little snuggling and watching a movie, or taking care of Tomas when he was sick, or Tomas making me dinner when I was working on a deadline. With him, it was all appearances and nothing inside—like the beautiful porcelain Royal Doulton figurines my grandmother would collect, the hole in the base revealing their empty interiors.

I wanted more in a relationship—inside jokes, crossing places to visit off a shared bucket list, getting a little bungalow together. Caring for someone—though maybe not while they were unconscious. It would've been nice if they could conduct a conversation. I would've preferred to start with a hangover, or the flu. And perhaps with someone who liked me and whom I actually liked, not like my actual nemesis.

Whom I happened to be spooning, nearly naked, my arms wrapped around his chiseled chest, my bra pressed against his back.

Oh Ben.

I had always been a go-getter, someone who took charge and made things happen—like standing in Roberto's office four days ago, taking the film-permit issue into my own hands. I got things done myself because I knew what to do. But now, stranded in an abandoned farmhouse, I was the only one who could fix this problem, but I had no idea what to do next. I hugged Ben tighter, and wrapped my bare legs around his. My frozen toes were beginning to feel a little less icy. Simon sauntered over and nuzzled my neck. Then he turned around once, twice, and settled down beside me.

For months, this film had been the most important thing in my life—so important that anything that wasn't the film was put on the backburner. I'd said no to beach days with friends, a girls' trip to Cabo, lunch dates with colleagues, even nights out on the town with Tomas. I hadn't even committed to seeing Stella during my Christmas break. And now look at me. I was thirty and sandwiched between a dog and a small-town mayor on the floor of an abandoned farmhouse in the middle of nowhere. I'd always told myself that my professional success was the most important thing; that it didn't matter if I missed *another* holiday with family, because one day, once I was married and had kids, I'd be home for Christmas. I'd get the big house with the fireplace. We'd cut a tree and hang stockings. I'd make a gingerbread house. I'd start the traditions I'd longed to have my entire life, once I met the right person and got married and all that. And that just hadn't happened yet, so, for now, I'd focus on work.

When Tomas and I were together, I'd just do whatever he wanted to do for Christmas. Two years ago, we celebrated December 25th on a beach in Aruba; last year, we'd gone parasailing in Cancun. These were amazing experiences, and I'd loved them, for sure, but what did I have to show for it in this moment? And now my movie was in major jeopardy because of this guy I was lying next to, whom I couldn't even help? What was the point of all my ambition if I was just going to die out in the Quebec wilderness?

But I couldn't think like this—I had to focus on this moment and what I was going to do right now. I couldn't change any of the details that had led up to us being here, and I certainly couldn't predict the future.

Action is the antidote to anxiety, I reminded myself as though I were scrolling through cheesy inspo quotes on Instagram. I closed my eyes and thought about my film, playing through scenes. Ruby and Jacques's story always kept me going, kept me focused, whenever I felt beat down by other aspects of my life. It would get me through now, too. Could I incorporate some of the details of the past few days into the film? I felt my mind starting to clear and a sense of purpose and motivation creeping in. I looked around the farmhouse, picturing it as the cabin Ruby rented for the holidays. The far wall, with the clock, transformed into a roaring fire in an old stone fireplace surrounded by a hearth of rough-hewn logs, casting a golden light across the room. I could almost feel the heat, could nearly smell the woodsmoke. The crackle of logs filled the air. I looked around, letting my imagination consume me. The pot in the sink was dirty because Jacques had made hot toddies for him and Ruby after they'd wrapped all the gifts for his many cousins. Wait—Jacques didn't have cousins; *Ben* had loads of them. I considered it, but maybe it would be a nice touch for Jacques to have a big extended family. As he and Ruby sipped their drinks and talked about their favorite Christmas traditions on the cozy and comfortable couch, Jacques would fall asleep, and after a few minutes, Ruby would curl up beside him, resting her head on his shoulder. She wouldn't let him spend the night—what would her girls think?—but she didn't want to wake him up just yet, didn't want to let him go.

I yawned. It was likely only two or three in the afternoon at this point, but because it was so dark outside, it felt like night. Not to mention that the stress of the accident, of getting Ben to the farmhouse, had made me so tired. I tightened my arm over Ben's warm chest and rested my chin on his shoulder.

Even if he was grumpy, and kind of rude and selfish, and was stopping me from achieving one of my life's goals, he was probably a good guy. People seemed to like him. He had stopped a really drunk guy from harassing me, and he seemed very close to Xavier and his kids. He'd taken over his father's business. And he was mayor of Chelsea when he was so young. But he'd wasted my time in the town, when he knew without the town permit there was no way I'd be able to make my film. Though he'd tried to get me to Wakefield. He'd genuinely seemed like he wanted to help me—provided it wasn't in his town. But he was also stubborn and self-righteous and utterly maddening. But he was so good-looking and fit. So were lots of guys. So why was I so attracted to him? What was it about him? I could feel Ben's chest rising and falling against my skin. His skin was so soft. He smelled so good.

I sighed, and closed my eyes.

CHAPTER ELEVEN

Tuesday, December 23, 3:30 p.m.

Ben stirred, causing my eyes to fly open. He made a low groaning sound. I untangled myself from the sleeping bag, stood, and promptly tripped over Simon. I got myself vertical again. Ben's eyes were open, and looking at me.

"Oh thank god," I said, not hiding my relief.

Ben scratched his head. "Why are you in your underwear?" I looked down. There I was, half-naked, for all the world to see. Or at least, for Ben to see.

"It was an emergency," I said, flustered, then turned around, looking for my bag. I bent down and rummaged in it for dry, warm layers. Yoga pants, a tank top, my UCLA hoodie. While I dressed, Ben's attention was on Simon. He stretched and rolled over onto his back, baring his white underbelly. "*Bon chien*," he said, scratching the dog's midsection.

"*Qu'est-ce qui s'est passé?*" he said, his voice low and gruff. Then he looked around the room, blinking several times.

"I still don't understand French," I reminded him. "How are you feeling?"

"I'm fine," Ben said, seemingly unaware he'd been unconscious. "Where are we?" He rubbed his face. "Oh, I remember. The storm." He looked at me. "Zoey, what time is it?"

I looked around for my phone, then remembered it was dead. "I'm not sure. My phone's dead, and there's no service anyway. I put yours in my pocket." I walked over to my coat, which was hanging on a hook in the wall. It was still wet. I reached into the pocket, and pulled out Ben's phone, then handed it to him.

"*Tabernac*. It's dead, too." Ben stretched his arms over his head. "I fell asleep?"

"Sort of—if you call getting into a car accident and losing consciousness 'falling sleep,'" I joked. "Don't fall asleep again, okay? How do you feel actually?" I studied his face. He looked okay—not like he'd been in an accident earlier that day.

"Weird," he said slowly. "Like, just sort of out of it. Disoriented. I was unconscious? We got in an accident?" He stretched his neck this way and that, trying to loosen the tight muscles.

"Be careful. You might have broken something. Or, I guess, more accurately, I might have caused you to break something," I added, biting my lip. "Sorry."

"Oh man, I'm just so stiff." He rubbed the back of his neck.

I studied him. "Do you know your name?"

He raised an eyebrow. "*Mon nom*? Emile Benoît Deschamps. Oh wait, that's my dad's name." He grinned, winking at me. "So does that mean I *have* amnesia or I *don't* have amnesia?"

"Don't joke. You could have a concussion, and my only training for that is the time I directed a film where the hero had a concussion and lost his memory and the heroine had to help him get it back by Christmas Eve or—"

"Or what? Christmas wouldn't happen that year?"

"They wouldn't be able to get *married*, as per her long-standing tradition."

"Ahh, the old marry-someone-who-doesn't-know-your-name-on-Christmas-Eve tradition. How could I have forgotten?" The corner of his lip curled up.

Sarcastic Ben was back. And yet his edge was dulled. "Wow, you *must* be okay if you're making fun of me."

He raised an eyebrow. "I'm teasing, Zoey. I was always teasing."

"Hmph." I looked around the room. Outside the window, the clouds were dark. I shivered. Without the warmth of our bodies together, I was reminded how cold it was in the farmhouse.

Ben looked down at himself. "What happened to my shirt? My pants?" My eyes went to his bare chest. I could still feel his soft skin on mine. He cleared his throat and I realized he was staring at me, but he looked more amused than annoyed.

"They were soaked through. I was worried about hypothermia."

"You were worried?"

I scowled at him. "Obviously. I'm not a monster."

"So you . . ." His voice showed interest.

"I didn't look." My face heated up, and I hoped the farm-house was dark enough that he didn't notice.

"Removing my clothes with your eyes closed. Did you go to magician's school for that particular skill?" he teased.

I rolled my eyes. "You know what? You're *welcome*."

His smile disappeared and he looked me deep in the eyes. "Thank you," he said so genuinely that it felt like there were champagne bubbles in my stomach. I shivered again, but this time not because I was cold.

He stood up and walked around the room. I tried not to admire his legs, which were long and muscular, dark hair running their length. "So, where are we?"

"Not the Beverly Hills Hotel, that's for sure," I said jok-ingly. "Did you see that farmhouse right before we crashed?"

Ben turned back to me, his eyes wide. "What—or who—did we hit?" Lines formed between his eyebrows.

My expression softened. Right—we could have hit some-one. We could have *hurt* someone. "Just a tree."

"Okay. So we were driving, the storm was bad. I do remem-ber sliding. But how—where . . . ?" He scratched his chin.

"It got really icy, really fast," I explained. "And then we hit the tree. And then your truck slid into the pond. Well most of it anyway."

"How did you get me in here?"

"I dragged you," I said simply.

"But *how*? I weigh so much more than you." His eyes showed concern.

"I don't know. With the energy generated by my guilt about how it was my stubborn insistence we keep going that almost killed you?"

"Wow." He closed his eyes.

"Wait! Don't close your eyes. What if you fall unconscious again?"

His eyes opened and he laughed. "I'm standing. I'm not going to lose consciousness." He rubbed his head, on the left side, above his eyebrow, at his hairline. I leaned closer to him, examining his forehead. "It looks like you have a bump. You may have hit your head on the steering wheel." I reached out. "Can I . . . Can I touch it?"

He nodded, not saying a word. I held my breath as my fingers grazed the goose-egg bruise on his brow.

"Does this hurt?" I whispered.

His eyes were on mine. "A little. But, I think it's fine. I'm fine, Zoey. Don't look so worried."

I blinked. "I was worried. I'm still a little worried."

"You saved us," he said quietly. "You know what that means?"

My heart stopped. "What?" What was he going to say? What was he going to do?

"We're even." Then he laughed and my stomach dropped. I lifted my hand to punch him in the shoulder but he ducked out of the way in time, taking my hand in his. It was warm. We stood for a moment, my hand in his, before he let go.

He cleared his throat. "All right, so I assume no one's coming to get us, since we have no cell service. Right?" Even though this wasn't news to me, hearing Ben state the situation aloud was sobering.

"Right. And this place doesn't appear to have a landline." I tried to keep my tone light, but I could feel anxiety rising in my gut.

"Okay. So we're on our own then. Or, rather, we're in this together?" Ben looked at me expectantly.

"For sure," I said, my eyes meeting his. We were in this together. People died alone—not together, right? Especially not with an adorable dog by their side?

Ben walked to the middle of the room. "We should get out of here." Simon nuzzled his leg.

"What?" What was he talking about? "Where are we going to go? And how? And what if it's not safe for you to be walking around? Can't we just wait this thing out? It's really nasty out there." My voice was full of worry. I couldn't help it. Ben was finally awake, and, all things considered, we were safe where we were. I didn't want to think about leaving.

Ben grabbed one of my hands. "Zoey, you're freezing. And we probably only have an hour or so of daylight left. There's no food in here—we need to eat, so does Simon. We can't stay here. And tomorrow's Christmas Eve, *Réveillon* . . ." He trailed off.

That didn't matter right now. "Where are we going to go?" I asked again. Maybe he knew exactly where we were. Ben had grown up in these parts—he probably knew every street, every path, every cabin, every house, every abandoned farmhouse. He probably knew everyone who lived in this area. Maybe he also knew the owners of this place, and where they'd gone to. Maybe they had a new house just up the road, a place where we could get warm and then get home from.

"I'm not sure where we are—"

My hope deflated. *Scratch that optimism, Zo.*

"But," Ben continued, "we should be able to get somewhere safer than this place before it's too dark."

"But it's freezing out there," I protested. The hail and sleet had let up a bit, but the wind was making the branches crack loudly as it shook ice loose, sending large pieces crashing to the slick ground below. "I'm not leaving."

Ben turned to me, ready to fight, but he must have seen the panic in my eyes because he softened, setting his palms on my shoulders and looking into my eyes. My stomach fluttered. "Listen, Zoey. We absolutely have to go. The longer we wait the worse it's going to get out there—more and more trees and branches will start to collapse under the weight of the ice." He looked down at himself. "Aaaaand, whether we're leaving or not, I should probably put some clothes on." He reached into the emergency kit, rummaged around, and then pulled on the pair of jeans I'd seen earlier, and added a gray waffle shirt. Then he ripped open a small package. "Here, eat this and then let's get out of here." He broke off half the granola bar and handed it to me.

I took a bite, realizing the moment I tasted the bar how hungry I was. "Thanks."

Reluctantly, I began collecting the clothes I'd hung over the rocking chair and table to dry and stuffed them in my suitcase.

Ben walked to the far wall, to a flimsy door. He opened it, revealing a small closet. He emerged with a pair of snowshoes. "Ah, here we go," he said, as though this were all part of his plan. "Let me see if I can find another pair." I watched as he went back into the closet, then noticed a pile of slushy snow that had come in through the open window. Ben was right— we couldn't stay here.

A moment later, he came toward me, the wooden frames of another pair of snowshoes in his hands. "Ever snowshoed before?" he asked with a smile.

I took them from him. The shoes were weathered and worn from use, but I could still make out the faded patterns and symbols. The webbing was a deep gold, frayed in places. I was no expert on what modern snowshoes looked like, but I was pretty sure these would've been right at home as ancient artifacts in a museum.

"All the time. Snowshoeing on Malibu Beach is de rigueur," I said. "So these snowshoes—they're our plan?"

He nodded excitedly. "Yep. Trust me. This is exactly what we need. And what kind of luck that there just happened to be snowshoes here?"

"Huh."

"Come on." Ben placed the snowshoes down.

"Oof," he said a second later, touching his hand to his forehead. In answer to my questioning look, he said, "Dizzy."

"I bet you have a concussion."

He shrugged. "Something to consider later on," he said gruffly, as though I'd suggested he might have a hangnail. "Let's figure out what we can take and what we need to leave behind."

"Leave behind?" I didn't want to leave anything behind.

"We can't carry all this stuff with us, Zoey. We need to be light so we can move quickly. Consider it temporary. We can always come back."

This felt like the time I used the KonMari Method to organize my closets: Put items I wasn't sure about in a "maybe" pile, and then revisit them in a few months. If I had missed them, they were there for me to put back in my closet; if I hadn't, I donated them. I had to admit that this tactic worked, so I assessed my belongings. My cross-body bag was a must—not because it was my favorite, but because while it couldn't fit much, I could at least put in a change of underwear, some dry socks, and a scarf. And I could sling it over my body. My wool coat had dried enough and was now more damp than outright wet. My UGGs remained sodden, though they weren't as cold as they had been before. I pulled them on.

"Do you want a scarf?" Ben tossed it to me as I was pulling my hair into an elastic I'd found in my bag. It was handknitted red and blue. "Thanks." I wrapped it around my neck twice and tied it in a knot. It smelled of soap and pine—like Ben.

Ben grabbed a small lantern, the sleeping bag and some other essentials from the emergency kit and shoved them, along with the sleeping bag, into the bag for the sleeping bag. Then he looked at me. "Is that the only coat you brought? Nothing more sensible?"

I looked down at my creamy white coat, the one I'd been so excited about when I'd found it the day before leaving for Chelsea. It was now pilled and dirty, more gray than ecru. "No, this is it," I mumbled, shaking my head. "I think maybe I dressed for—"

"A holiday movie filmed in July?" he said.

"How was I supposed to know there'd be an ice storm?" I said defensively.

"Fair point," Ben said. "All right, you ready?"

A few minutes later we were standing at the door, Simon next to us, his tail wagging. He looked to Ben and made a noise, almost as though he was trying to speak. Ben nodded as though he understood. "Just a minute, boy." Ben slung his arms through the drawstrings of the bag for the sleeping bag so that it was a backpack. The rest of our things—the things we were leaving behind, for now—were organized into a neat pile on a dry spot in the middle of the room. Then he nodded to the snowshoes. "Let's get these on."

I looked down at them. The snowshoes were lightweight but surprisingly sturdy given they looked like they were about to fall apart. I wondered who had worn them before me. "So we're just going to steal these?"

"I'm pretty sure the owners aren't going to mind," Ben said, dryly. "Besides, we're leaving a bunch of our stuff as collateral."

"I'm sure they'll appreciate my Dyson hair dryer."

"I'm sure they will," Ben said. "Okay, first things first." He picked up one of the other snowshoes. "You want to hold it like this, with the toe facing up and the heel down."

I watched as he demonstrated, grateful he wasn't leaving me to figure it out myself.

"You want to place your foot in the center of the snow-shoe, with your heel in the heel cup and your toes pointing toward the front," Ben continued, his voice low.

I did as he instructed, crouched on the floor, but I couldn't figure out the straps. Ben already had both feet strapped into his snowshoes.

"Can you—I can't seem to . . ." I fumbled over the words.

He nodded and leaned over, his hands brushing mine as he tightened the bindings around my foot and ankle. The touch felt like snowflakes dancing on my skin but instead of having chills, I felt warm. "Just make sure they're secure, but not too tight, so you're able to walk." His breath was warm in my ear.

I nodded, my heart racing as I finished lacing up the first snowshoe. "Okay, now let's do the other one," Ben said, his face turned toward me, his eyes locked on mine.

I fastened the second shoe, my fingers trembling, then stood. Ben clapped his hands. "All right, you ready?" He looked around, his brow furrowed as a branch broke free from a tree outside the window.

"Do I have a choice?" I was nervous. What if we got lost, or one of us got hurt? What if Ben wasn't well enough to be snowshoeing in this weather? "I feel like this is a bad idea. We have shelter."

Ben looked around. "I know it seems crazy to go out in this weather, but the storm's only going to get worse. Yes, we could stay here for a few hours, melt snow for water, but we don't have anything else. At some point we have to eat. And we have enough time to get somewhere before dark. This farmhouse isn't in the middle of nowhere, I know where we are. It's not far to more homes and cottages. Ones where people actually live."

He sounded so confident. And what did I know?

"Come on," Ben said, leaning into me and nudging me. "Snowshoeing is actually pretty fun."

"We seem to have two different perspectives on what 'fun' is."

"Okay, *more* fun than walking without snowshoes through that mess out there. How's that?" he said with a wink. I knew there was no way he was actually this happy about being stranded in this storm, but he was trying, if not only for himself, then for me, too.

He trudged toward the door and grabbed the knob to pull the door open, but the door instead fell right off its loose hinges. Simon sniffed at it and Ben looked back at me. "Definitely time to get the hell outta Dodge."

CHAPTER TWELVE

Tuesday, December 23, 4:00 p.m.

Walking with snowshoes felt like I was walking on ice with surfboards strapped to my feet.

The cold air blasted my face, so cold it felt like hot irons were being pressed to my cheeks. I pulled the scarf up to create a makeshift balaclava, the only opening for my eyes.

"You okay?" Ben yelled. Though he was next to me, the wind was so strong he had to shout to be heard over it. I nodded, though I didn't feel okay. I felt weak being back out here, fighting the wind and in the cold. I'd always thought forests were supposed to make shelter, but even though there were snow-covered trees in every direction, the wind seemed to blast through them like they were merely toothpicks.

"So the key to snowshoeing is to take small steps and distribute your weight evenly across the snowshoes," Ben yelled over the howling wind, then demonstrated.

I watched, and followed his lead, trying to mimic his movements. Simon, happier than I'd seen him all day, raced across the slushy ice-snow like he was born for this weather—which he probably was.

"I feel like a penguin," I said.

Ben turned, watching me. "Yep, you look like one, too."

I scowled from behind my scarf. "Not helpful."

"What if I said you look like a cute penguin?" Ben called back. "Is that better?"

I was thankful he couldn't see my face redden. Was he *flirting* with me? I was thankful for the heat that rushed to my face—at least, for a brief moment, one part of my body was warm. I looked down, focusing on my steps. One foot at a time. That was the plan.

When I looked up, Ben was already at least three body-lengths ahead of me.

"How are you so good at this?" I called to him.

He turned and stopped to wait for me. "Tapping the trees for maple syrup!"

"I don't get the connection."

"I wear snowshoes to get around. They're like sneakers to me."

"Huh. I see." I took another step, keeping my legs as wide as possible, so the snowshoes wouldn't knock each other.

Simon sniffed along the snow as though he knew we were debating the route and wanted to help us.

"Stay behind me. I'll try to break the wind for you." Ben's voice was barely audible over the wind, but I could tell it was serious. I nodded and followed, trying to keep up with him, but with each step I fell farther behind. The entire forest was a sheet of ice. The wind picked up, as though someone were controlling it with a dial; as if they were saying, *You think this is wind? I'll show you wind!*

"You okay?" Ben called back.

"This is a lot harder than I thought it was going to be," I responded loudly, feeling tears welling in my eyes. I fought them back, but not quick enough. They froze, making my lashes stick together. Simon, who was up ahead with Ben, turned and lumbered back toward me. He stayed by my side for a bit before catching up to Ben again.

Buck up, Zoey. Just imagine this is a scene in the movie.

```
FADE IN
INT. Jacques's cottage—Chelsea—morning.
Jacques and Ruby stand in the
kitchen, sipping coffee from mugs.


              JACQUES
Want to take a walk before breakfast?


Ruby nods.


EXT. Cabin—day—sun shining, fresh snow.


              JACQUES
    Hey, what's that?


Jacques points past Ruby. She turns
to look and he scoops up a mound of
```

snow, rolls it into a ball and tosses
it at her. It brushes her shoulder.
She squeals and turns, her face showing she knows he tried to hit her
with the snowball.

                    RUBY
                    Hey!

Ruby laughs and runs toward a tree,
taking cover behind its thick trunk.
She retaliates with her own snowball,
hitting him square in the face. She
throws a hand to her mouth in surprise.

                    RUBY
            I have bad aim! Promise!
            I meant to hit that tree!

Jacques laughs and runs toward
her. She squeals and races away.
He catches her and wraps his arms
around her waist.

                    JACQUES
            I have bad aim, too.
            I meant to hug that tree.

Jacques nuzzles her ear.

I sighed happily at the thought.

Suddenly, my left foot slipped on a patch of ice, sending me flying into the air before landing me on my tailbone—hard. A moment later, Ben was crouched by my side. "Are you okay?" he said softly. He put a hand on my back.

"I don't know," I said, feeling sorry for myself. I pulled my left leg in, and then my right.

"Move slowly," he said.

I tried pushing myself up again, but my left foot shot out in front, and I slammed down into the ice. I let out a frustrated groan.

"It's just walking. What is my problem?" I said, feeling angry. I sat up. "I can do this."

Ben laughed. "I know you can. If there's anyone who can do this, it's you. I think you're about the toughest person I've ever met."

Under the scarf my face heated up again. My neck, my arms, my fingers, too. Ben thought I was tough?

He stood and held out a hand. "But you can still let me help you up."

I took his hand and pushed off the ice with my left hand, digging my feet into the ice and leaning into Ben as he pulled me up.

Once I was standing again, I brushed my hands across my butt, and then pushed my shoulders back and took a breath.

"You're the one who was unconscious an hour ago, yet you're taking care of me."

"We can take turns," he said. Just like there had never been any *taking care of* with Tomas, there had never been *taking turns* either.

"Deal." I pushed Tomas out of my mind. "Let's do this."

"Let's do this," he said, mock-seriously.

We started off again, but this time I tried to stay in step with him. I put more of my focus on my thighs, steadying myself with every step. "I think I'm getting the hang of this," I said a few minutes later. I was moving more quickly now, putting my whole body into it and I was warming up as though I was lightly jogging along the Malibu Beach boardwalk.

He turned to me and grinned. "I think we're going to make it home for *Réveillon* after all. I can feel it."

"All right, let's hear it. More about this *Réve*-whatever you keep bringing up." Simon looked at me and made that husky-talking sound.

Ben sighed happily. "All right, all right. For most people who celebrate Christmas, it's all about the day. But for us, in Quebec, it's all about Christmas Eve. It's a whole night of family and festivities and Christmas music and gifts and good food. And it all starts with Midnight Mass. We'd all go—even the little ones."

"I've heard of that but I just thought it happened in—"

"Small towns?" he said with a grin.

I smiled back. "The 1800s, actually. Midnight Mass? That's crazy. How do the kids stay awake?"

He shrugged. "It's one night and they've waited all year for it. They're so excited, because everything starts *after* Midnight Mass. Well, traditionally, of course. Now we do start earlier—before Mass. We can't wait. And we listen to carols, always 'Chanson de Noël' and 'Il Est Né, le Divin Enfant'—"

"So . . . no Mariah Carey then?" I interrupted.

He looked disapprovingly at me. "I hope you're joking. Surely you've experienced Christmas carols at a church before."

I shook my head and shrugged. "Not religious."

"I'm not particularly religious either. But I like believing in something. It's been helpful recently, in dealing . . ." He trailed off. *In dealing with the death of his father.* I opened my mouth to say something—what, I wasn't sure—but he spoke again. "Plus, it's important as the mayor to be part of the church. Obviously." There was that pompous veneer again.

"Obviously." I mimicked his tone. I couldn't help it. It would be one thing if he was so *into* being mayor, but it didn't feel like it was his idea, more like just another example of him doing the right thing without making his own decisions or carving his own path in life. Instead of telling him what I really thought, I thought of home. "I can't imagine the mayor of LA showing up at Midnight Mass."

"That's why it is so great to live in a small town. It's a *community*. I can't imagine LA at Christmas," he said with disdain.

I hadn't spent a Christmas in LA in years, so I couldn't say for sure what it would be like either, but something about his tone rubbed me the wrong way and I defended it.

"There's nothing wrong with LA. LA is *great*." If I'd had a choice about how to spend every Christmas growing up, it would've been like that one magical Christmas in Chelsea. And once I had kids of my own, I wanted them to experience traditions like what Ben was describing. But there was no way I was going to give him the satisfaction of thinking that he was right.

"Uh-huh. That's why you're here, not there, right?"

"I'm here for my movie," I said, then realized my window. "You know, I live and breathe holiday movies and never once has one featured *la Réveillon*."

"Le *Réveillon*. *Le*. Not *la*."

"See? I don't even know if it's *le* or *la*. But we could change that. Help others experience Chelsea, the people, the traditions."

He turned to me. "Seriously? You're pitching me in the middle of an ice storm?"

I shrugged. "Seems pretty appropriate. Think about Delphine," I said, hurrying to keep up to him. "I bet she'd love to hear—from you—that there was a romantic holiday movie filming in her hometown. You could tell her when you see her." *Why? Why would I bring up Delphine at a time like this?* Because I was blatantly playing with Ben's emotions for my own self-serving purposes. It was shameful, really. I wasn't proud. But if Ben *was* trying to get back together with Delphine, how swoon-worthy would it be for him to say that he, the big ol' important mayor of Chelsea had agreed to allow a Hollywood holiday movie to be filmed in his town? Unless, of course, Delphine wasn't a romantic. Or was on Team No Tourists, like Ben.

"Delphine's opinion is irrelevant," he said, to my surprise.

That sounded like there was history. Of course there was history—she was his ex. But was there still something there? "Really?" I said, hoping he would continue. I loved hearing about people's relationships. And as sexy as Ben was, it wasn't like there would *ever* be any chance of us hooking up. We were *so* different—he was stubborn and unyielding . . . and I guess I could be those things, too, but only when it mattered, like getting my movie made. Oh, and that was another difference: He was stopping me from doing my job.

"There's nothing to tell about Delphine," Ben responded after a pause.

"Oh, come on. I make movies about holiday romances for a living," I said. "And yours sounds pretty cookie-cutter." I knew it wasn't, but I also knew saying that would get his back up, make him talk.

"It's not *cookie-cutter*." He furrowed his brow at me. "What does that even *mean*?"

Bingo.

"All right, then give me the twist. Tell me what's different about you and her. Convince me your story isn't like every other holiday movie I've seen and directed."

"No." He picked up his pace.

"Well, what about Australia?" I asked, hurrying to keep up again. My foot slipped, but I lifted it before it went out from under me. Light touch, light touch. "You did go and visit her a few months ago. And you were supposed to pick her up at the airport. So there must be something."

"There's history," Ben said with a shrug. "And obligation, I suppose."

Obligation? "Sounds sexy. Tell me more." The temperature felt like it had dropped even further. The wind burned my exposed cheeks.

He looked back at me from below his thick lashes, which were frosted with ice. "It's anything but."

"Well . . . she's coming back to Chelsea. What does that mean?"

He exhaled, as though resigning himself to spilling it all to me. "Delphine and I grew up together. We've known each other since we were kids. Her parents' home was next to ours. Her parents and my parents were good friends. Her mom would borrow an egg, we'd swim in their pool. Play shinny in winter. I have tons of cousins but no brothers or sisters, so I spent a lot of time hanging out with her and her sister, Noémie, who you met at the diner. And it's a small town. Eventually, Delphine and I ended up together."

Oh, so Noémie was Delphine's *sister*. I knew there was history when Noémie asked Ben to pick up Delphine, but I certainly wasn't expecting that history to go back decades.

We reached the edge of the copse of trees that led into a more wooded area, and almost instantly the wind died down. It was a Christmas miracle.

"You guys didn't just 'end up together'—you and Delphine were friends to lovers."

"What?" Ben sounded confused.

"Friends to lovers. It's a popular romance trope." The tie on my left snowshoe came loose. I bent down to retie it.

"Do you define everything in life by romance movies?"

My fingers were so numb I couldn't feel the leather ties in my hands, which made it almost impossible to grasp them. "Mostly."

Ben leaned down to help me. I tried to picture Jacques and Ruby out in the snow, maybe bent down, just like Ben and me, building a snowman together. Jacques would help

Ruby when the bottom snowball got too big and heavy to push in the snow. Ruby would find two thin branches for arms. When they were finished, Jacques would sling an arm over Ruby's shoulder and pull her close as they admired their work. She'd lean into him and he'd kiss her on the forehead, then she'd tilt her face up toward him and stand on tiptoes in her boots to kiss him on the lips.

He whipped off his gloves and quickly tied the straps, then double-knotted them, and stood up. "Thanks," I said, standing, too. "Go on, tell me more about Delphine."

Ben sighed. "And here I thought you might forget what we were talking about."

"Not a chance." He could've just told me he didn't want to talk about Delphine anymore, but he didn't. "So yeah, we were friends and then we just sort of fell into being a couple. Like people always assumed we were, and then sometime in high school, we just were."

"I feel like you're brushing over details. Like, you were in love, right? Friends to lovers can be tricky because the spark isn't instant. But she was your . . . first?" A branch whipped toward me and I ducked.

"How long have I known you?" I had fallen a bit behind, and Ben had to turn his head almost 180 to meet my eyes.

"Does it really matter?" I grinned.

"Yes, she was my first."

"Thank you. So you're prom king and queen or whatever—"

"We were *not*—"

"I'm kidding. But you're together through high school. Then what?"

"Then CEGEP, that's what you do after high school, before university. We went to the same one, same as most of our friends. And then it came time to apply to university. And out of the blue she says she doesn't want to go."

"Not everyone wants to go to college," I said.

"Right. It's fine, but she didn't have another plan. It just seemed shortsighted. Not to even apply. Not to even give yourself options for the future."

"True. So what happens—you go away and she doesn't?"

"Right. She gets a job at a pub."

"The Pub du Village? But her parents own it? So it's not that different from you."

"No, the Manchester Pub, down the road. Which is—" He shook his head.

"Oof. A big f-you to her parents?" I suggested.

"She didn't see it that way, she saw it as showing her independence, getting her own job. But I don't know, I didn't love it. It felt a bit immature—"

"She was young. Not everyone can be as responsible as you."

"But I supported her. Even when her parents didn't speak to her for months. Not sure that was the right move though, frankly, but it was a long time ago." A few beats passed where it was just the sound of our snowshoes hitting the ice, in sync. Off to the right the crash of a falling tree limb created a loud bang. I jumped.

"That sounded like a big one," I said, suddenly aware that at any point, these massive branches that were sheltering us from the wind could come crashing down.

Ben nodded. "We should keep up our pace, get through this as quickly as we can. So anyway, I went to McGill University, she stayed in Chelsea." I knew he was talking to distract me, but it was working. "We took a break. I dated other people, she dated *un mécanicien* in Aylmer, and a journalism grad at Carleton." I noticed that he sounded neutral, not jealous or bitter, about Delphine's exes.

"Did you guys see each other though? When you were home? Did she come to visit you?"

"*Bien sûr*," he said, with a trace of sarcasm. "It's Chelsea. Everyone sees everyone when you're in town."

"Right."

"But she never came to visit me. Didn't like to travel, didn't want to be far from home, or her friends. I did a term in Paris, I wanted her to come then, but she just had no interest."

"So you two were . . ." I looked over at Simon, who had found a stick and was carrying it in his mouth.

"Friends, not friends, together, not together, it was an awkward phase, for sure. But we got through it. Anyway, I graduated, I moved back home to work on the farm, so that my father could be freed up to be mayor. And I just sort of fell back together with Delphine. It was easy and I definitely thought it was what I wanted." He paused. "I'd been *with* her more than I'd ever been apart from her. It was like . . ." He trailed off, seemingly at a loss for words.

"Friends to lovers?" I offered.

Ben grimaced. We approached a clearing, where the wind kicked up. I dug my chin into my scarf, trying to shimmy it back up over my cheeks.

"I wanted to get married, start a family," he finally said. "She said she wanted the same, and didn't want to leave Chelsea, so it made sense that I came back. I liked Montreal, but I also wanted to be with her. And I loved the area, I loved the community, and I loved being around my family and friends. I was happy to continue the family business, what my father and grandfather had worked so hard to build. Me and Delphine, we made sense."

"But then something happened." The truth was, I wanted him to stop talking about Delphine. I regretted bringing it up. There was something about him talking about his life, planning it out, marriage, kids . . . It made me feel sick. And yet, I wanted to know exactly what had happened.

"First, she grew tired of working at the pub. Then one of her friends was planning a trip to Australia and she decided to go with her." A fallen tree trunk blocked our path and Ben surveyed it, stepped over it. Simon ambled over it. I sized it up, set a single snowshoe on the bark and then paused, trying to figure out where to step next. Ben held out his hand to me. I took it. His grip was firm, his arm strong. I leaned into him as I brought my second leg over the log.

"And you had a problem with that?" I asked.

"Not at all. I love traveling and I was so happy that she wanted to leave Chelsea, see another part of the world. That she wanted to travel. But she wanted to do it alone. I tried to be understanding. I'd had my time to explore and figure things out at university, and doing an exchange in Paris."

"Okayyyy," I said. "So what was the problem?"

"It was supposed to be a two-week trip. That turned into a month, and then two. After a few months of her being away, I suggested I go over to see her. I missed her, and I wanted to travel *with* her. I thought we could tour around, see parts of the country she hadn't seen. But when I got there, she didn't want to leave the small town on the west coast she and her friend had been in since they arrived. She didn't want to travel around, she didn't really want to do anything. She had re-created her Chelsea life in a small town in Australia. That worked for her, but it didn't make sense to me. If you're going to live in a small town, why not live in the one where you have roots? Family, friends?"

Ben looked at me and shrugged. "The point is to grow together, to try new things. Or at least, that's what I was looking for in a partner. And it felt like we grew apart. We had nothing in common anymore. I'd been holding on for so long, and I wasn't even sure why. We broke up on that trip and she's stayed in Australia ever since."

"I get that," I said softly, thinking about Tomas and me. I never felt that we were growing in the same direction. The older he got, the more money he had, it seemed the less he wanted to settle down.

A gust of wind came at me, sideways, throwing me off-balance. I reached out for Ben, and he steadied me.

This relationship really did sound just like *I'll Be Home for Christmas*, where the main character returns home and gets back together with her ex. The perfect holiday romance for the TV screen, but it made my stomach hurt thinking about the possibility of Ben and Delphine getting back together. Why did I care, though?

"Guess this is all helping confirm small-town stereotypes, huh?"

I shook my head. "I was born in a town of eight thousand people, in Virginia," I said. "I'm not against small towns. Why do you think I set my film in Chelsea?"

"Oh." He didn't hide his surprise. "I just assumed . . ."

"What?" I said. I wanted to know what he assumed about me. But then another loud crack shook me out of the moment. Simon yelped and raced forward. I looked up as a branch as thick as my thigh and twice as long as my height embedded itself in the snow mere inches from me. I gasped and looked at Ben, frightened. He stepped closer to me and kept his gaze on the tree canopy above us.

"We need to keep an eye out for shelter. We'll need to stop soon," he said quietly. "We're almost out of light. And this is only going to get worse."

"What do you mean? I thought you knew where we were going?" Wasn't Ben leading us to a place he knew we could stop for the night? Where were we walking to?

"General direction, yes. And I was hoping we might hit a strip with some homes, but I'm not feeling very positive about that now, not when it's so close to dark. And we must be farther than I thought we were when we slid off the road. Ideally, we'll find a cottage, occupied or not. Just in case."

"Just in case of *what*?" I hunched forward to push against the wind but it felt like I was pressing against a cold metal wall. I couldn't feel my hands or my toes. My eyes watered, but I didn't know if it was because of the cold or because I was scared. I wriggled my toes. I wriggled my fingertips, too. Tears ran down my cheeks, freezing to my skin. Simon sniffed at my hand, then licked it.

"You can do this," Ben said, and I realized that he was beside me. And that I was no longer walking—instead, I was sitting on the frigid ground. Why wasn't I standing? And was Ben saying the same words over and over or was I imagining it? I blinked a few times and tried to focus on what he was saying. His breath was warm on my ear, then Simon licked my face. I closed my eyes and tried to imagine Jacques and Ruby curled up by a roaring fire, Jacques's dog by their feet, warmth radiating from the flames.

"We can do this. Just a little farther. Come on. You can do this," I heard Ben say. It sounded like he was very far away.

I opened my eyes, then Ben lifted me up to standing. "Come on, we've got to keep moving," he said.

"Why do we have to keep moving?" I asked. I truly had no idea anymore. Everything felt foggy. The wind was so cold it felt hot on my face.

"We still have a bit of light, but soon these woods will be black. The temperature will drop. The wind will pick up."

"And what?" My voice wavered.

"There are wolves out here," he said.

"What?" A pit formed in my stomach. "But . . ." My throat closed up. I couldn't get out the words.

"We're going to be okay. But we've got to keep moving." Ben reached out and touched my arm. Then he set off. I didn't move. Part of me wanted to follow him—he was getting farther and farther away. The other part of me just wanted to stay where I was; to sit against a tree and maybe go to sleep. Maybe if I fell asleep I wouldn't feel so cold.

I must have sunk to the ground. Closed my eyes. Then Ben's breath was hot against my ear again, his voice soft. "Come on, Zoey. I know you can do this. We've just got a little bit farther to go." I felt his arms around me. "You wrote a screenplay. You've directed tons of films. You just snow-shoed for the first time in your life. You're too determined to give up now."

I heard that last line clearly, louder than the wind that was wailing around us. Ben was right. I was not going to give up. I straightened my frame, took a deep breath, then squeezed my eyes shut. After a moment, I opened them wide again. I could do this. "Let's go," I said.

The wind was getting stronger by the minute, it seemed, but Ben stayed by my side. "We're just going to go one step at a time. I step. You step."

"We step?" I said.

"I love your sense of humor," he said, then quickly cleared his throat, as though realizing what it sounded like. *Did he say that he* loves *my sense of humor?* It felt like I was suddenly wide awake, my heart beating fast.

I opened my mouth to say something, but decided against it. Together we led Simon for some paces, Ben's arm looped through mine, holding me close. Another gust blasted at my entire body. Just as we were about to step around a gnarled tree, the entire trunk tipped away from us. I felt myself suddenly rising up as though the ground below us was rising. Ben pulled me backward.

I screamed. "*What* is going on?"

The ground was *lifting up*. I was no geologist, but this did *not* seem good. "It's the weight of the ice on the branches," Ben yelled over the wind, grimly looking up at the trees above us. "The ice is pulling down the forest. This is just the start. Come on!" Simon barked and ran ahead. They always say that animals can sense natural disasters before humans can—did even Simon know that it was unsafe to be here?

The wind was so strong that it was hard to stand upright. My right foot slipped but caught on a branch poking out of the ice, and I regained my balance before I fell.

"I'll go first, to shield you from anything that goes flying," Ben said. "Stay right behind me." My face was being pelted by what felt like tiny pebbles. I squeezed my eyes shut and silently nodded.

"Keep your head down!" Ben called. I buried my chin into my coat, looking up only enough to see that I was right behind him.

Something else hit my shoulder, throwing me forward. My hands flung out automatically, to break my fall, my knee smashing into the ice, my snowshoes tangling my feet. Ben was by my side instantly. I turned back to see what hit me— another massive branch by my side.

"Are you okay?" he shouted, his voice barely audible over the roar of the wind.

I nodded, trying to shake off the pain. I stood, bracing my legs in case I was pushed over again. Every second I spent falling or lying on the ground was a second longer we had to be out here in the storm. There was no way I was going to let that happen. As soon as Ben could see that I was moving again, he seemed to pick up the pace, and I kept up. My legs burned, but I forced myself to put one foot in front of the other.

Clomp, clomp, clomp. Every step took Herculean effort— and an hour, at least, it seemed.

"Look! There!" Ben yelled, breaking the spell. Simon sprinted ahead, tail wagging as though he knew there was something to see. I looked up, but couldn't make anything out through the blowing snow and ice. The sky was dark gray now, but I tried to focus on where Ben was pointing. Slowly, as we got closer, I was able to make out a small shape in the distance.

The cottage was small, with a peaked roof that gave it a storybook feel, like the cottage Hansel and Gretel found. It blended seamlessly into the snowy landscape, as if it had always been part of the woods, and the trees had been forced to grow around it. The exterior was made of dark cedar logs and looked as though each one had been hand-selected and slotted into place to create a seamless wall, not a slit of light peeking through. The roof was covered in a thick foot of snow, but from its center burst a brick chimney. I pictured a twirl of smoke lazily wafting upward, and my entire body flooded in a shock of warmth. I quickened my pace toward the front porch, which wrapped around the front of the cottage, the wooden deck sheltered by the sloped overhang.

Ben turned to me. "You see that, right? Tell me it's not a mirage?" But Simon had already made it to the porch. He happily looked back at us, impatiently wagging his tail.

"Mirage or not, I'm getting inside that cabin as fast as I can," I said, moving as quickly as I could.

CHAPTER THIRTEEN

Tuesday, December 23, 5:00 p.m.

We knocked and knocked, but there was no answer, the windows dark. I rattled the doorknob, but the door was locked tight, a drift of snow creating a tall seal against the bottom half. I hadn't come this far only to die of frostbite outside a cottage. But I also didn't have any idea what to do next. I collapsed into one of the rocking chairs on the porch and untied my snowshoes.

"What do we do?" I turned to Ben, hoping he had an answer. I felt dangerously on the verge of tears.

"We figure out how to get inside." Ben's voice was even. Instantly, my worry quelled. Even though that wasn't *really* an answer, I trusted he had an idea.

I moved over to one of the windows. It didn't budge. Out of the corner of my eye, I caught sight of the red handle of a shovel. I quickly maneuvered past the rocker and grabbed it, bringing it to the front door.

"Here, let me," Ben said, and immediately got to work shoveling the snow away from the door. Because it had been sheltered by the overhang it was still mostly soft snow, not completely iced over the way the rest of the forest was. Within minutes the bottom of the door came into view, and Ben let out a triumphant cry. In front of the door, on the porch, was a tan rattan mat that read *Baby, It's Cold Outside*.

"*I really can't stay,*" I said meekly.

He looked at me for a moment, his eyes wide.

"The song. One point for me," I explained with a small smile.

Ben looked relieved and exhaled loudly. "Oh," he said. "I thought you were, I don't know, telling me this cottage didn't meet your standards or something."

I laughed. "Standards? At this point, my standards include anything that's not us being outside any longer. I would go back to that farmhouse. Hell, I would *live* in that farmhouse."

"Let's not go back to the farmhouse, huh? Especially when there's a very good chance we could be inside this place instead." Ben used the shovel to chip away at the corner of the frozen welcome mat. It came loose and he knelt down, using his gloved hand to check the underside.

"You really think there's going to be a key under the mat?" I said doubtfully.

A second later, Ben held up a shiny silver key, then stood, throwing his arms around me. Tears that had been balancing on the lower rims of my eyes for what felt like hours broke free and I hopped up and down in excitement. He inserted the key in the doorknob and a moment later he pushed the door open. He gestured for me to go in. "Ladies first."

I wasn't about to complain about patriarchal tradition.

Inside was immediately warmer. Ben followed me in, but Simon pushed through at the same time and Ben caught a toe on the doorframe, lunging forward. I held out my arms to stop him and he fell into them, his face brushed up against mine. We stood still for a moment, his musky scent and body heat so close. I tried to find the words to say *something*. It felt so nice to hold Ben . . . And then the tears came. I'm not sure why. Relief? I threw my other arm around him and let the tears course down my face.

"Oh my god, I thought we were going to die," I cried. I was filled with emotion—relief, happiness, but also something else. As I sobbed softly, Ben tightened his arms around me.

"We did it. Man, you are so tough," Ben said softly. I felt myself warm at his words and relaxed deeper into our embrace. "But . . ."

I pulled back to look at him, holding my breath. What was he going to tell me—that he was going to leave me in this cottage, alone, while he and Simon continued to look for help? That it wasn't going to stop snowing for weeks, and I'd be stuck in Quebec, in this cottage, until then? "What?" My voice sounded nervous.

"Just so you know, you didn't get a point back there, because you sang the lyrics from *before* the line *Baby, it's cold outside*. What you *should've* sung was *I've got to go awaaaay*," he said, forcing a tune. "So one point for me." His eyes sparkled as he fixed them on mine, and my stomach dropped like I was on a roller coaster. I bit my lip and laughed, then blinked away tears. I was a mess.

I tore my gaze away from him, and turned to take in the space. The room was dark and it was hard to see, but my eyes quickly adjusted to the dim light shining through the window, casting shadows across the hardwood floors and the landscape paintings that hung on the walls, which were decorated with brightly colored handwoven rugs in rectangles and ovals. We were standing in a large open space, a stone fireplace taking up half of the far wall, its hearth dark. A string of lights ran across the mantel and there was a collection of wrought iron tools.

The furniture was simple but comfortable with an old floral couch and matching armchair facing the fireplace. Draped on the couch was a cream-and-rainbow-striped wool blanket. On the coffee table were crossword puzzle books, one opened to a puzzle, with a pencil nearby. Next to the mantel stood a bookcase stacked with board games and dozens of books, the spines cracked and wrinkled.

The other half of the main room was a small kitchen, a tiny window over the sink looking out into the forest, a rustic oak table the centerpiece for five mismatched chairs, painted in soft pastels. A rack over the counter held pots and pans by their handles.

My thoughts went to Jacques and Ruby—my default. The two of them spending cold winter nights huddled around the fire for warmth.

"You think whoever lives here is going to come home?" I asked Ben, unclipping the strap of my cross-body bag and letting it drop to the floor. I immediately peeled off my scarf, gloves, and coat, tossing them over one of the chairs.

Then I put a hand over my mouth. "What if they're here right now?" I whispered through my fingers.

"*Bonjour?*" Ben called out happily, and I laughed in surprise at his approach. Then he shook his head. "I think we're safe. That ruckus we made to get in—no one could sleep through that. Besides, there were no tracks outside. And no one could stay in here long without heat or a fire."

I could almost feel the heat of a fire radiating on my skin. "Please tell me you know how to make one," I said. I'd made a fire a few times in my life, thanks to Girl Scouts, but surely this had to be Ben's specialty.

"I would be an embarrassment to myself if I couldn't make a fire. So, yes, I've made a few fires in my lifetime," he said, moving toward the fireplace.

I reached out to flick the light switch on the wall to the right, but the room stayed dark. "The power's out," I confirmed, worry bubbling in my stomach. Of course the power was out. The storm was serious. And yet, I realized that I'd been holding out hope that maybe, just maybe, this cottage would miraculously still have power.

Ben looked over. "Yeah. I figured." His tone was soft, though, as though he realized what I'd been thinking. "But it'll be warm in here in a minute. So there's that."

I sat down and took my UGGs off. They were dripping wet, so I carried them to the rug near the door. "I could really use your grandmother's *poupons* right about now," I said over my shoulder. Ben chuckled, and I turned. "Don't say it."

"What?" he said, holding up his gloved hands in defense, but he was grinning. "That those Australian shoes aren't winter boots?"

"Yes. That." I shook my head, but I was laughing, too. I was too happy to finally be safe to bother being upset with him.

Ben sat down on the stone hearth and pulled back the metal doors of the fireplace screen. Simon, who'd been sniffing out the place, returned and sat down by Ben's side.

"Looks like it's in working order," Ben said, shuffling soot around in the base of the firebox with a wrought iron poker. "But I'm going to have to find more wood and kindling."

"I thought I saw a shed," I said. "Want me to go?" I added half-heartedly. The last thing I wanted to do was go back outside—but it wasn't fair that Ben had to.

"It's fine, I've still got everything on." He stood and brushed his gloved hands together then picked up the blanket and tossed it toward me. "You try to warm up." I caught the blanket, grateful for the dry fabric in my hands. He pulled his hood over his hat and slipped back out the front door. Simon looked at him, then turned back toward me, studying me for a moment before hopping onto the couch. For a split second I considered wrapping myself in the blanket and tucking in next to him, but I wanted to be useful. Ben didn't want to keep working any more than I did—and he had had an actual injury! I pulled the blanket around my shoulders and grabbed my bag and fiddled with the zipper, which had started to thaw, leaving it wet and difficult to grip.

I cleared away the remaining ice and snow and then moved the zipper enough to slide my hand inside and feel around for the tea lights from the emergency pack I'd thrown in there right before we'd left the farmhouse. I removed one at a time, then found the matches, which were miraculously dry. I set everything on the coffee table.

```
     INT. Jacques's cottage—brightly lit.
     Ruby's kids are playing a board game
     by the fire. Jacques hands Ruby a glass
     of wine. She takes the glass, then has
     a sip and looks around the room.


                   RUBY
     Don't you know the power of a tea light?


     Ruby finds a handful of small candles
     tucked into the back of a drawer in
     the kitchen and lines them up on the
     coffee table, lights them, then flicks
     a switch on the wall.


                   RUBY
        See? Isn't that so much better?


                  JACQUES
                 (sarcastic)
     So much better. I was almost going
     to leave my own home. Just give up.
```

With the tea lights providing a soft glow the cottage felt warmer, more inviting. I smiled, nearly forgetting the reality of the situation—that this wasn't a scene in a romantic holiday movie.

The wind howled behind me, and I turned to see Ben pushing his way through the front door, his arms laden with logs. My eyes widened. He looked . . . so sexy. There was something about seeing him carrying wood, his stubble creating a sexy shadow over his chin, his eyes on me, that made my entire body quiver. I swallowed and tried to ignore what I was feeling. I was tired, very hungry, probably delirious—I was clearly vulnerable. I'd probably be happy to be safe inside with anybody—man, woman, ogre.

"The candles are a nice touch." He made his way over to the fireplace, bent down, and unloaded the logs into a loose pile on the floor, then removed his boots and coat. He looked at Simon, who was stretched out on the couch, fast asleep. "Poor guy's tired," he said fondly, gently rubbing Simon's head.

Ben's biceps flexed as he picked up each log, moving it into the fireplace. He arranged one log this way, one log that, building them on each other with the confidence of someone who'd built a thousand fires, probably more. *Had he made fires for Delphine?* Where had *that* come from? I must have been more tired than I thought.

"All right." He rubbed his hands together and turned to look at me. *"The logs on the fire."*

Fill me with desire, I thought, finishing the line to "Merry Christmas, Darling" in my mind. I looked away.

"Where did you put the matches?" he asked. I held them up. "Ah, great." I passed the box to him, then made my way over to the bookcase, tilting my head to take in the colorful spines, a mix of fiction and nonfiction, classics and modern, a collection of poems, and a few paperbacks you'd find in the grocery store. I reached to pull out a copy of *Little Women* and flipped through the pages, feeling the weight of the book in my hands. I remembered reading Louisa May Alcott's novel over and over again as a kid, losing myself in the story of Jo and her sisters, relating to Jo's fierce ambition and independence, to her not feeling like she really fit into the family she was assigned even though she loved them fiercely.

"Any chance you see any old newspapers in there?"

"Just books," I said. "But we're not burning books. Oh, wait a sec." I walked over to the rolltop desk in the corner, opening the drawers. I sorted through the main part of the desk, found only personalized stationery that felt too special to use, then bent down to the low shelf where a straw basket held magazines and papers. "Jackpot," I said.

The newspaper was the *Montreal Gazette,* and the date gave me pause. It was five years old. Five years ago in TV was a lifetime. Five years ago, I was with Tomas. Five years ago, I was second-assistant director, still scouting locations, still doing grunt work, still trying to prove myself to Elijah, and hoping for an opportunity to step up, to take on more responsibility. Back then, if it hadn't worked out in Chelsea— if Ben had told me *no way, no how* on the film permit—I would've given up and gotten on the next flight back home.

I wouldn't have tried to drive to Wakefield, especially not with a storm looming. But things were different now.

This was *my* film. *My* first film.

Ben's teasing interrupted my thoughts. "Any chance you're going to give me those papers, or shall I make you a hot toddy while you read the news from 199-whocares?"

I snapped to and pushed the papers into Ben's arms, along with the box of matches. "Sorry. This paper's from a few years ago. Made me think about what I was doing then."

Ben paused to study the papers, then let out a low whistle. "Five years ago—wow. Seems like yesterday, in a way, and also a lifetime ago." He crumpled the papers and set them under the logs. He struck a match and brought it to the papers. The flame caught immediately, and Ben began fussing with the logs, blowing on them and coaxing the spark to grow. Soon enough, the fire was crackling, flames a foot high. Ben stood, wiping his hands on his pants.

"All right, that's one thing done," he said, satisfied. "But I'm soaked through. You?"

I nodded. "Yeah. My pants were frozen solid, and now I think I've made the blanket wet too." I pulled it off my shoulders and held it up in the air, then draped it over the back of a nearby chair. "But that's a *tree*-mendous fire."

Ben winked. "Thanks. What if you look for something for us to eat and I try to figure out a way for us to get some dry clothes?" he suggested. That sounded great to me. I nodded, and Ben disappeared down the narrow hallway that separated the sitting room from the nook where I'd found the newspapers. I walked over to the kitchenette and tried the door of the old china cabinet that stood in the corner. It stuck, but then popped open, and I peered inside. The shelves were bare. I stood on tiptoe to run my hands along the top shelf, which was too high to see. My fingers found only dust. I twirled around, selected one of the dining chairs and dragged it across the floor, then stood on it and peered onto the top shelf.

"How's it going on the food hunt?" Ben called.

"Great, if you're in the mood for dust bunnies."

"Gourmet rabbit. A delicacy."

"I think there's a good chance the people who own this place haven't been here in a very long time," I said. "It's also really hard to see," I said. In the time that we'd been inside the cottage, what daylight there'd been was now gone.

"There's a lantern in my bag," Ben called. A moment later I'd found the lantern and turned it on. Miraculously, it worked. Back on the chair, I moved aside a box of coffee filters, and tucked in the back corner of the shelf was a package of spaghetti. I reached for it, feeling like I'd just found a bag of unmarked bills.

"Jackpot!" I whooped with joy, startling Simon awake. "Sorry, buddy."

I stepped off the chair, then pulled open the doors to the cupboard above the sink. A few random jars and cans occupied the space: Pinto beans. Evaporated milk. And a single can of tomato sauce. I grabbed all three and placed them on the counter. I was dizzy just imagining a big bowl of hot pasta. Reaching up above the counter, I pulled down a medium-size pot, and brought it to the stove. We didn't have power—was the stove going to work? Biting my lip, I placed the pot on a burner and turned the knob for the gas. Nothing happened. I turned the knob to off, walked back to the fireplace and picked up the box of matches, then tried the stove again.

This time a flame burst, sending me stepping backward in shock.

"Yes!" I shouted. I turned the burner off and went to the sink to fill the pot. I flipped the handle on the tap back but nothing happened. No water.

"There's no water," I called to Ben, then set the pot on the counter.

"Oooh, pipes may be frozen," Ben called. "But in good news, I just found clothes."

"I'm not wearing some strangers' worn clothes," I called back.

"Really?" His voice was closer. I turned to see him walk into the kitchenette, holding a folded stack of items. "You'll break in, eat their food but not wear their clothes?"

"It's weird."

"Their very dry, very cozy, warm clothes?"

I squinted. "Are they clean?"

"As a whistle. Whatever that means." He grinned.

The idea of putting on dry clothing seemed so appealing.

Ben tossed a mound of clothes my way and I held out my arms to catch it. Flannel shirt, wool sweater, some jeans that may or may not fit, and a pair of socks.

The flannel was soft and glorious. The cable-knit sweater had a weight to it like it had been made by someone's grandma. Ben set his selections on the floor. Then he stripped off his gray waffle shirt, revealing his taut stomach. Was it possible that he looked better now than he had a few hours ago when I'd *last* seen his naked chest? Or was it the fact that I didn't feel so bad about looking now that he was alive and well? His stomach was well defined, every inch of his six-pack outlined. I'd never seen a *mayor* with a six-pack. Not that I'd seen many mayors shirtless.

I forced my eyes upward, trying to meet his. If he noticed I was staring at his half-naked body, he didn't show it. I realized that I hadn't seen myself in a mirror since I got ready in my hotel room in Chelsea that morning. Ben barely had a hair out of place, and I probably looked like a mad scientist. I smoothed a hand over my hair and confirmed that it was a matted mess.

"So . . . are we eating a bird then? Squab? From the nest?" He nodded at my hair. My jaw dropped. "Well, I *was* going to make you pasta, but now that you said that, forget it." I shot him a dirty look.

Ben frowned, apologetic. "I'm sorry, I was teasing. Please can I have pasta?"

"You're just apologizing because you want pasta."

He gave me a half smile. "Clearly."

"No." I pointed to the tap. "Gas stove but no water."

"Well, *water* ya gonna do?" His voice was muffled as he pulled on his own find, an off-white Irish fisherman's sweater. It fit perfectly, hugging his chest. Was he going to take off his pants, too, and replace them with the jeans? As if reading my mind he unbuckled his jeans and I held my breath. But the sweater was just long enough that it covered his boxer briefs, so I was denied a show. I couldn't help staring at his knees, though, like they were absolutely captivating. What was going on with me? This was the guy who was effectively stalling my career and putting me in a position where Elijah could *fire* me for wasting company time and resources with this jaunt to Quebec. But this was also the guy who'd probably saved our lives by finding this cottage. Let's face it, I'd been in a romantic drought for weeks, even months, now. And then of course, there was the fact that he was—

"There's a forest of snow outside our door," Ben said, interrupting my train of thought as he pulled on the dry jeans. They fit him well except for the bottoms, which billowed at his ankles. "The world is our water. Here—" He held out a hand. "Give me the pot and I'll go grab snow while you get out of your wet clothes. Then we can get going on our *primo* course." He pulled on his coat.

"Sorry to dash your dreams but I'm pretty sure it's going to be our *only* course." I laughed, grateful that he hadn't noticed me practically salivating over his torso.

"Well, I'll take whatever you're serving," he said, looking up from his winter boots that he was lacing back up.

"Who says I'm serving?"

Ben winked. Then he turned and headed out the front door again. What did he mean by that wink? Contemplating the various options, I picked up the lantern and walked down the hallway of the cottage, taking in the rustic wooden walls. On my left was an open door and I poked my head inside. The room was homey and inviting, with a large four-poster bed that took up most of the space. The bed was covered in a thin patchwork comforter and two lace-trimmed pillows. To the left of the bed was a small nightstand with a

Victorian lamp, and the window behind the bed was covered in soft, gauzy curtains that rustled lightly with the movement of air in the room, revealing a draft in the window. Feeling like an intruder, I backed out of the room and turned. On the other side of the hallway, a door was closed. I opened it and stepped inside, finding myself in a small bathroom: small wooden vanity supporting the sink and a toilet with a wooden lid. To the right was a claw-foot tub that looked inviting but given there was no water, it was out of the question. I set the lantern and my dry clothes on the vanity, shut the door, and stripped down. I grabbed one of the thin hand towels hanging on the towel rack to dry my skin before putting on the change of clothes. The flannel felt even softer once it was on. Same with the sweater. The jeans were a problem. They were about ten times too big, the legs hanging several inches past my feet, but I didn't care. I rolled up the hems, folded down the waist. I draped my wet clothes over the edge of the tub, then leaned in to look at my reflection in the oval mirror above the sink. My eyes widened in horror. After the day we'd had I didn't expect to look like I'd left the salon, but this was worse than I'd imagined. My face was red and blotchy. Mascara had created football-player smudges under my eyes. And my hair: It truly could have been on display in an aviary. I grabbed a tissue from the shelf over the toilet and swiped at my eyes. Then I pulled open the top drawer of the vanity, found a brush and elastic, and pulled my hair into a loose braid.

Ben called out, "We're in business!"

In the main room, Ben was at the stove, setting a lid on the pot. An orange flame flickered beneath the burner.

Ben turned and looked me up and down, which made the hair on my arms stand on end. "Wow," he said. "You dress up nice."

"Not so bad yourself, Mayor." A lump formed in my throat. *Stop talking, Zoey.* Was I . . . flirting with him—the guy who still wouldn't give me the film permit? Not that I'd been trying very hard to convince him in the last few hours, I supposed.

I peered into the pot to see a snowball melting into clear water.

Ben took the pack of pasta off the counter and tossed it at me. "All right, you're back in business. And I've got to tend to the fire."

Minutes later, I added the noodles to the boiling water. On a quest for salt in the cupboards, I found a particularly heavy can. "You won't believe it," I said, and held it up. Ben looked over.

"Dog food?" I opened the drawer next to the stove and found a can opener and a spoon. In another cupboard I found a metal bowl, which I emptied some of the food into.

I nodded. "Come here, Simon," I called, and the dog looked up from his spot on the couch, where he was blissfully curled up. I slapped my leg and he came over, tail wagging. I placed the bowl on the floor in front of him.

Simon made quick work of the meal. I returned to the same cupboard, trying to remember what it was I'd been looking for in the first place, when I spotted the tall dark bottle near the back. I pulled it out to examine it more closely. "*Do you hear what I hear?*" I asked Ben.

"*Said the night wind to the little lamb?*" he responded, sounding confused.

"Wait, what? The line is night *wind*? I thought it was night wine." I laughed. "Anyway, that's what I found." I held up the bottle and did a little happy dance.

"Open it!" Ben beamed. I opened other cupboards, searching for wineglasses, but came up empty. Mugs would have to do. I twisted open the wine bottle and poured some into each mug, then walked over to Ben and handed him one. "Cheers." He clinked his cup against mine. The acidic liquid burned the back of my throat and I coughed. "Wow. I hope you're not a wine snob."

· "It's not good?" he said, his voice full of surprise. He sniffed the mug.

"No, it's *terrible*. No wonder they don't own wineglasses." I made a face but took another sip. "Not to speak ill of the people who have just unknowingly lent us their home and their food," I added, sitting down on the couch next to Ben.

Ben took a sip and winced. "It really is bad."

"Maybe it'll get better the more we drink?"

"I'm willing to give it the ol' college try." He took another sip. "Still terrible."

"It's warming me up."

"It's probably my fire." Ben grinned and pointed to the flames. "That's a good one, if I do say so myself."

I looked over at the flames dancing. There was something familiar about this moment, about this me, sitting on the couch, drinking wine, with Ben and his dog two days before Christmas. It was . . . *perfect.* My stomach felt like it was doing snow angels. *What was it about this moment?* It hit me: It was almost exactly like the scene I'd written in the screenplay, of Jacques and Ruby and the dog curled up together at Jacques's place. That was a good thing: It meant audiences would relate. Maybe if Ben drank enough wine, I mused, I could convince him to give me the film permit. I smiled to myself. It was amazing what twenty minutes of being warm and dry could do for my focus. Not to mention the prospect of some food.

"Delicious. You made a great spread," Ben said a few minutes later, after I'd handed him a plate of steaming pasta. I returned to my spot on the couch, pulling my legs up underneath me. "Seriously, I know we're making light of this situation, but I think we need to appreciate that we found a cottage, firewood, a gas stove, pasta, *and* wine? I'd say—"

"We're lucky? Isn't that what you always say?" I smirked as I took another sip of wine.

"I was going to say what you always say—jackpot." He took a bite of pasta and then sighed. "This is seriously so good."

The fire, the first bite of food in hours, the compliment— it all warmed me.

"I think we're both just starving," I said modestly. "It's like when you go camping and *anything* warm tastes like it came out of a five-star restaurant."

"That's true," he said, then cocked his head, surprised. "You like camping?"

I nodded. "Actually, yeah. I really do. I haven't done it in years, though, because . . ." I paused, considering how much I wanted to share.

"Because?" He sounded curious.

"My ex, Tomas, didn't like camping. He was more of a white-glove-service kind of guy."

"So you stopped going camping?" Ben's voice was challenging.

"Well, it's kind of hard to *force* someone to go camping," I said, feeling a bit defensive.

"But you could've gone," he said before putting another forkful of pasta in his mouth.

"Mm-hmm," I said with a nod. "Yep, I could've." He was right. I could've gone camping. I used to go camping with my college friends. Why did we ever stop?

We were silent for a moment, taking sips of wine between bites of food. Simon wandered over and rested his head on my knee and I scratched him behind his ears. "So did you always want to be the mayor? And own a Christmas tree farm, *and* produce and sell maple syrup?"

He gave me a sidelong glance. "Yeah, the dream was always to juggle three jobs." I rolled my eyes, making Ben laugh. "Okay, Zoey. You really want to know?"

I nodded, twirling spaghetti onto my fork. Simon returned to his spot in front of the fire, curling up and completing the picture-perfect scene.

"I grew up on the tree farm. It was my grandparents' place before it became my parents'. My grandparents bought it back when it was just acres and acres for miles. They planted the balsam firs themselves, down on their hands and knees."

"Wow," I said, reaching for my mug and taking a sip. The pasta must have cut the acidity, because the wine really wasn't quite so terrible as the first sip.

"Then my dad came along, the oldest of three sons," Ben continued. "He started helping out with the business when he was old enough to, then, when he was a teen, he and his brothers thought they should be replanting cut trees with other varietals. People were asking for it, but my grandfather wouldn't have it. Balsam firs or nothing." He got up and retrieved the bottle of wine from the kitchen table and poured himself another mugful. When he offered to top me up, I nodded, holding out my mug.

"Isn't one of the rules of business to give people what they want?" I asked.

"Maybe that's how it works in movies—"

"Actually, I take back what I said," I interrupted. "People don't always know what's best. That's why I don't want to make *I'll Be Home for Christmas*."

"You don't want to make your own movie?" Ben looked puzzled.

"That's *not* my movie." I waved a hand. "Anyway, we weren't talking about me. We were talking about balsam firs or nothing. Go on." I took another sip of wine. I wanted him to continue telling me about the farm, about his family. I wanted to know more about him.

"Right. Well, my grandfather reasoned that balsam firs are the best. At least in Quebec. No need for anything else. It was like suggesting they make pinot grigio in Champagne."

"You *are* a wine snob," I teased.

Ben's eyes met mine, the corners crinkling. The glow of the fire and tea lights created golden flecks in his hazel eyes. "*Anyway*, my dad's brothers kept pushing my grandfather to reconsider, to the point that when it came time to figure out what to do with their lives, they both decided they didn't want to work at the farm."

"All because of balsam firs?"

"Not just that. It was because of every little decision. They second-guessed my grandfather on it all, but he was right," Ben said with a shrug. "Other tree farms opened of course, some of them the kind where they just ship trees in from all over Canada and the U.S., but people keep coming back to us for the balsam firs. I think we'd be far less successful if we added other varietals."

"What happened to your uncles?"

"One went to work in a paper mill. The other became a doctor." Ben took a sip of wine.

"And so your dad took over the farm." I studied his face, feeling slightly nervous to bring up his father. I remembered his call with Paul earlier in the day.

Ben nodded. "And then came me. I loved working alongside my dad. A lot of other kids hated being around their parents, and helping out around the house, but I loved it. Until I was a teen, obviously."

I smiled at him. "They must have been great parents." I thought of my own mother, more like the character Cher played in the movie *Mermaids*, who considered boxed mac and cheese a gourmet meal.

"They really were. My mom is still that same woman, and now I appreciate those homecooked meals again. They wanted a whole brood of us, but they were never able to have more kids after me. So they put all their focus on me." Ben turned his head and gazed into the roaring fire.

I couldn't imagine not having a sister. It was weird. Ben was an only child but had a huge, close, extended family. And I had Stella, but really no one else. "Wasn't that hard, though, being an only child? Did you feel like you *had* to take over the farm?"

"For sure," he said, looking back to me. "They didn't say it, but I knew. I think that's why I rebelled as a teen—went to work at the *dépanneur*, a kind of convenience store we have in Quebec—mostly so I could get free beer." He grinned. "But eventually I was happy to know that I could keep the family business going."

"So . . . when did the mayor stuff come into play?" I'd cleaned my bowl and put it on the coffee table, then twisted on the couch, putting the pillow behind me, and leaning back.

"When I was at college. Things were starting to change in the town. My dad decided he could either go along with it, or resist it—and so he decided to run for mayor, and make sure the town stayed the same as it ever was."

"Most people go into politics to effect change—not the other way around," I said, bringing my mug to my lips. If I thought Ben was traditional, his dad sounded practically prehistoric.

"Sometimes ensuring change *doesn't* happen is as important as making change happen." He downed the last of his wine and then reached for the bottle. He added more to both our mugs. "Anyway, I got back from McGill," he went on, setting the nearly empty wine bottle back on the table, "ready to take a bigger interest in the farm, and it turned out to be good timing. My dad and I worked for a few years side by side, then my dad ran for mayor a few years ago, and I was able to take on the farm full-time, with both of us feeling confident about it all. Things had been running smoothly but then he got pneumonia last winter. And didn't make it." His eyes clouded over.

"I'm sorry," I said, leaning forward and resting a hand on his knee. "That's awful." He looked at me and smiled sadly. "Thanks. And then I sort of fell into the mayor thing. They opened up a temporary election and I could just hear my dad's words over and over again in my head: *We don't want anything to change Chelsea.* So I ran, mostly to honor my father's memory."

I raised my eyebrows. This Deschamps family seriously loved Chelsea. I could understand why—it was a really special place. Hell, I visited once when I was a kid and loved it so much that I set an entire movie there.

"I didn't actually think I'd win," Ben was saying. "I thought I'd get a mediocre show of votes, but that I could tell myself I'd done what he would've wanted. I just wanted to focus on the farm, you know?" He looked over at me and I nodded. "But it turned out people in town felt loyal to my father, or maybe they also wanted to ensure that Chelsea stayed the same. Maybe they thought voting for me would make that happen, I don't know, but here I am. So now I run the farm and . . ." He trailed off.

"The town."

He nodded.

I cleared my throat. "So what's the long-term plan? Pass the farm to your, uh, own kids?"

He shook his head. "I don't know. I really did choose to do this myself. I love the farm. But if my dad were alive and asked me to run for mayor, I wouldn't have. But he didn't ask for a lot, and keeping Chelsea the same was high on his list so . . ."

"Which is why you're pushing back on the developers who are barking at your heels." I was beginning to understand why it seemed Ben was so stubbornly against everything—the development, and my movie.

He nodded. Then, as if reading my mind, he said, "And that's why I can't issue the film permit to *you*, either."

I swallowed, my heart racing. I put the mug down on the table and clasped my hands. "Right, but, Ben, the thing about your father was that he had strong beliefs. And because he believed so strongly, and had his reasons, others rallied behind him. He was a true leader. But all your reasons for 'protecting' Chelsea aren't really *your* reasons—they're your dad's. I haven't heard you say what *you* believe. So that makes you a follower."

The words tumbled out more harshly than I intended, and I held my breath while I waited for Ben's response.

But he didn't seem offended—more intrigued. He mulled over my words and then said, thoughtfully, "I guess I'm still trying to figure out where I stand when it comes to the town. Take into consideration various views and opinions, but ultimately make the decisions I think are best for the future of the town," he said, his eyes on the fire. "And that takes a lot longer than fifteen minutes with a stranger who walks into my office with a proposal." Then he walked over to the hearth, and added a log to the dwindling flame. There was a finality to his tone—but the night was young.

"So you want to hear why I want to make this movie? How's now? You have more than fifteen minutes now," I said. He stood and turned.

"Why don't you tell me why you wrote a Christmas movie when you're clearly not a Christmas person."

I blinked. "Not a Christmas person? I *love* Christmas. I don't think you could meet someone who loves Christmas more than me."

Ben was skeptical. "You said that before. And it's clear you love Christmas *movies*," he said, sitting on the couch again. "And Christmas songs. But you don't love *Christmas*, you can't. You didn't have Christmas plans."

"That doesn't mean I don't love Christmas," I argued. "I just—it's different."

I gulped my wine.

He twisted on the couch to fix his eyes on me. "What is?"

"I live in LA," I said, throwing up a hand. "I *want* the snowy house in the forest, the Christmas tree and the lights and the hot cocoa and all that, but I also want the family that goes with that. And right now, I don't have that. So until I do, this is my life." I reached over and grabbed the bottle of wine, splitting the remains between our mugs. "Anyway, one day when I meet the right guy and we get married and have kids, then I'll have a reason to do the rest. I'll get the house, make the gingerbread cookies, and write *all* the notes to Santa. We'll leave cookies and milk for him, and carrots for the reindeer. I want my kids to believe in Santa for as long as possible." I looked down and played with the hem of my sweater. "I want us to wake up at the crack of dawn because we're all too excited to sleep. I have this idea of putting a special ornament from somewhere we traveled that year in each of my kids' stockings, so that they'll have a memory they can put on the tree and also take with them when they're grown up—you know, so they can carry on the tradition with their own kids . . ." I looked up and Ben was staring at me. "What?" I suddenly felt very self-conscious.

He put his mug down and reached for my hand. "That sounds incredible." His hand was warm and soft, and my heart skipped a beat.

"Oh. Well, yeah. Because I *love* Christmas. Duh." I laughed nervously.

He didn't join in on my laughter. "What are you waiting for?"

I pulled my hand from his grip. "Uh, do I *look* pregnant? I know this sweater is big, but seriously."

"You know what I mean, Zoey."

"No, I don't." I avoided his eyes and instead turned my attention to Simon, who was lolling by the fire.

"You're waiting until all the perfect elements fall in place before you allow yourself to enjoy this holiday. Your dream, everything you imagine, sounds incredible. So *do* it. Fine, maybe you're not wrapping gifts from Santa, but rather the gifts from you, Zoey. Do you ever have your friends over? What about your sister?"

"My sister's husband is Jewish, so they don't celebrate Christmas now."

"So? You want to. If she invited you for Hanukkah dinner you'd go, right? So invite her to your Christmas. Make it happen. What are you afraid of?"

I nodded, but it was just to get him to stop talking. "Listen, I need to use the bathroom." I stood and walked down the hall into the bathroom and shut the door. Then I slid, my back against the door, to the floor. I needed a minute.

Ben had no idea what he was talking about. He had no idea what I wanted, and just because I didn't celebrate Christmas the way I wanted to yet didn't mean that I was *afraid*. I loved Christmas, but it was *hard* for me—it made me think of my parents and Stella, and one of the few times that I could remember us being happy together. Was it so bad that I just wanted to build these memories with the right person? He just didn't get it.

When I returned to the living room, Ben was sitting on the floor with his back against the couch and legs outstretched. Instead of settling down next to him, I went back to my spot on the couch and also extended my legs. For a few minutes, neither of us said anything. I watched the fire and Ben rubbed Simon's belly. Despite the tension between us, I could feel my body relaxing.

"So what's it like being a director?" he asked, breaking the silence just as I was dozing off. "Did you always know you wanted to do that?"

I looked at the ceiling. "Yep. Ever since I learned what a director does. I love movies, but I love stories most. I love hearing about other people, I love sharing other people's experiences. I'm that person who hears a great story and retells it so many times at parties that eventually I end up telling it back to the person who told it to me in the first place."

Ben laughed. "I doubt that."

"No, it's true," I insisted. "I've done it multiple times, in fact. It's embarrassing. Anyway, lots of people love movies, I guess. It's not *that* special."

Ben put his hands behind his head, so that his elbows were resting on the couch, inches from my legs. "Yeah, people like movies, but it doesn't mean they *make* movies for a living. What you do—it's cool."

"You're right," I said. "I think stories were so comforting to me as a kid. My parents were always fighting, and breaking up, and then my sister and I would be shipped back and forth between them. Movies were the constant. Stella and I would watch them to drown out the fights and the loneliness. Escaping into someone else's story meant . . ." I trailed off.

"Being able to escape your own?" Ben asked, turning his head to look at me.

"Exactly. Twelve-year-old me didn't recognize that, of course, but now I do."

"I'm sorry about your parents," he said softly. "That must've been tough. You were so young."

I nodded. "Yeah. You know how in the movies the divorced parents are always fighting to have custody of their kids?" Ben nodded. "Not in our house. My mom and dad didn't fight about whose time it was *with us*, they'd fight about whose time it *wasn't*."

"Zoey. That's awful." Ben reached over and touched my leg, but then quickly pulled his hand away, like my skin was hot. He cleared his throat. "So what about the Christmas movies?" he prompted.

I smiled widely. "They're the best kind of comfort. No one ever watches a Christmas movie and is disappointed. We give them what they want. You know there'll be drama and excitement, but also swoony romance and an epic kiss—and a perfect happily ever after, right on Christmas Day." I breathed a sigh of satisfaction. "And that's what people want."

"But is it realistic?" Ben sounded doubtful but his face was curious. "Do you think it perpetuates these unrealistic notions of love and relationships?"

"In some form," I admitted. "Or maybe it's just that it's a tweaked version of what you *hoped* for. The movies always brought me so much comfort, and they also gave me ideas for what I wanted my life to be like, when I could control it. They brought me—they *bring* me—so much hope and I don't want that to end. I want to make sure we're still bringing that kind of hope to other people, whenever they need it. Being a director means I get to help shape those stories. It's not *that* different from your work as mayor. You want to provide comfort and stability and continuity to the people in the town, but you also want to pave your own way." I considered *I'll Be Home for Christmas*. It wasn't fresh. That was why I wanted *my* movie. I was about to tell Ben this, to make my point, as a last-ditch chance to convince him—but then he changed the subject.

"So why Chelsea?" he asked.

"You don't really want to know."

"Why wouldn't I?"

"Because maybe if you hear, you won't be able to deny me the film permit," I teased.

"That ship has sailed. To Wakefield, remember? But tell me anyway."

I stretched my arms over my head and told him about the Christmas I'd spent in Chelsea. How our parents had dropped us off at the school playground so they could do some last-minute shopping together. We'd never experienced a playground in snow. How the snow was so high we were able to carve out a tunnel from the top of the play structure to the base, the plastic slide running through it. How back at the cottage all four of us had been able to snuggle on the sectional couch because it was so big, something we'd never been able to do at home, and watch *It's a Wonderful Life* together. How I still had the beautiful snow globe of the main street in Chelsea my parents had given me that Christmas. When I was younger, I kept it in my bedroom year-round, shaking it to watch the snow float up and settle back down, wishing in July for another magical Christmas that year. And then, years later, how I tucked it away when I moved from Chicago, where I'd lived for years after university, to LA, from apartment to apartment, taking it out only at Christmas, my lone decoration, keeping it on my nightstand. How I hoped that one day I'd have it sitting on the mantel over a fireplace in my home, where my children could take it down to shake the snow free themselves. I didn't intend to share that part with him but it spilled out before I could stop it.

He let out a low whistle. "Wow. I wasn't expecting that," he said.

"Yeah, well, you asked," I said, my eyes filling with tears. I blinked them back. I'd just shared it all with Ben and I didn't know how to feel.

"Yeah," he said softly. "I did." He cleared his throat. "So your characters, do they make *la tire*?"

"*La tear*?" I repeated. "Like . . . crying?"

Ben shook his head. "No, no. But I'm shedding a tear at the thought you don't know about this tradition either. We need to get you some French lessons!"

"What is it?" I sat up and turned to face him.

"It's spelled like tire like on a car, but pronounced *la teer*. The full name is *tire sur la neige*. It means pull on the snow but it's actually maple syrup on snow. And I've never seen anyone having *that* in a holiday movie."

"I thought you said you never watched holiday movies." I crossed my arms and smiled at him.

Ben slapped his leg. "Okay, I have an idea. We'll make *la tire* for dessert. Any chance you saw maple syrup in the cupboard?"

"They were pretty bare bones," I said, shaking my head, then remembered the jar of amber liquid. "Actually, there was something in the top cupboard, but in a mason jar." I pointed to the cupboard to the left of the stove.

"Probably from my farm," he said. He stood and made his way across the floor to the kitchen. I followed him.

"You say that as though every cottage has maple syrup, and there's a good chance it's yours."

He shrugged. "We make the best maple syrup around, remember?" He opened the cupboard and felt around, then pulled out the mason jar and inspected it. He twisted off the cap and took a deep whiff. "Ah, yep, it's maple syrup all right."

I leaned against the counter and watched him. "So we're . . . just going to drink maple syrup?"

"No. *You're* going to heat the maple syrup on the stove while I go outside to get snow."

"More snow?" I frowned. "I think I've seen enough snow to last a lifetime."

"More snow."

Seconds later, another gust of cold air whipped through the cottage as he slipped out the door. I found another pot and poured the amber liquid into it. As it slowly heated, I ran my finger along the edge of the jar, then tasted the sticky liquid. I was no maple connoisseur—did IHOP even serve the real stuff?—but the syrup burst on my tongue, a perfect balance of maple and vanilla.

Soon Ben returned with the bowl of snow. "All right, now we need a tray," he said, shaking off his coat. "Like a cookie sheet."

Hmm. Where would I keep baking trays, I wondered. I opened the drawer under the oven and found a well-worn tray that, judging from the patina of darkened stains on the surface, had clearly seen countless batches of cookies. The corners were bent, the surface rough and bumpy. "This okay?" I held it up for Ben to see. When he nodded, I slid it onto the counter toward him.

Ben gave it a quick wipe with his hand, then dumped the snow on it. He reached for a spatula in the ceramic jar by the sink and used it to spread the snow into a thin, even layer on the tray. I turned to the stove and inspected the syrup, which was slightly bubbling. "Should I stir this?"

Ben leaned over my shoulder. "You're a good student."

"Good teacher, though I'd love to know what the final result will be."

"You'll see." I closed my eyes and inhaled. He smelled like the fire. I almost leaned back into him, but then remembered that this wasn't Ruby and Jacques. This wasn't a date.

Ben turned off the burner. "All right, now you're going to very carefully pour the maple syrup in thin ribbons on the snow."

I reached out for the pot handle, but just as I was about to touch it, Ben put his hand on mine to stop me. "Don't touch that!" he warned, pulling my hand away. I turned in surprise.

"It's metal. You'll burn yourself," he said, his eyes concerned. My stomach flip-flopped. Was it the near-touch of the hot handle or Ben's hand on mine?

Ben let go of my hand and turned his attention back to the pot. He found a tea towel in the drawer at his hip and used it to pick up the pot.

"My father taught me how to make *la tire* when I was little," he said as he created two ribbons on the snow. "We make it for guests when they come to cut their tree. Though it's mostly Gérard, who manages the tree farm, who does it. He and his son. Maybe I'll have time, one day—"

"When you're not *also* the mayor?" I asked sardonically.

Ben gave me a look. "I was going to say, when I'm a dad. For now, he enjoys doing it." He turned. "All right, typically we would have some sort of stick, like a Popsicle stick, but since we don't, we'll use spoons." He pulled open a few drawers, then held up two metal spoons, passing one to me. "Let's roll." He placed his spoon, round side down, on the syrup, which had hardened on the snow. Then he slowly rotated the spoon, the syrup sticking as he moved it from one end of the cookie sheet to the other. I followed his actions, rolling my spoon over the second ribbon. Ben held his spoon in the air. "*Et voilà! La tire.*"

I touched the cold, hard taffy to my lips. The rich flavor of the maple syrup seemed more intense when cold. I never thought I'd want to taste anything cold after how many hours I'd spent in the cold today, but it was delightful. "This is incredible."

Ben smiled. "Good enough for a scene in your film?"

"My very authentic, must-shoot-in-Chelsea film?"

"Although I have to question the authenticity of this so-called Quebecois film if you don't already have a scene with *la tire*."

"Maybe I need a script consultant." I leaned against the counter and licked the sweet and sticky clumps of melting ice resting in the hollow of the spoon.

Ben sat down on the kitchen table opposite me. "So in your film the heroine returns, but you didn't return before you wrote the script, did you?"

"Why?" I said, confused.

"Never mind."

"What?" I prodded.

"I was going to say that I don't remember you, if you'd come back last year or whenever you were writing the script, but I know how that sounds." He gave me a sidelong glance.

"How does that sound? Like you know every single person in town? It's a small town but . . ."

He shrugged. "I'd have remembered you, if I'd seen you. I would've wanted to meet you." He put his spoon to his lips.

I stared at his mouth, then blinked, trying to refocus. The combination of the wine and the sugar was making me feel light-headed. I was probably reading too much into what Ben was saying. Besides, I could never really *like* him. He was so infuriating. I found him attractive, no doubt—in fact, he'd be the type of guy that I'd date, I think—but I also found him stubborn and arrogant. "Why?" I challenged him.

"Because you're *that* kind of girl. You're beautiful, and you're sexy as hell. And you're this incredible go-getter who doesn't care if her hair gets messy."

My mouth dropped open again, but for a different reason this time. Did he just call me beautiful? And sexy? And did he basically say that he *liked* how determined I was? I was convinced that was the part about me that annoyed him the most. "Oh," I said, at a loss for words. I suddenly didn't know what to do with my hands, but I needed to do something with them. I gripped the counter behind me. Ben stood and walked closer to me, reaching out and gently uncurling my left hand from its grip on the edge of the counter, and curling it into his.

"You *think* that?" I whispered. I blinked, searching his face.

He nodded. He looked down at my hand in his and rubbed his thumb over it. "But I know that you think I'm just this jerk who won't give you what you want."

I nodded. "It's true." I bit my lip.

"You're probably really mad at me," he said softly. He took a step closer to me.

I nodded again. The air between us felt charged with energy. "Uh-huh."

"So it's a real conundrum," he said, his voice low. "Because I want to kiss you, but you probably don't want to—"

I reached up and put my hand behind his neck, pulling his head close to mine. My fingers disappeared in his thick hair as I pressed my lips to his—hard. All the pent-up feelings I had toward him—the wild attraction, but also the resentment and anger for standing in my way—fueled the kiss. As our lips pressed together, Ben took another step toward me, closing the space between us, so close that I could feel his legs between mine. I moved my other hand to his face, tilting my head to the side so I could pull him in even closer. His hands found my hips and pressed against them, his thumbs on my hip bones. My tongue traced the inside of his upper lip. I deliberately pressed my body closer to him, wanting him to feel how much I wanted him. His body felt taut against mine.

He pulled his face away from mine, ever so slightly, meeting my eyes with his. "I've been wanting to do that since you slid under my truck," he said hoarsely.

My breath caught in a small gasp. "Me too," I admitted softly. The words surprised me—I hadn't even known it was what I wanted, but I was telling the truth.

Ben found my hand and laced his fingers with mine, then led me toward the couch. "Hang on," he said. He took the cushions off the couch, then spread them on the floor. Simon looked up, seemed to get the memo that the mood in the room had changed, and scooted away, disappearing around the corner.

Ben looked at me again, desire in his eyes, and stepped toward me. Within seconds, his lips were on mine. His hands moved to my waist, his fingers finding their way under my sweater and shirt to my skin. He ran his hands up my sides, sending tingles through my body. He stopped kissing me for a moment to ask, "Can we take this off?"

I nodded, then let him work the sweater, and then the flannel shirt, over my head. For a split second I felt self-conscious but then his lips caught mine and I could think of nothing else. I unbuttoned his flannel shirt. This time he wasn't unconscious, and I didn't feel bad looking at him. I reached out to lightly trace the tree tattoo on his biceps with my finger before moving my hands down his chest until they met the top of his jeans. I tugged on the waistband and pulled him close, so that his bare chest, his taut stomach were pressed against my stomach, too.

Our lips met again, and then Ben lowered me down to the cushions. I stretched out on my back. His eyes flitted over my body, taking in every inch of me, and a slow smile spread over his face. "You got a sneak peek of me earlier today, but I've been imagining this moment for hours," he said, then lowered himself on top of me. His lips grazed my ear, then tugged on my earlobe. I moaned softly.

I held on to the tops of his muscular arms as his lips worked their way to the spot behind my ear, then to the curve of my neck. His tongue traced a line along my collarbone. My back arched involuntarily, like I was trying to get even closer to him.

I drew my fingers up his stomach and to his face, pulling him tight and pressing my mouth to his. Our tongues met, our kisses breathing into each other. My whole body was aflame. I couldn't believe that I was kissing *Ben*. Ben who, yesterday, I wanted to throttle. Ben who, for the last thirty-six hours, had been the opposition. Now kissing him felt so . . . right.

We continued like this, kissing between ragged breaths, until Ben pulled his lips from mine and worked them down my body—my collarbone, my shoulder, between my breasts. In this moment, my body was a maze, and Ben's tongue a pen. I wasn't sure where his tongue would go next, but it all felt so good, like wherever he moved was exactly the right way to go. I tangled my fingers in his hair, moaning with each kiss, each flick of his tongue on my skin.

When he got to the top of my borrowed jeans he tugged at them with his teeth, then knelt between my legs. I lifted my hips so he could shimmy the denim down past them. When they were finally off, he looked at me with appreciation. "You are beautiful, Zoey."

I blushed. "Okay, your turn. Fair's fair," I teased, and he stood, stripping down to his boxer briefs, kicking his jeans to the side to join mine.

"How's that?" he asked.

I drank him in. His creamy, smooth skin, his defined muscles, fine, dark hair running up and down his legs and arms. "Pretty good," I said. He crouched down, but instead of laying his body back on top of mine, he began working his tongue up my right leg, along my shinbone, then all the way around my knee. Higher and higher his mouth climbed, pushing me deeper into pleasure.

Eventually, his tongue worked its way up to my inner thigh and I held my breath in anticipation. Gently, he pushed my underwear to the side and brought his lips to my center. I gasped, then opened my legs wider to give him more access. For minutes he pleasured me, bringing me closer and closer to the edge. Just as all the tension of the past few days was about to release he stopped and moved up until his body was beside mine.

"How was that?" he asked, his voice thick. He kissed me once again, pushing his tongue into my mouth.

I moaned with contentment, then, without answering, I maneuvered myself between his legs and shimmied his boxer briefs down his legs and over his toes, then flung my own underwear to the ground, too. Stretching out beside him again, I pressed my body into his and wrapped my leg around him. I slipped my hand down into our tangle of legs, reaching until I found what I was looking for. With a groan, Ben climbed on top of me, and I arched my back, slipping him inside me as a sob of rapture escaped my lips. He moved his hands to either side of my head and then sank himself into me. I used his biceps as leverage, to press myself toward him, holding on tightly as our bodies moved together. Every part of us seemed fused—I'd never felt anything like this. We moved in rhythm until, finally, his body released, and then mine did, in the most perfect way. We collapsed around each other. And then we stayed like that, our bodies intertwined, Ben touching my hair and me tracing his tattoo until, eventually, warmed from passion, contentment, and the fire, we fell asleep.

CHAPTER FOURTEEN

Christmas Eve, 8:30 a.m.

The sound of a motor revving woke me from a deep sleep. I opened my eyes, confused, and closed them again, trying to return to my dream, which was filled with snippets from the night before. Ben's kisses, on my lips, my collarbone, my stomach, my legs, then between my legs. His hands on my bare skin, our bodies intertwined, like it was the most natural thing in the world. Falling asleep beside him, my head in the crook of his arm. Then waking up a few hours later and doing it all over again until, tangled together, the blanket over our naked bodies, we'd fallen back to sleep.

Now I opened my eyes—again—and smiled up at the wood ceiling of the cottage, wondering what time it was, and also thinking, who cares? That was the best sex I'd had in months, years. Maybe . . . ever? There was just something about being with Ben. It was passionate and exciting, but also easy. We just . . . *fit* together. I stretched and looked around and only then noticed that Ben's spot next to me was empty. Surprised, I sat up. There was no sign of Simon. I stood, pulling on the cotton shirt, then looked out the window to the frozen wonderland, relieved to see Ben by the shed. Simon was nearby, hopping and sliding on the ice. For a moment the scene looked peaceful, but the next minute there was a crack, and a large ice-covered branch broke off from a massive maple, and crashed to the icy ground. Ben jumped and turned, then looked around. When he saw me watching him through the window, he raised his arm in a wave. I felt caught, but smiled and gave a small wave. He disappeared around the side of the house, and I chewed on my lip. Were things going to be weird between us? What had happened last night—that wasn't a common occurrence for me. Was it for Ben? I didn't know if it was no big deal, us hooking up, or if things would suddenly be awkward.

A moment later, the cottage door opened and Ben entered, Simon at his heels. A cold gust of air whipped through the cottage. He pulled off his coat and hung it on the hook behind the door. He was wearing the oversize sweater, jeans, and boots, as well as a huge grin on his face, which was red from the cold.

"Hey!" I said a little too excitedly as though he hadn't just seen me staring at him. *Not awkward at all, Zoey.*

"You won't believe it," he said, his eyes sparkling. "I found something out there that's gonna change our entire trip."

"Uh, let's see," I said, pretending to think very hard. "A magical reindeer. Attached to a sleigh that's going to get us out of here."

Ben dangled a set of shiny keys. "No. Better. There's a snowmobile out behind the shed. And I found the keys. I'm surprised it didn't dawn on me when I saw the helmets in the little utility room at the back last night—not that it would've done us any good in the dark. But now? It's our ticket out of here." He disappeared down the hall, Simon following him, and I took the opportunity to scooch into my jeans. *Out of here?* The suggestion provoked a surprising mix of feelings. I'd become used to the idea of being stuck here, in the cabin with Ben. Being forced to spend Christmas here, with Ben, all to myself? That sounded like the Christmas present I wanted.

"Why are we trying to leave?" I called out to Ben. "It's warm and empty, and we could just wait out the ice storm until the power comes on, couldn't we? Then we charge our cell phones and call for help. Perfect plan."

He came back into the main room, and looked at me like I was crazy. He carried two helmets—one matte black, one red with a skull on the side—and a mound of shiny fabric, which he let fall to the ground. He handed me the helmet with the skull. It was heavy, made of hard plastic with a thick lining of red insulation. I ran my fingers over the smooth surface, then brought the helmet to my face, inhaling the smell of gasoline and rubber. "It could be days before the power returns, and there's no more food in the cupboards. There's no water, and even if the power does come back on, the cell phone lines could be out for days."

Now I felt self-conscious. Was either of us going to mention what had happened last night?

"Plus, it's Christmas Eve. I have to get home for *Réveillon*."

I pointed a finger at him. "That's the *real* reason," I said accusingly.

"Oh Zo," he said, using my nickname. It made my heart flutter. "There are so many reasons."

Why was I acting like it was so wrong of him to want to be with his family on Christmas Eve, rather than stuck in a cabin in the woods with me? We'd had sex—great sex, all night long—but I was still a near-stranger. Why did I care if he wanted to get back home to his family? I still wanted to find the Wakefield mayor, secure the permit, keep the job of director on my film, a role I'd worked so hard to get. So why did it matter that Ben wanted to leave? Because I wanted to stay. Here, with the snow and the cushions and the sex and the fire . . . And I wanted him to stay, too. And I felt hurt that he wanted to leave. Well, at least I was self-aware.

I pulled on the helmet to mask my complicated mix of emotions. What would Stella say to do in this situation? Should I tell him how I felt? I concentrated on the weight of the helmet instead. It was bulky, and blocked my peripheral vision, but through the visor Ben was clear.

"Quite the look," he said, then pulled on his own helmet and flicked up the dark visor. I fiddled with mine, but it wouldn't budge.

"Need some help?" Ben asked, stepping closer. I nodded, the helmet moving reluctantly, and making me feel like I was underwater. His head close to mine, Ben smoothly lifted up the visor with a quick flick of his wrist. "There you go," he said, his breath warm. The smell of the helmet was replaced by Ben's now-familiar scent of pine and soap—how did he still smell *so* good? My heart skipped a beat, remembering how it felt to have his body on top of mine last night.

I swallowed and gestured to the shiny fabric on the floor. "What's that stuff?"

"Snowsuits!" Ben beamed. He pulled at a bright red suit and tossed it to me. I caught it and held it up to look at it. It was thick and padded, with a hood and a full-length zipper that ran from the collar to the ankles. Ben was already pulling his on, so I stepped into the legs and then pulled it up over my body to slide my arms in. I couldn't decide how to feel. On the one hand, this was promising, particularly if Ben knew how to drive a snowmobile. But on the other hand, leaving the cottage felt like an ending to what had happened last night, which had been incredible. I needed to find the right time to talk to him about it. I needed to know if it meant anything to him or if it was just a one time, in-the-moment thing.

"How does it feel?" Ben asked, once I was zipped up.

"Great!" I said. Ben seemed focused on the moment and the task at hand. I didn't need him to think that last night was a big deal if he didn't think it was a big deal.

"Great, huh? Remember yesterday when you were all up in arms over wearing a stranger's clothes?" he teased. "Look at you now, Zoey Andrews."

I rolled my eyes. "Whatever." My stomach grumbled. Okay, maybe we did need to get out of here, if only to get some food.

Ben took a breath. "All right, we just have one issue."

"One? That's it?" I held out my hand, counting on my fingers. "There's an ice storm. We're in the middle of nowhere. There's still no power. No cell service. The ice on the trees is either hurtling the branches to the ground or pulling them over. We're starving. And we have no idea where we're actually going to go once we get on the snowmobile. That's what—seven issues right there—should I go on?"

"Talk about waking up on the wrong side of the couch cushion. Not a morning person, huh?"

I bristled. "I actually *am* a morning person, but I like to wake up and have my coffee in a proper bed and then start a well-planned-out day. So this"—I waved at my outfit—"is not really how I thought I'd be starting the day." I knew I was grumpy and taking it out on Ben, which wasn't fair, especially when he'd found us a way out of here.

But it wasn't about the snowsuits or the snowmobile or any of it. It was about last night. I'd had a great time—it certainly hadn't felt like a mistake to me, but maybe he felt differently . . . though Ben didn't seem like the kind of guy who'd just have sex with anyone. But this wasn't a normal situation. And he probably thought he was never going to see me again anyway.

Ben put his hands on his snowsuit-covered hips and looked around. "No, the issue is gloves. It's freezing out there and our still-wet gloves aren't going to cut it. But where there are snowsuits and helmets, there must be gloves." He disappeared into the back hall and emerged a moment later, tossing me a pair of thick gloves. "Jackpot!" he exclaimed with a wink.

I yanked off the helmet and set it down on the table. Ben might be eager to get going, but the place was a mess. "So we're just going to steal more stuff?" We'd worn these people's clothes, and now their snowsuits, helmets, and gloves, too. Not to mention eating their food, drinking their wine . . . Was this okay? It didn't *seem* okay. When he didn't answer, I picked up the copy of *Little Women* and replaced it on the shelf. "At least let me tidy up a bit before we take off."

I gathered up the mugs and brought them over to the sink, bending down to look for dish soap in the lower cabinet. It was all incredibly awkward in my snowsuit, but I refused to take it off, as though keeping myself in this ridiculous getup was somehow punishing Ben. As though I wanted to get out of here as quickly as he did. I flicked the tap on, moving it toward hot water, forgetting that there was no water—hot or cold. Groaning, I pulled on my UGGs, but something was stopping my feet from sliding easily into them the way they normally would. I reached down, and pulled out crumpled newspaper from inside. "Why is there newspaper in my UGGs?" I grumbled.

Ben looked up from replacing the couch cushions onto the couch. "Are they dry?" he asked. I left the crumpled paper in a pile and pulled the right boot on. Miraculously it was.

"I'll take the silence as a sign that your feet are living in the lap of luxury," he said with a big smile. "Dad trick," he added. The mention of his father reminded me that he was probably eager to get home to his mother and grandmother. I sighed. It was his first Christmas without his dad, but it was his mom's first Christmas without her husband, and his grandmother's first Christmas without one of her sons. And here I was, bitter that he wasn't professing his eternal love. I'd been a warm body in a cold place last night, and he'd been the same for me. Right?

"Thanks," I said loud enough for him to hear, before grabbing the pot we'd used for the maple syrup in one hand and the bigger one I'd made the pasta in, in the other, and trudging toward the door.

Outside, the sky was still gray. The wind whipped across the front porch, and the trees cracked and crinkled their icy sheaths. Though I'd hoped a new day might mean slightly warmer temps—say, really cold rather than absolutely freezing—it actually felt colder than ever. Every breath felt like I was inhaling tiny pins. I gritted my teeth and quickly filled the pots with clean snow from the corner of the porch to use to wash the dishes. At the sink I made my way through the pots, bowls, cutlery, and mugs, stacking them on the counter to dry. I watched out of the corner of my eyes as Ben used the metal poker to break up the remaining logs in the fireplace and a small shovel to scoop out the ashes, placing them in a metal container and taking it outside. Then he refilled the fireplace with a fresh supply of logs and kindling, which I thought was so thoughtful.

I made my way over to the writing desk and pulled out a sheet of personalized stationery and a pen. "I'm going to leave a note to the owners explaining that we're borrowing their snowmobile and helmets. But that we'll return everything."

"Tell them who I am and leave my number. And that I'm happy to reimburse them for anything we used," Ben said, joining me at the table and leaning over my shoulder.

"Why should *you* have to?" I said it more harshly than I meant.

He gave me an amused look. "Because you're American and it will feel complicated to them. I'm close by and can easily drive back here to sort things out once the ice melts."

I knew what he meant—why would I return to this cottage in the middle of nowhere?—and yet, it highlighted the point: that I'd have no reason to return. No reason because I had no film. But more than that: No reason because what happened last night was nothing. That Ben couldn't wait to get out of here, to get on that snowmobile and get back to Chelsea.

If Ben sensed it though, he didn't say anything and instead of confronting him with my feelings, I busied myself tidying the rest of the cottage.

"Well, I guess that's it," Ben said, picking up his makeshift backpack and slinging it over his shoulder, then holding the door open. Simon barked and ran outside. I pulled on my cross-body bag, then looked around once more before I put on the helmet. I walked outside, bracing myself for the cold.

"This way," Ben said, leading me down the ice-covered front steps. Simon raced ahead, slipping and sliding on the ice. Ben held out a hand to help me down the slope, but I ignored it. I took small steps on the icy ground, using my arms for balance instead. I followed him toward the shed, then around to the back. Sure enough, there it was: a snowmobile, black and white with a red stripe down the side, the glossy paint catching the light.

I looked at the leather seat. It was small, maybe big enough to fit one and a half of us, but both of us? We'd have to sit close. The thought of sitting behind him on the snowmobile made me start to sweat under my thick outer layer. A flash of him on top of me last night made me weak. "Is this going to fit both of us?" I asked, my voice strained.

"No. You're right. There's just space for Simon and me. Good luck, it was nice meeting you."

I swatted at him with my gloved hands. "Come on," he said with a laugh. "I'd think that after last night, us sitting close together in snowsuits on this thing wouldn't be that big a deal, would it?" He looked at me curiously.

And there it was. My heart thumped and I felt a bit of relief. Okay, it was going to be easier to talk about last night now that he'd brought it up.

"Anyway," Ben continued, "of course we're going on this together. We're a team now, you and me. You can thank yourself for that, for not leaving me to die in the truck." He put his arm around me and squeezed me close to him.

I couldn't help but smile. "But what about Simon?"

"I'll go slowly. The snowmobile should break the ice and create a path for him to follow." Simon barked as though he understood and Ben reached down and patted him on the head.

"So do you actually know how to drive a snowmobile?" I waited nervously for his response.

Ben twisted around to face me and flipped up the plastic visor. His cheeks were squished together, making his face puffy but somehow he still looked so good. "What do you mean? I was counting on you to drive this thing."

"*What?*"

He laughed and swung a leg over the seat. "Come on, get on. In these parts, driving a Ski-Doo is something you learn about the same time you learn to walk."

I heaved one puffy leg over the seat and positioned myself behind Ben. He turned around. "Hang on tight, okay?"

I nodded, wrapping my arms around Ben's waist and clasping my gloved hands together. I leaned into him. He felt safe and warm, and for a split second I was transported back to last night.

Ben inserted the key into the ignition. With a quick turn, the engine roared to life, the sound of it echoing through the ice-covered forest, the same familiar sound that had woken me up.

"So what's the plan?" I yelled. "To find the main road, wherever that is?"

Ben nodded, then slipped the visor down. "Exactly." He adjusted the throttle and checked the mirrors—so we didn't run into anyone? We could be so lucky. Then he glanced behind at me and gave me a nod, and I clasped my hands around his waist even tighter.

We set off slowly. As Ben predicted, the skis easily broke through the ice. I turned to make sure Simon was okay, but it was as though he'd heard the plan. He tromped along happily in the tracks we created for him, his mouth wide and tongue wagging. He looked so happy and excited to be on an adventure.

While at first glance it should've seemed easy to speed through the forest, the storm had created a series of road-blocks every few feet—hidden dips and bumps that could easily throw the snowmobile off-balance and fallen branches that could easily throw us off. The wind, which had felt strong even while we were standing still, was ten times worse now that we were moving, and devilishly clever at finding the gaps in my gear. I tucked my head closer to Ben's back and I tried to relax. We were getting out of this ice storm and closer to safety. I tried not to let myself think about anything else: the fact it was Christmas Eve and I was over 2,700 miles from home; that I was so hungry, I would eat absolutely anything at this point; that the moment we got back to Chelsea, Ben would probably dash off to be with his family . . . and Delphine?

And what would I do? I had nowhere to go and none of my belongings except my wallet, my passport, and a few personal items. I had no plan, and Stella was probably worried sick about me. I felt awful for not responding to her last text yesterday morning. I also had no movie permit. I was going to make my way back to Los Angeles with nothing to show for this trip—none of my things, no happy Christmas memories, probably a bit of heartbreak and a lot of confusion about Ben, and no holiday movie.

The snowmobile skidded and slid along, bumping up and down as it broke through ice in some spots and skimmed the surface in others. Ben fought the handles to keep it in a straightish line, his head moving back and forth, scanning the horizon. The wind was still whipping all around us, and it was just as cold as yesterday, but I felt a bit of hope that we were getting out of here. The forest couldn't possibly go on forever. Eventually, we'd have to reach a road. And roads led somewhere—that was the whole point.

"How far do you think we are from the main road?" I yelled to Ben. He didn't answer, but slowed the snowmobile. When it stopped I saw the reason—a tree limb that blocked our way. He slung his leg off and stepped toward the obstacle. Before he could look up at me, in appeal, I was by his side, heaving the frozen wood in unison with him until our path was clear. He turned to me, rubbing his gloved hands together.

"Nicely done. And . . . twenty minutes?" he said. I tried to ignore that he was responding to my question with a question, because it didn't make me feel very confident. I had no idea how far we were from the main road—so why did I expect him to? As we climbed back on the snowmobile, I had a realization: There was a good chance we were nowhere near the main road. What if we'd been heading in the wrong direction this whole time? I hoped my geography was wrong, because I had the terrible thought that if you went in a certain direction, from Chelsea, the next major landmark was the Arctic Circle.

"I'm looking for spots where it looks like the trees have been cleared," Ben shouted, as though he could read my mind. "Could mean it's a road."

I could feel my hands getting sweaty in the thick gloves,

but since there was nothing more I could do, I tried to take in my surroundings. In spite of the ever-present layer of OMG-we-are-lost-in-the-woods, it really was beautiful out here, with tall trees everywhere and the most pristine white snow I'd ever seen. In the last ten minutes or so, as my mind had spiraled, a stillness had fallen, and the wind had died down a bit. Looking out at it from behind the plastic lens of my snowmobile helmet was like looking into a snow globe right before it's been shaken.

If I ever got out of here, and back to LA, I vowed to treat myself to a day off. A day on the beach. Drinking margaritas—lots of margaritas. Sure it was winter and wouldn't be *that* warm in Malibu, but it was still warmer than this. And surely I deserved a break after this?

And then the snowmobile sputtered and slowed to a crawl. I craned my neck to see if there was another obstacle but the span of snow and ice in front of us looked clear. "What's wrong?" I shouted just as the snowmobile died. The roar of the motor was replaced by complete silence.

"I'm not sure." Ben twisted the right handlebar, but the snowmobile just sputtered for a moment, then died again. *"Tabernac."* He flipped up his visor.

"Oh no. That bad?"

"It's definitely not good." Ben leaned forward, his face close to the dashboard of the snowmobile. "Pretty sure we're out of gas."

Simon caught up to us, passed us, then turned back and looked at us expectantly.

My stomach sank. "No."

"Yes." He slung a leg over the snowmobile, holding on to the handlebar. He held a hand out to me, and I took it, climbing off the seat.

"But this was the plan."

He tilted his head. "*Was* is the key word." He frowned. "Dammit."

"There go the margaritas," I sighed to myself.

"What?" Ben said, sounding annoyed.

"Nothing. It's just so frustrating." I turned around and paced a few feet in front of me and back again. I was stating the obvious, but Ben didn't chastise me. Instead, his tone was kind.

"We can do this, Zoey," Ben said, trying to sound encouraging. "We've come this far. And this snowmobile got us farther than we would've gotten skiing or walking. So now we walk."

"No." It all felt like too much. I pulled off my helmet and slammed it into the ground. The ice cracked, and the helmet rolled on its curved surface, then stopped. I stared down at it. Without the helmet my head was freezing. I bent down and picked up the helmet, then put it on my head and flipped up the visor so I could see more clearly.

Ben looked amused, but then, when he saw my face, which was anything *but* amused, he sobered.

"We weren't even far off the main road to start. I don't understand how we're *so* lost. For all we know we're even farther into the woods. I'm done. This is pointless."

"So you're just going to live here?" Ben waved a hand around. Simon jumped at it, thinking he was playing a game.

"Maybe I am," I spat back. I knew I was being irrational, but I didn't care.

"Don't be ridiculous," he said harshly. "You'd last two hours out here in this cold."

"You know what, Ben? Everything about this entire trip has gone wrong from the start. Not just this, not just the storm, but long before that. Coming to Chelsea. My movie." With each word my voice rose. "I'm mad at myself that I didn't check the weather to see there would be an ice storm. I'm mad I didn't rent a stupid car with stupid snow tires. I'm mad because I didn't wear the right clothes for this trip, or that I didn't pack snacks. I'm mad that I came to Chelsea without calling you—the mayor—and hearing you say on the phone that you weren't going to give me the permit for some ridiculously small-minded reason before I got on a plane. I'm mad at myself for last night. I'm hungry. I'm thirsty. And I wish I'd never met you." I threw my hands up and glared at him.

And Ben laughed. It wasn't a *Trevor Noah is hilarious* laugh, more of a light chuckle, but it still made me mad. "Stop *laughing* at me," I yelled, stamping my foot into the ice. I stamped it again. And again. And again. Over and over until the ice cracked and my foot went straight through, getting stuck.

Ben laughed harder, then asked, "Do you feel better?"

I shook my head, the helmet moving a half second behind, like it was on time-delay. A tear escaped my eye. Then another, until I was full-on sobbing.

"Hey, hey, hey." Ben looked alarmed and was at my side in an instant, wrapping his arms around me. "Everything's going to be okay, Zo."

"You don't know that," I mumbled.

"You're right. But I don't know it's *not* going to be okay." He pulled away and looked at me. "So you pick your side. And also, I *do* know that stomping on the ice isn't going to get us out of here, though it probably felt pretty good."

I sighed, wiping my face with my gloved hands. "Okay. What's the plan now?" I asked, then shook my head. "Sorry, I don't know why I expect you to have all the answers."

"It's fine," Ben reassured me. "I don't mind—I'm taking it to mean you trust me." He brought me in for a hug. "And," he said, pulling back, "we *are* going in the right direction. I know it doesn't seem like it but remember how long we drove away from the highway to start? We've made great headway on the snowmobile, and we'll get there soon." He paused, waiting for my response. I nodded. "Anyway, now we move on to the next leg of Ben and Zoey's Amazing Race. This is actually a very easy task to accomplish. You need no equipment. And there's little risk of failure. You just put one foot forward. When you've done that, you put the next foot forward. Again and again. It's called walking. Let's give it a try." He grinned and winked at me, and butterflies fluttered in my stomach. He could be very charming some-times, even in the most intense, will-we-survive moments.

I started walking. "You're doing great," Ben called encouragingly.

"I have a few decades of experience," I teased, then realized he wasn't beside me. When I turned around, I saw that he was back beside the snowmobile. My heart raced. "Wait, you're not *coming*?"

"I'm coming. I realized I should push this thing somewhere that I can remember where it is." He looked around the forest, which looked pretty much exactly the same in every direction. "In theory, anyway." He leaned into the handlebars of the snowmobile and pushed it a few feet forward, toward a trio of trees. He removed the keys from the ignition and slipped them into his backpack, then pulled out his scarf and wrapped it around one of the tree trunks.

Then he caught up to me. "Now we walk." We set off, side by side, but I was sliding with nearly every step. Instead of losing my composure, I leaned into the sliding motion. A moment later, Ben started sliding, too.

"Good idea," Ben said as we shuffle-slid along. Simon ran circles around us seemingly impervious to the cold, the snow, the ice, or even the stress emanating from me.

"It's going to take forever at this rate, but at least we're upright," I said, just as one of my UGGs slipped a little too far ahead. Ben grabbed my arm, steadying me before I wiped out. "Do you think we should go back for the snowshoes?" I asked, even though the thought of walking back the way we came seemed worse than continuing on.

Ben shook his head. "Definitely not. And we're in these superwarm outfits. We don't have to go fast; we can just take our time. Enjoy the beauty of the ice storm."

"People die in ice storms," I said. "You said yourself I wouldn't last more than two hours out here."

"Most of the trees that will fall, have fallen. And remember what happened last night? Well, I want another chance at that, so we're going to *have* to make it somewhere so we can get these ridiculous clothes off."

I turned to stare at him, my mouth hanging open. He grinned back at me.

"I wasn't sure . . . ," I began, suddenly feeling shy.

"Wasn't sure about what?"

"Well, you didn't say anything."

"You didn't say anything either," he pointed out. "But I guess I was focused on us getting home for Christmas Eve."

"Right," I said. Of course he wanted to get home, for all the reasons I'd already considered: on top of loving the holiday, to be there for his mom and grandmother, too. This wasn't about me or us—even if we did have an amazing night together.

"You're the mayor," I said, trying to be positive, "and the mayor is missing! Do they send out the armed forces or something?"

"To rescue people in the ice storm—actually yes."

"Really?" I said hopefully. He took my hand and held it in his.

"Yes, but it could take days for them to find us. We're better to save ourselves."

We continued slide-shuffling along.

Simon had darted farther into the forest, and was trotting back toward us now, a large stick in his mouth.

"Remember when you were all like, who would ever spend Christmas somewhere warm?" I said.

"I'm not sure those were my exact words."

"Well, I just have to say, isn't there a tiny little bit of you that wishes we were doing this on a deserted island? Like on *Survivor*? Why is *Survivor* always in hot destinations?"

"Bikinis," Ben said wryly. "No one looks sexy in a snow-suit." He turned to me and raised an eyebrow. "Present company excluded, of course."

Simon finally reached us, and Ben took the stick from him, then threw it back toward the forest. Simon raced after it with an energy I didn't feel.

"Tell me again. How do you know we're going the right way?" I said.

"The sun is over there. Rises in the east . . ." There was no sun in the sky, though the sky where Ben was pointing did seem slightly more illuminated—maybe.

"Yes, but how do you know the *road* is to the east?"

"Well . . . ," Ben said. I waited for him to go on but he was silent.

"How do you know the road is to the east?" I said again, panic rising in my chest. "You're supposed to know this stuff." But did he? I just assumed Ben had this area memorized and knew where we were going. "You *don't* know, do you?" I said, my voice barely above a whisper.

Ben sighed, looking at me. "I have an idea, but no, I'm not totally sure," he admitted.

My eyes widened. "Ben. What if we're supposed to be going *that* way?" I flailed my arm off to the left.

He nodded. "Yep. There is a chance we should be walking in the opposite direction."

"What?" My voice rose two octaves. *"What?"*

Ben caught my arm and held a gloved finger up to the front of his helmet.

I glared at him. "Do *not shush* me, Ben. I—"

"Shh!" he said, then pointed to the left. I turned my head just as something moved in the distance. It wasn't Simon— he was next to us. I brushed the ice from the front of my visor and gasped. "What is it?"

The creature was majestic, its coat so deep a shade of brown, it looked like velvet. It stood as tall as Ben, its antlers reaching high.

"It's a reindeer," I said. "Isn't it?"

"Basically," Ben said. "Caribou, but same animal. She's a female—the male would've lost his antlers by this time of year."

"But when we say reindeer, in the stories and the songs—"

"Yes," Ben said. "That's her. Dasher or Dancer or which-ever ones were female."

Now the reindeer raised its head and looked at us with an air of patient assessment. She seemed to be evaluating us. Some moments passed. Then with a snort she turned and headed across our path, and off to the right. That was the moment I caught the flash of white on its flank.

I let out a breath I didn't know I'd been holding. "I swear I've seen her before," I whispered as she moved farther into the forest. "I thought it was a deer. I didn't know she was a reindeer."

"What?" Ben said, intrigued.

"I almost hit her, when I first came to the town. And then again, she led me to the farmhouse when I was going to give up. When you were unconscious. I think we should follow her," I said.

Ben's gaze followed the reindeer's path. "But she just went that way"—he pointed to the right—"and I think we should head that way." He pointed to the left.

I nodded. "I know. I just have a feeling."

I expected Ben to disagree with me. Instead, he flipped up his visor, watched me for a second and shrugged. "Okay."

The reindeer's antlers moved through the trees in the distance. Simon seemed to see her, but stayed close to us. "*Allons-y*," Ben called to the husky, and Simon followed us. I focused on the reindeer, which stayed a stone's throw ahead. The focus energized me. Quicker steps, staying just on my toes, helped me better regain my balance when one of my feet slid out from under me. Ben fell behind. "Come on," I called back. "We don't want to lose her."

"I'm with you," Ben huffed. Another noise, however, made me pause.

"*Do you hear what I hear?*" I called out. It sounded like the rumble of a car engine.

"*Said the night wind to the little lamb,*" he finished, but I waved him off.

"No." I held a finger up. "That. Do you think that's a car?" My heart thumped and I willed it to quiet down so I could hear the sound. "Come on."

Our path led on a slight incline. I raced as fast as I could. Every third step it seemed, I'd slip, grabbing a branch or putting a hand on the ice—but I kept going. And then the forest cleared. There was a ditch, then a white strip that continued on into the distance, and another ditch opposite. A road. Finally. I squealed and turned to look at Ben, who beamed at me.

A faint rumble sounded through the air.

"It's—it's a truck!" I yelled.

"Maybe a van," Ben guessed. We sprinted forward.

Ben called for Simon, who was up ahead, and he sprang back toward us. He looked at the dog, then pointed toward the approaching vehicle and said something in French. And then added: "*Allons-y!*"

The dog shot off in the direction of the car, barking, steam from his mouth creating a trail in the sky above his head.

Ben followed behind. Within seconds he was well ahead of me. With my UGGs slipping and sliding and breaking through the crust, tripping and falling and getting back up again, I stayed as close as I could. The van, a battered red Econoline with the legend *The Sweeping Santas* emblazoned on the side, sped past us just as Ben reached the gravel shoulder. Simon barked. Ben jumped and waved his arms.

"*Arrêt!*" I shouted, a few paces behind.

And . . . nothing. The van's progress continued. Simon gave chase. Ben and I watched as the van continued along the road.

"Maybe another car will be along soon?" Ben said.

No way. This was our only hope. I cupped my hands to my mouth. "*Arrêt, s'il vous plaît!*" I pulled the useful phrase from somewhere deep in the back of my memory. I jumped up and down, flailing my arms.

A screeching whistle pierced my eardrums.

I whipped my head around toward Ben.

"Sorry!" Ben said sheepishly as he removed his fingers from his mouth. "Should've warned you." The van disappeared around a corner, leaving Ben and Simon and me alone with the forest.

Then I heard a distant whine. The van appeared at the curve, reversing now toward us. As it backed up, Ben kept whistling. I waved my arms. The van got closer. Ben threw his arms around me, his helmet hitting mine. "You did it," I said. "You saved us." I tried to plant a kiss on his lips, but our helmets clanked together first. I laughed.

"*You* did it," he said back, his eyes meeting mine.

Simon raced toward the van, reached it, and turned right back toward us again.

The van slowed to a stop a few feet down the road and I bit my lip.

"What on earth," I said, my eye on the sign on the side of the van, "is a 'Sweeping Santa'? Please tell me it's not like a cleaner—getting rid of dead bodies."

Ben pulled off his helmet and slung an arm over my shoulder.

"That seems a bit—Hollywood horror flick."

"You know what? At this point I don't even care. Just so long as they're not murderers."

"We're not going to get in a van with murderers," Ben assured me.

"I might be willing," I said. I caught a flash of movement to the right and turned just in time to see the reindeer disappear out of sight.

Ben and I came up along the passenger side. The front passenger window rolled down. A guy with weathered skin and kind eyes, white hair that escaped his green toque, bushy eyebrows and a beard, poked his head out the window and gave us a hearty belly laugh and a toothy grin. He looked *exactly* like a storybook Santa Claus.

"Greetings, Earthlings," he bellowed.

I collapsed against the side of the van, then removed my helmet.

"We've had a run of bad luck," Ben said, then held out a hand. "Benoît Deschamps."

I sprang to life. "He's the *mayor*. Of Chelsea."

Ben raised an eyebrow, looking at me weirdly.

"What?" I said. "If there's any time to pull the celebrity card it's now."

"What the heck!" Santa roared. "Mayor?" He turned to the driver. "You hear that?" Then he turned back to us. "Wait, are we in trouble?" He roared with laughter again. "You can't be pulling us over for speeding. But if it's for having too much beef jerky in the back, well then, guilty as charged." He held up his hands.

"We're not trying to pull any strings," Ben said politely. "We're just looking for a ride. To the next town. Anywhere, really."

"Well, where are you headed on Christmas Eve?"

"Chelsea."

"Ahh," Santa said knowingly. Then he turned to the driver. "You know where that is?"

He turned back to us. "Never heard of it, but we're on the way to Ottawa for the Barbershop Bonspiel. Any chance it's thataways?"

"Ottawa?" My heart did a triple toe loop. "That's so close, right, Ben?" That was where this all began a few days ago.

"Chelsea's right on the way," Ben said. "Would you mind?"

"Mind?" Santa bellowed. "We'd love to drive you. An audience for our warm-up."

I was confused. *Warm-up for what?*

"We'd love a warm-up," Ben joked.

The door opened and Santa ambled out of the van. Beside him, in the driver's seat, was another guy, about the same age, with thick, shoulder-length black hair extending from his blue toque, his black beard highlighted with strands of silver. "Add it to our claim to fame of celebrities we've given rides to," he said in a Jamaican accent. "It's not a long list, but it's a quality list," he said. "You"—he pointed at Ben's chest—"and Taylor Swift."

"You gave Taylor Swift a ride?" I asked.

"Yes, for a while," the original Santa said. "While we thought it was Taylor Swift. Turned out it was *Tyler* Swift. But arguably the most impressive Taylor Swift–impersonating drag queen out there." He stuck out a gloved hand. "I'm Graham, by the way." Then he pulled on the side door to the van and two more men, also with beards, appeared.

"Bet you didn't think you'd see two more of us!" an East Indian gentleman said from the back seat, sticking out his hand. "I'm Alfie." He was wearing a red sweater with a picture of Rudolph on it. His beard was dark brown with only a few strands of white. The fourth man waved. He had translucent, peachy skin, a full head of white hair, no toque, and his white beard was so long it brushed the top of his green sweater.

"Let me guess," Ben said as he looked from one Santa to the next. They rearranged themselves to make room. Ben offered his hand to me so I could climb in. "You're a Christmas-themed punk rock quartet?"

"No. Close!" Alfie exclaimed. "We're a barbershop quartet slash curling rink. That's curling lingo for 'team.' We sing in harmony and then we get on the sheets. The ice, you know? We're the Sweeping Santas from Shediac Bridge, New Brunswick." I maneuvered myself into the back row. I sank into the seat and leaned back. It felt like I was lying on clouds. And that this was a dream. Were we really out of the forest, in a moving vehicle that was going to take us back to civilization, to our lives? Was this whole nightmare about to be over? I sighed happily, then noticed Simon hopping into the van, squeezing past the middle row of seats. I patted the rough fabric at my hip and he climbed onto the seat, taking up more than half the back row, leaving barely a sliver for Ben to sit. I laughed and rubbed the dog's belly.

"That's Zaphod." Alfie thumbed at the guy beside him, then pointed to the driver. "And Samuel."

Samuel gave a "hi-ho."

Ben squeezed into the third row beside Simon, shaking his head at the dog. He looked up, his eyes meeting mine, then reached over to rub my padded leg. "Looks like we made it."

Not a Christmas song, I mouthed. But I was grinning.

Ben chuckled, then turned his attention back to the rest of the van. "Look at you fellas!" Ben exclaimed.

"Look at us? Look at you three," Alfie roared. I looked to Ben and then down at my own outfit, remembering how ridiculous we likely looked, in our retro snowsuits, helmets in hand.

"Snowmobiling," Ben explained.

"Snowmobilers without a snowmobile."

"It's a long story."

Samuel started the engine.

"We've got time," Alfie said.

"Speaking of—what time *is* it?" Ben leaned forward between the two seats.

Alfie pointed to the retro clock in the middle of the dashboard. One gold hand pointed upward, one down. "Just about one thirty."

Ben looked to me. "No wonder I'm starving. You must be dying," he said. "And yet . . . we weren't fighting. Does this mean we're making progress?" The corner of his lip turned up. "Any chance you fellas have anything I can give Simon to eat? Poor boy hasn't had anything since last night either."

Graham opened the cooler between his and Samuel's seats. "We've got water, beer, and beef jerky. All the provisions you need to drive across three provinces."

"They don't call us the Prepared for Anything Quartet for nothing," Alfie said, then turned back to us. "They don't call us that at all."

"Could we charge our phones?" Ben said. "Back to reality, right?" He looked at me. "Your sister's got to be wondering where you are."

I bit my nail. "Right," I said.

Samuel belly-laughed. "Does it *look* like this is the kind of van that would have iPhone chargers? Besides, cell service hasn't been working since the storm hit."

"Right," Ben said. "Well, it's not that big a deal, I guess. We'll be home soon enough."

You'll be home soon enough, I thought. The joy I'd felt just moments earlier about being rescued, about being in the van, about being on our way back to Chelsea was replaced with the realization that this weird adventure was coming to an end. Disappointment fell over me like light snowflakes: Faint enough to know they were there, but not substantial enough to be able to do anything about them.

CHAPTER FIFTEEN

Christmas Eve, 1:30 p.m.

"So what exactly brought you out in this storm?" Alfie asked, turning in his seat.

Ben laughed. "It all started with a maple syrup delivery."

"Actually." I put a hand on Ben's leg. "It *started* when Ben wouldn't approve my film permit and I was forced to take the icy roads that were completely unsafe for driving to Wakefield."

"Unsafe if you don't have studded tires," he said to me. His eyes sparkled.

"Let me guess: you slid off the road and a handsome stud saved you." Alfie winked at Ben.

"He did not *save* me," I said, frowning.

"She was having a great time sledding. I interrupted her. What a party pooper I am."

I reddened at the memory of Ben finding me at the bottom of the ice-covered hill. "So then he gave me a ride to

Wakefield but he drove *so* slowly . . ." I looked over at him, trying not to smile.

"That the mayor's office was closed," Ben said. "On account of the storm. We didn't make it in time."

"Darn it all," Samuel said. The road turned to the right, and merged onto another road, this one twice as wide. "Then what?"

"Well, Ben knew where the Wakefield mayor's cottage was and we were on the way there—"

"Plus, I was going to deliver some maple syrup," Ben added.

"Maple syrup!" Zaphod said.

"He owns a maple syrup farm," I bragged. "Taps the trees himself and turns it into syrup. It's famous. Even the restaurants serve *his* family recipe."

We went back and forth like this, tossing lines at each other like we were playing catch. And even though we were creeping along the road, the time flew by. We were lucky to have such a captive audience.

"And now you're here with us. Are you ready to help us warm up?" Samuel asked.

Alfie clapped his hands. "All right, all right, all riiiiight."

Samuel reached into the front pocket of his thick wool jacket and pulled out a red-and-white pitch pipe, then pressed it to his lips. He took a deep breath and blew into the instrument, creating a single constant note. The other three harmonized with a long "Ahhhhhhh."

Ben looked at me, mouthing *Oh my god*. I laughed.

Then Zaphod, his voice rich and deep, started off: *"Juuuuuuuuust hear those sleigh bells jingling, ring-ting-tingling too . . ."*

"Come on it's lovely weather," I sang along, looking at Ben, who was also singing. He flubbed the line, saying *snowy* instead of *lovely*.

"One point for me," I teased.

The other three Santas continued to sing, Alfie's tenor, clear and high-pitched, soaring above the others. The richness of the sound filled the van as they cycled through a verse of "Jingle Bells" and then transitioned into "Joy to the World."

I listened in awe. Zaphod's baritone added depth and complexity. Their voices melded together, creating a harmonious sound that echoed inside the van. We had a front-row seat to an unforgettable performance. And for a few minutes, it succeeded in banishing any thoughts of what was next for Ben and me.

When they eventually took a break, Ben and I clapped. Simon, who'd been sleeping, perked up at the excitement. Alfie turned around. "How'd you like that, lovebirds?"

"You guys are incredible!" I said, still clapping.

"Bravo!" Ben said, then leaned close to me.

"He called us lovebirds," he whispered. The four Santas started up again, Graham tapping the dashboard with his fingers, mimicking the sound of drums.

"You know," Ben said, "I think it makes more sense to skip my place and go straight to Xavier's, if you don't mind." He leaned forward, directing the next part to Samuel. "He's right on the way." He turned back to me. "Just realizing that there's not much good in going home to my place yet, given I won't have my truck to get over to Xavier's anyway." The more he talked through his own plans, the more distant I felt from him. Now that our adventure/nightmare was over, he was moving on with his plans. And I was disappointed. That his plans weren't my plans. That they weren't *our* plans. But not enough to say something. Because as much as I wanted to be with him, my pride was standing in the way. "Xavier's house is solar-powered," Ben was saying, which only irritated me. Was he *bragging*? "And I would've gone over early to help him set up for tonight. It makes more sense to just go straight there." He nodded enthusiastically. I nodded curtly.

"You tell us where to go and we'll get you there for Christmas Eve," Alfie was saying to me.

"I'll just grab a cab to the airport from wherever you're going in Ottawa," I said, leaning forward. Ben looked at me, his brow furrowed.

"The airport?" three of the four Santas said. "On Christmas Eve? After all the closures and cancellations? And why wouldn't you two be spending the holiday together?"

Ben turned to me, searching my face for an explanation.

"Christmas Eve is for family," I said, trying to act like it was no big deal.

"So you're . . . going to be with Stella?" he said slowly, then nodded. He was the one who told me to make plans with Stella, regardless of whether she celebrated Christmas. Did he believe I was taking his advice?

His jaw clicked. "All right then," he said, facing forward.

Neither of us said anything. If our van mates noticed our silence, they didn't show it, continuing to joke and laugh. And with Simon between us, we had a buffer. I wasn't sure if I was grateful or disappointed. Was this how it would all end?

♣ ♣ ♣

"We're getting close," Ben said, and I realized I'd dozed off for a few minutes on Simon. Ben leaned forward, between the seats, the better to direct Samuel. "All right, if you take a turn at the top of the hill, it's the second street on the right."

The road curved this way and that, lined with tall skinny evergreen trees covered in snow. We passed house after house decorated with Christmas tree lights, some on, some off. But then, suddenly, we saw a handful of the evergreens lit with hundreds of tiny white lights glowing in the gray sky. A break in the trees signaled a driveway and Ben called up to Samuel. "Right here."

The van turned and maneuvered between the two opening doors of a massive wrought iron gate. The drive had been plowed recently, with just a thin layer of snow on the winding pavement. Nestled in the quiet woods was the stucco and timber of a Tudor home standing tall and stately against the snowy landscape. Its steep roof and tall, narrow windows were adorned with intricate trim, adding to the charming old-world appeal. Smoke puffed from the chimney, a warm contrast to the frosty air.

Hundreds more tiny white lights dotted the trees, the eavestroughs, and even the wreaths that hung in every window. It was every bit as magical as the setting in a holiday movie. Oh, how I wanted to say something to Ben: *Ask me to stay! Can I stay? Let's not end this now . . .*

The van slowed to a stop and Samuel cut the engine. Simon looked up and as though sensing this was his stop, thumped his tail on the seat. Ben slid out of the van, and Simon followed him. I stayed put, unsure what to do. Was this the moment I would say goodbye to Ben, after all we'd been through together? And was I going to have to do it in front of this quartet? But what was the alternative—not say goodbye at all?

"*Don't want to say goodbye . . .* ," Alfie sang. Ben looked at me through the open door of the van, his eyebrows raised. But I wasn't in the mood to finish the lyrics—and for once I wasn't sure of the words anyway.

"*To Christmas yet,*" Ben continued, singing along with the others. Then he came over, offered me a hand, and helped me out of the van. The Santas piled out after me. The four Santas group-hugged. Ben turned to me. The others seemed to get the idea and climbed back into the van.

I turned to Ben. But I didn't know what to say, where to start. He pulled me away from the van.

"Stay," he said earnestly. "*Please* stay. With me. If this was the movie you were writing, you'd stay. This is the third act."

Was he really saying exactly what I'd wanted him to say? It felt too good to be true. I wanted to say yes, that I'd stay, but instead I shook my head.

"But this isn't a movie," I said sadly. I looked away, worried that I'd burst into tears if I held his gaze a second longer. *Say yes, Zoey. This is what you want.*

Ben stepped around so I had to look at him. "You're right," he said. "It's not a movie. It's better. You want Christmas traditions? This is it—a gift right in front of you. A huge Christmas celebration, with me." He looked over at the Santas, and swallowed, suddenly looking apprehensive. "Zoey," he said in a lowered voice, "what we had last night, that was special. What we just went through together, that was something intense and most people would not have survived it. I don't want you to go. I don't want to say goodbye to you."

"What do you *want*?" I whispered, holding my breath.

"What I want is for you to come inside with me, and meet my family and my friends and to spend *Réveillon* with me."

"But this is *your* tradition, not mine." What would happen after *Réveillon* was over?

"It doesn't have to be. It can be *yours*. It can be *ours*." He took a breath before speaking again. "I don't want to get ahead of myself, but what if this is the start of something real?"

"But what about Delphine?" I asked, biting my lip.

"What about Delphine?" Ben looked confused.

"Won't she be inside?" I assumed someone else had picked her up from the airport.

He shrugged. "Yes, probably, if she made it back."

I rolled my eyes. "So then . . . *what about Delphine?*"

"What about Tomas?" Ben countered, raising an eyebrow.

"What *about* Tomas?" I said, confused.

"You and Tomas broke up a lot more recently than Delphine and me. So why are we so fixated on Delphine?" His tone was gentle, and his eyes searched mine.

He was right, but I couldn't let it go just yet. "But Delphine might be here."

"And you're here. If you stay," Ben said. "Wouldn't that be better than running away?"

It was all I needed to hear. Besides, I didn't need to think about it. I didn't *want* to think about what would happen after *Réveillon* was over—tomorrow or the next day or anything else. I just wanted to be here with Ben.

I reached for his hand. *"D'accord."*

He grinned. "Now you're speaking my language!" He pressed his lips to mine, so quickly that it was over before I could register it. Like the most natural thing in the world. I felt like I was floating.

"God rest ye merry, gentlemen," sang the Sweeping Santas, behind us, and we turned toward the van, where the windows were all rolled down, and all four Santas were serenading us. I laughed and went in for another kiss—a better one, more passionate, and when we came up for air the whole first verse was done. Ben slung an arm over my shoulders, giving me a squeeze. Alfie passed our helmets to Ben, then Samuel started the van. I waved. "Thank you guys, so much! You saved us!" I called.

"But I heard him exclaim, ere he drove out of sight . . . ," Samuel called as they backed down the drive.

"Happy Christmas to all!" all four of them shouted. *"And to all a good night!"*

CHAPTER SIXTEEN

Christmas Eve, 2:00 p.m.

Ben squeezed my hand as we walked up the drive toward the house, Simon keeping pace with us.

A small path had been shoveled through the drifts, leading to the front door, on which a wreath of evergreens and holly berries hung. It reminded me of Mireille's wreaths. A brass lion's-head knocker was tucked into the center of the wreath. Ben set the helmets on the porch, lifted the knocker and let it drop three times, then turned to me. "You ready?"

I nodded, and took a deep breath.

The door opened, and a man about the same age as Ben stood in front of us. He wasn't quite as tall, and his hair was jet-black. I recognized him from La Jardinière.

His amber eyes widened when he registered who was standing before him. "Ben! *Mon dieu.*" He threw the door open wider and pulled Ben into a tight hug. "We've been so worried."

When they stepped apart, Xavier looked at me. "*Desolé*," he said, placing a hand to his chest, then followed it up with something very quick in French. I smiled and shook my head.

"Sorry, my French is *terrible*." I stuck out a hand, took it back, removed my glove, and stuck it out again. He took it in his warm hand.

"Xavier, this is Zoey," Ben interjected.

Both Xavier and I nodded. "We met. At Mireille's. It's so nice to see you again." He leaned in, then kissed me on one cheek, then the other.

Xavier said something in French to Ben, then motioned for us to come in. Simon scooched between our legs.

"Ah, Simon!" Xavier looked past us, said something else in French, then laughed.

"English, Xav," Ben said. "So Zoey understands."

"Right, of course, I'm sorry. How did you get here? And what on *earth* are you two *wearing*?"

Ben scooped up the helmets and motioned for me to enter the house. I stepped onto the mat, which was red and green, *Joyeux Noël* in white cursive font. I found myself in a bright atrium, round, with a large table in the middle, a crystal vase holding red and white flowers. Behind was a circular staircase up to the second floor. Two stories above, a skylight the size of a dining room table allowed a clear view of the cloudy sky.

"And where were you?" Xavier continued. "I was calling you and calling you—that is, until the cell service went out. I brought water to your mom. She's so worried. No one knew where you were."

"We didn't know either, to be honest," Ben said, then winked at me. "I'll answer all your questions, but first, we've gotta get out of these things." He unzipped his snowsuit as a female voice called something in French.

"Geneviève!" Xavier called back. "*Viens ici!*"

A moment later a woman with long, shiny jet-black hair appeared through one of the archways to the left. She wore a pristine white apron tied neatly around her waist over black leggings and a white shirt. Her skin was warm caramel, and her deep brown eyes sparkled. As she walked toward us, she carried herself with grace, but then rushed to us and grabbed Ben's face in her hands, kissing him on both cheeks. Then she threw her arms around him. When she untangled herself from him I could see her face radiated with joy. Then she slapped his hand. "We were so worried."

He shrugged and she shook her head, then turned to me, her smile just as big. "*Salut!* I'm Geneviève," she said with just a touch of a French accent.

Ben introduced me just as a small girl of maybe four or five rushed to the front entrance, appearing under the bridge of Xavier's arm. Her red dress sparkled with sequins, her hair curled into ringlets with a red satin bow holding her hair off her face. I recognized her as one of the two children Xavier had by his side that day at the florist.

"Sophie!" Ben bent down, outstretching his arms.

The girl squealed with delight and rushed toward Ben for a hug. He lifted her up and swung her around. "Who's excited for tonight?"

The little girl nodded, then wiggled out of his arms and bent down to rub Simon, who was on the floor, legs in the air. A few seconds later she skipped down the hall, Simon following her, tail wagging. Ben called after her: "Could you give Simon some food?"

"*Non!*" She giggled and ran away.

Ben shook his head. "The dog is starving."

"I'll make him a sandwich," Xavier joked. Ben stepped out of his snowsuit, then helped me from mine. When I looked up, Geneviève was staring at us, laughing. "We can wash those for the two of you," she said. "For the next time you want to wear them."

"Which will be never," I said, which only made Geneviève laugh harder.

"Well, I'm glad we could be so amusing to you both," Ben said, grinning as two boys, who looked like identical twins, about seven or eight, raced into the hall, Nerf guns in arms. They fired away at us, leaving a confetti of blue and orange foam bullets on the floor. Geneviève looked at Xavier. "They need to run off their crazies before everyone arrives," he said, but then called to them. They stopped their fight and introduced themselves as Jean-Patrique and Benoît. I shook their hands then turned to Ben.

"Got myself a namesake," he grinned. "Pretty cool, right?"

"Never mind that," Xavier said. "I want to hear what happened? There must be a story to this?" He pointed at our outfits on the floor.

"Well, Zoey learned to snowshoe. I got a concussion. We had wine by a fire," Ben said. "How's that for the movie trailer?"

"That sounds like a story to be told over some mulled wine," Geneviève declared. "I put a pot on the stove a while ago. It should be perfect right about now."

We followed the couple down the hall, through the archway into a kitchen. It was a masterpiece of modern design, with sleek lines and luxurious details. But it included a real fireplace built out of natural stone that was roaring, emitting heat into the room and creating a warm and inviting space, perfect for entertaining. When I walked over and held out my hands in front of the vents, I felt all the stress of the day dissipate.

At the island, Ben pulled out a high-backed stool, invited me to sit, then took the stool next to mine. We sat so close our legs touched. It felt right. Music played softly from every corner of the room, and Ben sang the words to the instrumental song. *"I know when he gets here, he will never go away . . ."* Ben nodded at Xavier and Geneviève. "They're probably thinking that about me."

"What?" I looked from Ben to Xavier.

Xavier shrugged. "I have no idea what he's talking about."

"The song," Ben said. "Carole King. 'Everyday Will Be Like a Holiday.' My point."

I shook my head. "It's instrumental—that doesn't count."

"Oh yeah?" Ben looked around. "Where's the rulebook?"

I bumped shoulders with him, then turned back to Xavier. He and Geneviève were staring at us, and suddenly I felt very self-conscious. Ben cleared his throat.

"You must be starving," Xavier said, clapping his hands together.

Ben turned to me. "That's probably an understatement."
I nodded. We hadn't had anything to eat today and I was
suddenly ravenous.

"Xavier, you make them roast beef sandwiches," Geneviève
said, picking up a rolling pin and continuing her work on
the pastry. Another little girl rushed into the kitchen, opening the pantry and making off with a box of crackers. "Stop!"
Xavier commanded, and she did. He said something to her
in French and then she turned to me.

"I'm Claire," she said, and I recognized her as the other
girl from Mireille's.

"*C'est beau, Papa?*" Claire asked.

"Yes, Claire," Xavier said, and then she dashed off into
another room. Geneviève called after her in French.

"How many kids do you have?" I asked in amazement.

"Too many to count," Xavier said, opening the fridge and
loading up on sandwich ingredients. "I'm always saying to
Ben, you see one you like, they're all yours."

Geneviève swatted at Xavier with a tea towel, but he
ducked out of the way. When he stood, he was grinning. He
walked over to the pot on the stove and lifted the lid, then
waved a hand toward his face and inhaled, closing his eyes.
"Ahhh," he sighed. "Heaven." He turned to me. "Will you
try the mulled wine?"

"Definitely," I said. "At this point I would drink or eat
almost anything, so mulled wine exceeds any expectations."

Xavier poured four mugs and passed them out. I brought
the warm mug to my lips and took a sip, closing my eyes
and letting the flavors dance on my tongue. The cinnamon

and nutmeg were prominent, with a hint of orange zest and a subtle sweetness from the honey. It was the perfect drink for a cold winter afternoon—though I'm pretty sure even tap water would've felt like a delicacy right about now. I sighed. When I opened my eyes, everyone was looking at me.

"I think it's safe to say she's happy," Xavier said, nodding to Ben, whose eyes met mine.

"I'm happy she's here, too," he said with a smile, and I smiled back, my cheeks flushing as I did.

"*Ça suffit!* Tell us about you two!" Geneviève interrupted. "How did you come to get stuck together in the storm and why were you wearing those ridiculous snowsuits?"

Ben threw up his hands. "All right, all right!"

Xavier finished assembling the sandwiches and passed them to Ben and me. Shaved roast beef piled high on rye bread. It was the best thing I'd ever eaten.

Ben and I took turns relaying the story between bites of our late lunch, filling in the gaps when the other forgot. Geneviève and Xavier looked back and forth between us, awe on their faces. It was only this time, now that we'd *actually* made it to safety, that I could appreciate just how much we'd been through.

"Well, it worked out," Geneviève said at the end. "And now you're here."

"Right," Ben said, slapping his hands on the bar. "We're here. Although I wish I could call Mom to let her know I'm okay. No cell service, but do you have Wi-Fi, since you have power?"

Geneviève shook her head. "No, the cables are apparently frozen. Can't get any service."

My stomach clenched. Even though my no news was bad news, I wanted to be able to check in with Elijah, to let him know *what* I'd been through. Beg for a few more days. Maybe after Christmas, I could get in touch with the Wakefield mayor again?

I shook myself back to the present. There was nothing I could do. "How can I help?"

Geneviève looked at me. "You can't. You're our guest and you must be exhausted." She paused, then looked at Ben. "You know, from hanging out with him."

I laughed. Ben shook his head but he was grinning.

Geneviève turned back to me. "Would you like a soak in the tub?"

"Are you kidding?" I said. "I would give *anything* for a soak in a tub." Then I frowned. "But are you sure? I should help you set up for the party," I said.

Geneviève held up her hands. "Absolutely not. Ben can help with setup while you relax." She winked at Ben.

"It's so fortunate that you have power," I said.

"We were lucky," Xavier said, taking a sip of wine.

"It's not luck." Geneviève rolled her eyes. "It's the solar panels, the gas-powered generator, the windmill. I always thought you were crazy, all your survival preparation for the apocalypse. But it sure came in handy in the storm."

Xavier slapped Ben on the back. "We'll get to work, but first, a little shinny with the kids?"

Geneviève clucked her tongue. "He built a rink in the backyard and has been dying for Ben to come over and skate with him and the kids."

"You said the kids needed to run off their crazies," Xavier reminded his wife, kissing her on the cheek.

"All right, all right." She called out something in French and within seconds small children seemed to appear in the kitchen from every direction.

Ben put his arms around my waist. "I'm really glad you're here. It's going to be a lot of fun."

"I'm glad I'm here, too," I said, standing on my tiptoes to give him a light kiss.

Once Ben disappeared to play shinny, I convinced Geneviève to let me pitch in. She accepted with an explanation. "We always host a huge *Réveillon*," Geneviève said, "but even more people will be here tonight since we're the only ones around with power. It's going to be twice the size it normally is." She paused, considering her words. "I hope you like crowds. Maybe it's better, actually. You won't be put on the spot."

I nodded, suddenly feeling a bit anxious at the prospect of meeting all Ben's friends and family.

Geneviève led me to the counter and handed me a red-and-white-checked apron. "Do you want to help me make the *bûche de Noël*?" she asked. "It's a traditional Quebecois dessert. A yule log cake. Chocolate with lots of icing. The kids love it, not surprisingly. I've already made three, but with all the extra people coming, I thought maybe I should make one more."

"How many people?" I asked curiously, tying on the apron.

"Fifty, maybe sixty?"

"You seem *very* relaxed."

She laughed. "I know. But I love hosting parties. And I love *le Réveillon*. Everyone gathered on one evening together. The stories you hear, the reconnections made between people who haven't seen each other in weeks, maybe months." She hugged herself. "It's magical. I hope that's how you'll feel, too."

I thought about the first time I visited Chelsea. I was so aware of the snow. It was like the snow globe my parents had given me that Christmas. I'd shake it and be so focused on the snow swooping up to the top of the bowl and then how it would find its path down to the ground again. But I never really paid much attention to the street scene—the little houses in the middle of the globe, or the details painted onto the tiny windows—illustrating tiny scenes inside. That was the real magic, that I only noticed years later, whenever I'd take that snow globe out at Christmas, to set on my nightstand.

Geneviève handed me a bowl and another spatula. "I never use a mixer for this. Everything's by hand." She laid out all the ingredients and tools on the kitchen counter—flour, eggs, butter, sugar, and chocolate—and instructed me what to do next.

"Everything seems to be by memory, too," I said.

"I'm thirty-two and I've been helping my own mother with *Réveillon* since I could walk. It's all up here." She tapped the side of her head and grinned. "Or most of it, anyway. Besides, it's a thing of pride to have your own family recipe. Never written down anywhere, for fear a neighbor or cousin will steal it. Or so the tradition goes." She shrugged. Then she turned serious. "It's very important not to overstir the batter. Got it?"

I laughed. "Got it."

"So . . . you and Ben . . . ?" she asked curiously.

I was silent, trying to stay focused on blending the butter and sugar. I also didn't know what to say. What *about* me and Ben? I didn't even know.

"He seems really happy," she prompted. "And he hasn't always been happy," she said. She cracked an egg and added the yolk to the bowl.

"Really?" I wondered if Geneviève knew Delphine, but of course she must—Chelsea was a small town, they'd all lived here, and they were likely all friends.

"Do you like him?" she asked.

I smiled. "I do." I *did* like him. A lot. I thought about everything we'd been through together in such a short time. I thought about how after tonight, I might never see him again. Because while there was obviously chemistry between the two of us, our lives were like oil and water. How could we mix? How could we end up together?

Geneviève then instructed me to pour the melted chocolate, the final ingredient, into the bowl and stir it. Then I poured the batter into a long, buttered pan and passed it off to Geneviève, who popped it in the oven.

She cocked her head and studied me. "You're sure that you and Ben just met three days ago?" She raised a perfectly groomed eyebrow, her eyes sparkling.

I nodded.

"So tell me—is there something . . . between the two of you?"

My heart raced. "I don't know. I mean, he's very fun, and funny and good-looking, and smart. And he's successful and strong. He challenges me, which is sometimes annoying, but I also like it. And we've spent so much time together over the past couple days. But—"

"What is the *but*?" Geneviève interrupted. "You've only known him three days and it sounds like you know him better than most people know someone after *months* together."

I bit my lip. *But I live in LA and he lives here. Our lives are so different. And he won't give me the film permit.*

I sighed, and she looked at me with worry. "Are you okay?" I nodded. "Are you missing your own family?" she asked. "It must be hard to be away from them at Christmas."

"I don't have—" I stopped myself. I *did* have a family, just not one that wanted to spend time together. "We don't do this kind of thing at Christmas. Although—I always wished we did," I added. "Anyway, that was a happy sigh, even though it may not have sounded like one."

I set to washing the sink full of dirty dishes, but Geneviève stopped me.

"Leave that, Zoey. Come on. Time for you to have a soak, and then you can change into something else for the party."

I laughed. "I would love to wear something else, but I didn't bring anything."

"You can borrow something of mine! I'll take you upstairs, show you my closet, and then you can have a long bath. We invited everyone much earlier this year than normal, since almost no one has power, but there's plenty of time until people start to arrive."

I followed her out of the kitchen past a large sitting room and into the rotunda. We climbed the rich mahogany staircase, and I admired the family pictures hung on the way up—photos of Geneviève and Xavier and every child, from birth to school photos.

"Your house is so beautiful," I said.

"Thank you. We're lucky," Geneviève said. "It's a wonderful place for the children to grow up, as long as we make sure they don't become spoiled by it all. That's why we make them shovel the rink before they play. That's what I told them when they went out to skate. You want to skate, you do the work first. Xavier thinks I'm too hard on them, but I think I'm just right." I smiled at her. Even though we'd just met, I wished Geneviève was my friend.

The floor at the top of the stairs was smooth oak, and decorated with area rugs. She pushed open a set of white double doors, revealing a spacious room with a giant bed in its center.

Geneviève waved a hand in the air for me to follow her. "This way."

On the far wall of the room were more family photos, candids and professional shots, including their wedding photo. Geneviève was dressed in a gorgeous silk gown that hugged her body, and Xavier was in a white tux, with a black tie. The backdrop was filled with evergreens. "Is this here?"

Geneviève nodded. "The home has been in the family for years. Xavier is the oldest child and we have the most children, so we decided to buy it from his parents. They live in the west wing. You'll meet them later, of course. Imagine growing up here? It's so massive. You need many children to fill it. I'm an only child and it was so lonely. That's why we wanted to have so many children. We started having kids right after the wedding. Actually"—she leaned close—"I was already pregnant at the wedding. We couldn't wait to get started." She laughed, and I smiled, then leaned closer to study the photograph. I recognized the young man standing beside Xavier—Ben.

"*Oui*, Ben was the best man," Geneviève confirmed. "The two are cousins, of course, but they've been friends since they were this high." She put her hand out flat, down by her knee.

"And her?" I said, pointing to the gorgeous woman on the other side of Geneviève. She was tall and impossibly thin, with long blond hair that cascaded over her bare, tanned shoulders. Her skin looked flawless, her smile radiant.

"Delphine," Geneviève said. "Ben's girlfriend." She caught herself. "At the time, of course, I mean. They're not together now. Obviously."

I nodded, trying not to be weird about it all. "Are you two close?"

She paused, then responded. "Yes. We still are, though of course it's been more difficult with her away. And I feel loyal to Ben because he's family."

"But you must feel sad to have lost that couple-friends feeling?"

"*Bien sûr.* Spent all the holidays together, skiing at New Year's, summers at the cottage on Lac McGregor."

"What really happened between them?" Even though Ben had told me about Australia, I was fishing for more.

Geneviève's eyes widened. "Ooh, so much. It was . . . eventful. And then—but that is for Ben to say, not me." As though to change the subject, she walked over to a door and opened it, revealing a massive walk-in closet.

"Now, I know I've just met you but I'm usually a very good judge of style. This sweater, however, it's really throwing me off the trail. I can't even tell what is happening underneath there."

"Well, I can tell you I'm nowhere near as tall or as lithe as you."

"I have been pregnant three times—once with twins. You better believe that these clothes in here range in many sizes." Geneviève began riffling through the racks. "Try this." She thrust a thin, shiny red dress at me. It was silky and light. She turned back to the closet. "Ooh, this might be even better. The green against your dark hair and eyes . . ." She handed me a green jumpsuit. "It needs a heel, obviously."

"It's too hard to pee in these," I said, and she nodded.

"*Oui, c'est vrai.*" She swapped the jumpsuit for a velvet dress. "Aubergine . . . *non*, everyone always looks tired in aubergine," she mused, holding up the velvet dress. "Ah, this is it." She held out a gorgeous ivory dress with a high neckline and bare back. I took it from her and admired it. "And a red shoe. Because it's the holidays." She pulled out a box and took off the lid, holding them out to me. "It's a heel, but it's not ridiculous. Just enough to make your legs look amazing. Try it on, just to make sure it fits."

I slipped the heels on—they fit—and turned to admire myself in the mirror. "Wow," I said, looking at my feet. Then I caught a glimpse of the rest of myself. It was a real look: Oversize sweater, and my hair—which I usually prided myself on keeping shiny and smooth—was a matted mess. Somewhere along the way I'd lost the elastic in it, I'd known that from touching it, but I hadn't realized it was *this* bad. My face was blotchy and uneven and I had dark circles under my eyes. I stared at myself, then started to laugh. Somehow, the laughter turned to tears.

Geneviève quickly put down the shoebox and wrapped her arms around me. "You just survived a *tempête de verglas*. This is nothing a little shampoo and some concealer won't fix. You're gorgeous," she said. "Inside and out. I can see why Ben is so into you."

I groaned. "It's not that—not exactly. It's everything. Before, it was simple. I had one mission: to get my movie made. To *direct*. But Ben is standing in the way of that. And yet, I think I'm falling in love with him?" Unthinkingly, I wiped my nose with the back of my hand. "It makes no sense."

"Life isn't supposed to make sense, Zoey," Geneviève said kindly. "Now, let me get you into this bathroom." She showed me out of the closet and across the room and into a room larger than my apartment. A large bathtub sat in the center surrounded by marble tiles and dim lighting. The floor was white marble, and I braced myself for the cold, but my feet were instantly warmed. Heated floors. I sighed.

"Help yourself to anything you like, and take your time," Geneviève said before leaving the room, shutting the door softly behind her. I was alone for the first time since this whole adventure began.

Beside the tub was a large window offering a picturesque view of the backyard. The vanity counter looked like a miniature New York skyline—bottles in various shapes, sizes, and colors creating buildings lined up against the mirror, which was framed in gold. A small shelf at eye level held rolled facecloths and a vase of fresh ranunculus. In the corner of the room was a small table, a tray holding a bottle of water, a candle, and a small lighter, and a stack of small books. It was as though Geneviève were prepared at any time to offer a guest a soak in her tub.

I stepped onto the plush white mat by the tub and ran the water, adding bath salts from a nearby jar. As the tub filled and the scent of lavender filled the air, I undressed, then climbed into the tub. Should I feel guilty that so many were without water and I was about to have the most luxurious bath in the most luxurious tub ever? But it was hard to feel guilty when the water felt so good—like it was touching every muscle in my body, instantly making me relax. I sank under the water, exhaled, then came back up.

My mind flitted back to that wedding photo—and Delphine. On a good day, if I was an eight, she was an eleven. And over the last two days? I'd been about a four. And sure, relationships weren't all about looks. But Delphine seemed to be more than just looks. Sure, the way Ben put it, she ran away from their relationship just when he was hoping they'd settle down and start a family. But he was clearly feeling influenced by his best friend who had four kids to his none. Who *wouldn't* be in a rush to catch up? And all Delphine wanted was a chance to see the world. To broaden her horizons. I didn't see what was so wrong with that.

So why did I feel jealous?

I leaned back and let the bubbles rise up around my neck, tickling my skin.

I thought about my colleagues and friends. Stella. Were they worried about me? Surely there must be some way to get word back? No cell service, Xavier's home the only one with power for miles. Xavier had said even the landlines were down. Adrift in the tub's luxurious warmth, I considered my other important life conundrum: my movie. And the options I had to get it made. For a moment I visualized stealing a car from Xavier's garage and speeding to the Wakefield mayor's cottage. Although why did I have to steal a car? Xavier surely would lend me one. I didn't know where exactly the cottage was though. Ben would come. So what was I doing in the tub? Ooh, but it felt so good. And had I said everything I could to Ben, to convince him?

I wasn't mad anymore. In fact, I thought I respected his decision. Maybe he *was* following his dad's footsteps rather than forging his own path, but he'd also lost his father, a man who'd shown him the way for so many years, a man in whose footsteps he *wanted* to follow. And it hadn't been that long. I didn't know how I'd react if I'd been in the same situation as Ben—and I'd never know.

So maybe I was okay with it all? But no. I wasn't. I had not given up the fight.

Eventually, sweat beaded on my forehead, and I slid down to submerge my head underwater, then washed and conditioned my hair. Then, reluctantly got out and dried myself off with a fluffy white towel. Clothed in my towel, I sat on the small vanity stool. My fingers ran over all the bottles—face creams and serums, eyeshadows and blushes, lip liners and lipsticks. I paused, then helped myself to a dab of rich face cream, a swipe of eye shadow, and a bit of gloss. Then I opened one of the drawers and found a hair dryer.

Next, I blow-dried my hair until it was straight with just a hint of flip at the ends. Slipping into the dress and heels that Geneviève had lent me felt like stepping into a new world.

I inspected my appearance in the mirror and smiled. I looked so different than an hour ago. I felt more like myself. Or, just possibly, better. I left the bathroom and headed for that spectacular staircase. As I descended, a low whistle caught my attention.

Ben stood at the bottom of the stairs. He'd changed as well. He wore dark jeans and a button-down blue shirt. His hair was tamed into submission and shined with gel. His beard was groomed. His eyes were on me.

"*T'as l'aire en forme,*" Ben said. And the way he looked at me . . . People talked about heartbeats quickening. They said fireworks went off when they saw "the one." And as Ben and I locked eyes, there was that, enough so that I became conscious of how thin the silk of my dress was across my chest. He looked so handsome. But there was also an awareness of allyship. No one but Ben knew the transformation I'd just undergone, because he'd just gone through it, too. Our shared experience kept us in on a joke that only we knew. And on top of all that was the sense that it didn't matter what I wore. I could have been in my snowsuit. Matted hair. And here was a man who would take me however I came. And look out for me. However I needed him. No matter what.

"You look incredible," Ben said, his eyes on me. I was sure that my face was turning the same color as the heels I was wearing.

"You look really good, too," I said softly, gripping the railing. The last thing I needed was to ruin this moment by tumbling down the steps.

"But be honest—you'd rather be back in that baggy sweater," he said with a wide smile. He held a hand out to me and I took it, more fireworks erupting.

"You want some eggnog? Cider? Wine?" he asked.

I gazed at him. What I wanted was to wrap my arms around him, to feel his body next to mine. And yet I felt nervous and shy. I shook my head no.

"So are you going to know everyone here?" I asked.

"Of course. Which is excellent, since I'll be able to intro-duce you to everyone." He nudged me with his shoulder. "That's maybe the best part. I'm glad you stayed."

"The only reason I stayed was the mulled wine. The cider. And the eggnog."

"I get it. It *was* good mulled wine," he said mock-seriously.

"All I want to do is kiss you," I exclaimed. My eyes wid-ened and my cheeks reddened, surprised at myself. I hadn't meant to be so blunt. "I was trying to play it cool, but I'm not sure I can."

He leaned close, running a hand over my back, then whispered, his breath warm on my ear, "Are you wearing underwear?"

"No," I whispered back, feeling an ache in my body. "It's one thing to borrow someone's dress and quite another to borrow their underwear."

"I like it. Now, this is what I wanted to do." Ben took my hand and led me toward the front door.

"Oh no, I'm not going outside again. Not like this."

"We're not going outside." He pointed up. My eyes fol-lowed his finger to a small sprig of deep green leaves suspended from a beam. Tiny white berries dotted the branches.

"*Oh, ho, the mistletoe,*" he murmured in tune, a hint of a smile playing at the corners of his lips.

"*Hung where you can see,*" I whispered back. Ben took a step closer, our feet in line, our bodies close. He cupped my face in his hands, his eyes on mine. I slid my arms around his back, then he leaned down and ever so gently pressed his lips to mine.

CHAPTER SEVENTEEN

Christmas Eve, 5:00 p.m.

"Zoey!"

Ben and I broke apart and I turned to see Mireille walking out of the kitchen. I let go of Ben and rushed over to hug her. She squeezed me tightly.

"I'm so happy to see you again." She looked from me to Ben and winked at me.

"Me too." I turned back to Ben. "You didn't tell me Mireille would be here!"

"*Bien sûr! C'est le Réveillon!*" he said.

Mireille squeezed my hand. "Come on, you have to see the others." She led me back through another doorway to the right that led into a den. The room was bright and airy with high ceilings and exposed wood support beams. A group of people were gathered around the fire, deep in conversation. In the corner an older couple—she with pearls, he in a tweed blazer—sat comfortably in a love seat, watching the goings-on. Standing to the side were a group of men in too-tight suits, as though they were their *Réveillon* suits, pulled out year after year regardless of whether they fit. A posse of pre-teen girls in sparkly dresses played Candyland on the floor.

"Renee! Lise!" Mireille called out, then wove through the crowd until we reached them. They were delighted to see me, hugging me tightly and admiring my outfit. A moment later, Ben appeared at my side. He held out one of the two glasses of red wine in his hands. "I took a wild guess that you like red wine. This one tastes better than last night's, at least I think so."

"Thanks." I took the wineglass, then clinked it with his.

"*Santé*," he said, bringing the glass to his lips. And for a moment he held my gaze, and I knew exactly what he was thinking.

"Can't leave her alone, hmm?" Mireille said, giving us a knowing look.

"I promised to introduce her to everyone, and I can't do that if you're hogging her attention," Ben explained, then looked at me. "And I want you to meet my mom."

My stomach jumped, but I nodded. "Okay."

Ben led me into another area, a sunken living room over-looking the backyard rink where many of the kids were skating or sliding in boots. Simon was outside, playing in the snow with another smaller fluffy white dog. To the right was a bonfire, with low benches made from trunks of trees. People gathered together, drinking and laughing, the fire creating a golden glow across the entire yard.

"*Maman,*" Ben said to a woman at the far corner of the room, sitting with other women, chatting animatedly. A woman with auburn hair turned and stood. She wore a skirt and top set in a gorgeous floral print. Her face lit up. "Zoey," she said, and I felt warm all over. She pulled me in for a hug. "Welcome. You look beautiful."

"Thank you, Madame Deschamps, so do you. I'm so happy to meet you."

"I'm so happy you saved my son and brought him back to me in time for the holiday," she said, making me blush. "I am so indebted to you. Particularly this year. And with the storm . . . thank goodness Xavier thought to prepare for such an event, and that he and Geneviève are such lovely hosts to take all of us in. This is heaven, isn't it?" She looked around the crowded room.

I nodded, still feeling so grateful to be here, for so many reasons. We chitchatted for a few minutes, until another woman, with gray hair in a neat bob, approached Ben, putting a hand on his arm. She had the same eyes, and I knew instantly she must be Ben's grandmother.

"*Mémère!*" Ben said, kissing his grandmother on both cheeks, and then stepping back to make room for me. "*C'est Zoey.*"

"I love your slippers," I said. She stared blankly at me, but her expression was kind. Ben's mother chuckled.

"*Mémère* doesn't speak English. Or claims she's too old to bother." He grinned, then turned and said something in French to her. She threw a hand to her heart and then outstretched her arms.

"Good one," Ben said as his grandmother pulled me into a hug. Though she looked frail, her embrace was strong.

As we made our way around the house, Ben alternated putting a hand on my back, or standing close to me. Eventually though he was pulled away by a group of friends. "You'll be okay?"

"I'm fine. You've introduced me to half the party—"

"How can I not? I'm *really* happy you're here." He gazed at me and then touched my face softly.

"Me too," I whispered.

He kissed me, then said, "Okay let's meet back here in an hour if we don't see each other sooner."

Mireille was back by my side within seconds. She raised her eyebrows. "You two are getting along," she said. "Does this mean he gave you the film permit?"

"We haven't talked about it," I said.

"Oh no, really?" She looked concerned. "I know how much the movie means to you."

A pit formed in my stomach. She was right. It made no sense. How could I feel this way about the person standing between me and my life's dream?

Mireille threw back the rest of her glass of wine. That seemed like a reasonable action in the moment and so I followed suit. We headed toward the bar in the hall by the kitchen. From there we helped ourselves to some food and joined some of her other friends in yet another room.

I made my way through a few rooms, keeping an eye out for Ben. When I reached the front hall, I spotted him. He was standing with a few other guys, drinking beer and chatting. The front door opened and another man, about Ben's age, entered, which caused all his friends to cheer loudly. He slapped hands and hugged, and then turned back as someone else came through the door. Her hair was long and blond, her skin smooth and her cheeks pink. I knew instantly who it was.

I watched Delphine place a large suitcase and a bag filled with wrapped presents onto the bench beside her. Then she hung up her coat, revealing a sparkly black turtleneck sweater dress that clung to every curve of her body. She changed out of her sensible winter boots into black heels that she pulled from the bag of presents. She was absolutely stunning. I swallowed, suddenly feeling like a little girl playing dress-up.

"I thought you'd never get here!" Noémie rushed toward Delphine, and threw her arms around her. I looked over and saw Ben watching. My legs turned to jelly. When the sisters finished hugging, Delphine turned, and that's when she saw Ben.

She waved a finger at him. "Well, *someone* didn't pick me up at the airport."

He took a step forward, moving through the throng of friends, and gave her a hug. I watched as she kissed him on both cheeks, my stomach twisting.

"I was stuck in an ice storm," he said.

"Oh, poor baby," she teased. "Well, I made it here, thanks to Antoine." The guy who had come in with Delphine pulled off his baseball cap and hung his coat on the rack. "And now, Antoine needs some of Ben's famous caribou," Antoine said.

Ben untangled himself from Delphine and gave Antoine a hug, slapping him on the back.

"Since when did you start referring to yourself in the third person?" Then he looked around. He seemed to be searching for someone. I held my breath until our eyes met. He smiled and started making his way toward me. Was he going to introduce me to Delphine? Did I *want* to meet Delphine? And if so, what was he going to say?

"Hey," Ben said just as a bell rang. He looked at me with excitement. "Oh, it's time for the gifts."

"Gifts?"

"For the kids. We don't give gifts for the adults, but we give all the little ones gifts on Christmas Eve, before it gets too late." Everyone moved into the room with the Christmas tree, the adults gathering around the periphery, the kids crowding around the tall balsam fir. Ben's hand grazed mine, and then he laced our fingers together. I peeked at him, unable to control the smile that spread across my face. He winked down at me.

Someone sat at the grand piano and began playing "Jingle Bells," everyone joining in when he got to the chorus.

"*Batman smells*," Ben whispered in my ear. I turned to him. "*What?*"

"The next line in the song. My point."

"That's *not* the next line and you know it," I whispered back.

"It was in the third grade and I stand by it to this day."

The kids took turns playing Santa's elves, handing out gifts to one another. At one point I noticed Delphine tuck gifts under the tree, then I watched as she sat with Geneviève, their heads close, laughing together. I reminded myself how long they'd known each other, and felt a stab of wistfulness, a desire to belong, to not feel like an outsider. I squeezed Ben's hand, and he leaned over and kissed my cheek, which made me feel nothing but joy. Ben had made me feel like I belonged; like I was exactly where I was supposed to be.

After we'd sung a dozen more carols and the kids had opened all their gifts, Ben said he'd go get us drinks. "More wine?" he asked, and I handed him my empty glass.

"I don't think we've met," someone said, the moment after Ben left. I turned to see the guy who'd come through the door with Delphine.

"Antoine, right?" I said.

He looked surprised. "Clearly, my reputation precedes me. Have I given you a ride?"

"Excuse me?" I laughed.

"I'm an Uber driver in Ottawa. Technically. Though not on one of the busiest nights of the year thanks to the lack of cell service. Also Xavier's brother. Ben's cousin. Mireille's godson. Stop me when I mention someone you know."

I laughed. "All of the above. I'm Zoey."

His eyebrows shot up. "Ahh, so *you're* Zoey." He threw out his arms. "I gotta give you a hug. Feel like I know you already."

We hugged lightly but then a tug on the hem of my dress caused me to look down to see Jean-Patrique, Geneviève and Xavier's seven-year-old.

"Look what I got for Christmas!" He held up a drone: the quadcopter, the remote, and the VR headset. I was very familiar with these, from using them on set for overhead shots. "Mom says I can't go outside with this without an adult. Will you come?"

"Sure, Jean-Patrique," I said, touched, even though the last thing I wanted to do—ever again—was go outside during winter. I turned to say goodbye to Antoine, and then followed Jean-Patrique. He led the way to the front door and rummaged around in the walk-in closet, somehow finding his coat, boots, hat, and mitts. Then I realized that all I had to put on was the ridiculous snowmobiling suit. I couldn't wear that—it would wrinkle Geneviève's dress. Jean-Patrique must have sensed my dilemma because he tossed me a Canada Goose parka. "This is my mom's. She won't mind. She has, like, a million. And also, call me J-P. Everyone does."

J-P was ready to go and I didn't want to disappoint him, so I pulled on the coat, found my UGGs and my bag and slung it over my body, rummaging in it to find my gloves as I followed him out the front door into what, with the light falling snow and the fog of our breath, seemed a winter wonderland.

J-P powered on the remote control, then flipped a switch on the drone. The four propellers spun, elevating the quadcopter into the air, to about head height, where it hovered. Then J-P focused on the remote. It had two joysticks. He explained that one controlled the altitude, while the other controlled the direction. He pushed one stick to make the drone fly forward and pulled another to have it return. Now he pulled on the VR headset allowing him to see exactly what the drone's camera was seeing. I squinted up at the buzzing device. J-P sent it up, atop the house, where it flew through the chimney smoke. He made the drone flip upside down and then right side up again. It zipped so high I couldn't hear it. Then it was back, dropping down until it hovered again, between the two of us.

"How did you get so good?" I asked, impressed.

"All my friends have them," J-P explained. "I race with theirs all the time." Then he pushed up the headset and looked at me. "Wanna try?"

It took some adjusting to get the VR display to fit my bigger head, but as soon as it settled on the bridge of my nose, I felt like I was back on set. Sure, we used them for filming, but at Epic, the crews passed the time as various shots were set up and broken down, with drone races. There was betting involved and several shoots back I'd joined in, as a pilot. And was surprisingly good. J-P handed me the remote and I recognized the controls, so similar to remotes I'd used before. I dropped the drone down, almost to the ground.

"Be careful!" J-P exclaimed. "Geez!" Then I zipped it up, just above our heads, flipped it in a spin, circled it around J-P, and sent it in and out of the cars parked all over the long driveway, into and out of view.

"Wow!" J-P shouted. "You have skills!"

Now I sent the drone high up over the house, where I took in the view of the backyard. At the skating rink, where a full-on hockey game was going on, I recognized Xavier on the ice, a handful of other adults, and a half-dozen kids.

I was maneuvering the drone past the skating rink when I saw them—Ben's broad shoulders and narrow waist. His thick hair. Her long blond hair, a coat over her turtleneck dress. Their bodies close. I steadied the drone.

"What's happening?" J-P asked. "Where is it?"

Their heads were a breath away from each other. She was talking. He was nodding. Then he was talking and she was shaking her head. *Don't panic, Zoey.*

I willed my heart to stop racing.

"You have to move the joystick," J-P said.

But I couldn't move the joystick. I couldn't take my eyes off the screen.

Delphine put a hand on Ben's arm. That same arm I'd taken so many times, when I was scared or worried. The same arm I'd kissed and touched last night. Ben scratched his head with his free hand, but didn't remove her hand.

And then Delphine leaned toward Ben. I stared, as the next seconds happened in slow-motion. She said something to him and he looked away, toward the bonfire. And then he turned his head back to her. A split second later, her hands were on his face, pulling it toward her. I tore off the VR headset.

"I've got to go," I said, looking around. "You get it back."

J-P took the headset. A moment later the familiar whir returned. J-P caught the drone when it was waist high.

"Come on," I said, hurrying back up the steps toward the house. My foot slipped on the still-icy path, but I caught myself before I fell.

I turned back to make sure J-P was with me. I didn't know what I was going to do, I just knew I had to get out of there. At the front door, my hand grasped the knob and I pushed it open to let J-P inside. Antoine was singing in the doorway. "*I've got to go away . . .*"

I thought of Ben and me, finishing the lyrics. But I was in no mood for that now.

Antoine hugged an older woman, then turned to leave. "You again!" he said. "It was great to meet you."

"You're leaving?" I asked.

"Sadly. My grandmother's in a nursing home in Ottawa. We always raise a glass at midnight."

I nodded and moved out of the way for him to pass. I stood, frozen, on the front doorstep. Should I go back inside, and face the humiliation of being at this party with Ben, while Ben and Delphine got back together? But how could I leave? Where could I go?

I'd been a fool to think I could fit in. This wasn't my family. These weren't my friends. This wasn't my town. I was a fraud. An interloper. It had been a huge mistake to stay.

I had to get out of there.

Antoine.

"Antoine!" I yelled, hurtling down the front steps. "Antoine!" I waved my arms. His back was to me. "Wait!"

He turned and I hurried toward him, my feet slipping on the thin layer of ice that had formed on the walk. He was standing beside a silver sedan.

"Can you . . ." I huffed. "Take me with you?"

"Avec moi?"

I nodded. "Yes. I'll go anywhere." I couldn't believe I was saying that. After all I'd just gone through with Ben. But I couldn't stay.

"You're leaving the party?"

"So are you," I said.

He held up his hands. "No more questions. All right, hop in." The lights on the car flashed as he unlocked the doors to the sedan.

I hurried around to the passenger side and climbed in.

"I'll just heat up the car while I'm scraping the windows," he said.

He started the car, then got out. As soon as he shut the door, the tears started to flow. There was no stopping them. Why had I been so foolish to let myself think that my moment with Ben would change anything? He could never want *me*, not when Delphine was still in the picture. They had history, a lifetime together. We had three days, and just one night.

And on another level was this *Réveillon*, this town, these friends, this family, this *Christmas*. How could I think any of it was for me? I'd tasted it, so many years before, that holiday in Chelsea. But clearly something I'd done, or something about me, my upbringing, my parents, some as-yet diagnosed darkness in my soul, was keeping such a holiday, and such happiness, from me.

The door opened and Antoine climbed back in.

He looked over at me. "All right, to the—" He stopped. "Oh no. What's wrong?"

I waved a hand in front of my face and then looked out the window. "Allergies," I mumbled.

"To heartbreak?"

"Something like that."

"You sure you want to leave? It's Christmas Eve."

I sniffled. "That's exactly why I want to leave!" I exclaimed.

"Well"—he shrugged—"then you're in the right place." He pulled on his seat belt and slowly backed out of the driveway. "So did you want to come with me to Grandma's?"

"Any chance you know where the mayor of Wakefield's cottage is?" I asked hopefully. Antoine looked confused.

"I'm afraid Ben is the only mayor I know."

"I was just sort of kidding anyway. Do you think you could take me to the airport?" I asked. "Maybe I can still get a flight out tonight. Or I'll just stay at an airport hotel till the morning."

"So you and Ben . . . ?"

I shook my head. "There's no sense competing with Delphine. You saw her."

He looked at me quizzically. "Yeah, I saw her. I also listened to her go on and on for hours, too. Man, that girl really likes herself. But she's Delphine. Everyone loves Delphine."

I nodded. "That's what I thought." I looked out the window, willing Antoine to drive faster.

"Zoey, who cares if everyone loves Delphine? Seems to me Ben thought you were pretty special."

"You talked to Ben?" I sniffed.

Antoine turned left, onto a dark road. I'd forgotten the power was still out. Being at Xavier and Geneviève's house had been an escape from reality. At least, for a bit. But it wasn't real life. It wasn't *my* life.

"Well, texted mostly. And it was mostly him. You know he asked me to go pick Delphine up, right?"

"He did?" My head was resting against the window, but at this, my eyes darted to look at Antoine. When did Ben text Antoine? We'd lost cell service so long ago.

"I see you looking over here with interest," Antoine teased. I looked out the window again, but I couldn't help smiling. "I wasn't supposed to be working until now. But there was no way he was going to go get her. Didn't want to send the wrong message to her—or you. He paid me my regular fare rate. I probably shouldn't have charged him, seeing as he's my cousin and all, but if I never charged someone who was related to me I'd never make enough to pay my rent. And I had to miss half the party."

I was still focused on the part where Antoine said that Ben hadn't wanted to send the wrong message. But what kind of message did he think kissing her sent to her—and me?

Had they actually kissed? I didn't know, of course, but her hands had been on his face. She wanted to kiss him. And it didn't seem like he was trying to pull away. Not that I'd stuck around long enough to see how that scene ended.

"Stop," I said.

"Huh?" Antoine looked over at me.

"Sorry, *can* you stop? Like, stop the car? I want to go back." I nodded as though agreeing with myself. "I *need* to go back."

Antoine stared at me for a moment, but then a slow smile crept across his face. "Thatta girl." He slapped the armrest between us and pulled the car to a stop, then threw it into reverse, looking in the rearview mirror. "Hmm. Actually, that's going to be a problem."

I looked out the window, trying to see what problem Antoine saw. Was the road too narrow to turn around? I twisted in my seat. A bright white light looked like it was moving toward us, and there was a roaring sound in the distance that got louder with every passing second. "What *is* that?" I said, craning my neck.

"Looks like someone's coming up the road behind us on a snowmobile. I'm gonna pull over, let them pass, and then we can turn around."

I nodded, trying to be calm, but inside I was full of nervous energy, like a kid on Christmas morning, waiting to open their stocking. I could barely keep myself from jumping out of the car and running back to the house.

I turned in my seat, watching as the single white light grew bigger and brighter. When it got close, it swerved off the road to the passenger side of our car. I thought of Ben and I, bumbling along on the snowmobile earlier today. Just a few more seconds and Antoine would be able to turn around.

The snowmobile stopped and the driver cut the engine. The figure was clad in a puffy black coat, black helmet. He flipped up his visor. And my heart lifted in relief.

Ben flung a leg over the snowmobile just as I threw open the door and stepped out into the snow. He removed his helmet and set it into the crook of his arm.

"What are you doing?" I said.

"I could ask you the same thing. Why did you leave?" His face searched mine for an answer. It was full of concern— more than I'd seen these past three days.

I looked for the right words. I wanted to ask him what had happened—or rather, *why* what I saw between him and Delphine had happened. I wanted to fight for him, to tell him how I felt about him, but only if he was going to be honest in return. What if he denied it all?

But then you'll have your answer.

"I don't know what you saw or if this is what you saw," Ben said before I said anything, "but Delphine and I didn't kiss. I want you to know that."

Tears welled in my eyes. Suddenly, I wasn't so sure I *could* fight for him. If he wanted to be with Delphine I wasn't going to convince him to be with me instead. But I also wasn't going to leave without telling him how I really felt— something I'd never done in other relationships. But I needed to. Relationships *weren't* equal. Someone often loved some-one more. All I could control was my own feelings for Ben. And I needed him to know. "I don't know how you feel about Delphine," I sniffled, "and maybe it was just when we were trapped together, the rest of the world blocked out, that you felt something for me. Maybe seeing her again stirred up emotions, or whatever, and that's beyond my control. But you should've thought about that before you asked me to stay. Before you sold me on this idea of a new type of Christmas. With your family and your friends. It wasn't fair to me to put me in that position. If I didn't already feel like an outsider, you made me feel ten times worse."

Ben's face crumpled. He nodded as though accepting that he had ruined whatever we might have had together.

Tears streamed down my face, like a frozen river suddenly thawed. Ben's eyes were glassy. He shoved his hands in his pockets. "I know," he said solemnly. "And I'm so sorry. And I'm glad you said that. You're right." I searched his face for more information. I might be right, but was I right that his feelings for Delphine were back?

He looked away, into the distance. I waited. What was he going to say?

He turned back to me, his dark eyes intense. "Delphine and I have such a history. You know that. And that's not something I'm going to pretend doesn't exist. We were together for a long time. It's a fact. But that's what it is now. History. Those years with her, and what she and I went through in the end were awful for me, because I felt like she ruined our plan. But if there's one thing I learned from Dad dying, it's that life doesn't go according to plan. And that I can only control a little bit of my life. And the rest, I've got to learn to adjust." Antoine cut the engine on the car. The air was silent.

"Delphine leaving felt like she'd taken a wrong turn off the road we were on together and I was trying to steer her back on course. But whose course? What I learned was that we're all just driving on our own. You can't drive your own car and someone else's at the same time. Or snowmobile or whatever you're in." His lip turned up slightly. "Sometimes people just need to take a different path and actually, it's for the best. Because what Delphine did was show me there are other paths out there, some of them leading to the same place, and some of them going in completely new directions."

The snow was falling more heavily now, forming a thin layer of white on Ben's brown hair. But there was no wind and it wasn't cold. It felt like being inside a snow globe. Though I'd always pictured that as a happy scene. And what was happening right now—I wasn't so sure how this was going to end.

"What I'm trying to say is . . ." Ben scratched his beard. "Delphine and I had our story, and it's over. Whether you'd been at the party or not, I wouldn't have kissed her. Because the story I'm focused on now, it's you. She knew that. I was telling her that. I think all she really wanted was one last kiss, but I thought of you. Our story. Delphine is my past. But you—Zoey, you're my right now." His eyes were fixed on mine. I wanted to look away, and at the same time, I wanted to look deeper into his eyes, to his soul, to know that what he was saying was true, that it was coming straight from his heart.

And yet—*right now*? That's what he was willing to give me? "Right now feels so *temporary*," I said between sniffles.

"And I'm not pushing you for more, but . . . actually," I swiped at my tears. "I am. I want more. I deserve more."

Ben nodded. "You do. And maybe 'right now' isn't the right thing to say. Maybe it doesn't feel big enough. But to me it feels real. 'Right now' is about living in the present. Being here together. Not letting this moment slip by, but also planning for the future. Because that present, it's ever changing, and we get to choose how we spend it. Every minute with you feels fresh and exciting and full of possibilities. You know I'm so trapped in tradition, but you make me want to break out of that, to try new things. To make our *own* traditions."

"I do?" I said.

He nodded. "Except Christmas Eve." He thumbed at the house. "Christmas Eve in snowy Chelsea? That's a must. As long as we're doing that together."

I shook my head and laughed. A snowy Christmas with Ben? Yes, that was what I wanted, too. "I guess what I mean is 'right now' is . . . now." He took a step closer. "And now. And now and—"

I put a finger to his lips, then stepped closer to him, the toe of my UGG touching the toe of his boot. "I get the idea," I said, biting my lip.

Snowflakes had settled on the tips of his lashes. I reached out and wiped them away with my thumb, then let my hand linger on the side of his face.

"So what does this mean? Will you take *right now*?"

"Right now sounds pretty perfect." I pulled his face toward me. His skin was cold, but his breath was hot on my face. Our lips met, softly at first, and then with more intensity. He wrapped his arms around my waist and pulled me closer. Eventually, we pulled apart, and I caught my breath. "*I don't want a lot for Christmas,*" he said.

"*There is just one thing I need,*" I finished the line, and smiled. "One point for me."

"Me too," he said, and then pressed his lips to mine again and I melted into the kiss.

CHAPTER EIGHTEEN

Christmas Day, 9:00 a.m.

"Merry Christmas," Ben said in my ear. I rolled toward him. He was sitting on the side of the bed, holding a mug, steam wafting into the air. His room was bright and airy, the sun streaming through the floor-to-ceiling window that looked out onto the balsam firs of the tree farm.

"Mmmm," I said, stretching and sitting up. "How did you know that coffee in bed is my favorite thing? Especially when someone else brings it to me."

"Oh this? This is for me." Ben lifted the mug to his lips. "You want coffee, it's down in the kitchen." He stopped before taking a sip, then smiled in that way that made my stomach do snow angels. "I'm kidding." He passed me the cup.

I held it with both hands and took a sip.

"But how did you—?"

"Power's on. It's a Christmas miracle." He leaned forward, his hands on either side of me, and kissed me. First on one cheek, then the other. And then on the lips. I sighed happily.

"Oh, that's great," I said, smiling as last night flashed across my mind. Ben and I sitting side by side at Midnight Mass in Chelsea's Gothic-spired church, listening to the choir sing "Chanson de Noël." Walking back along the main street to Rendez-Vous for hot cider over a bonfire that Lise and Henri had made out front of the café. Eventually, making it back here, to Ben's home.

"Mm-hmm. It means we can play Christmas music while opening our stockings." Ben turned and called for Simon. A moment later, Simon burst into the bedroom. In his mouth he carried a red knit stocking. His eyes were wide, his ears straight up, his tail wagged—as if he knew he was playing an important role in Ben's plan. I felt giddy. But also felt caught off guard, embarrassed that Ben had somehow thought to get me something—how?—and I had nothing for him.

"You got me a stocking?" I said in awe.

"I heard you love getting a stocking on Christmas morning. That it's one of your favorite traditions."

I nodded and sighed. "Yes, but—"

"But nothing. We celebrated Christmas Eve for me. Now we celebrate Christmas morning for you."

He took the stocking from Simon's mouth with one hand, and scratched him under the chin with his other hand. "Good dog." Then he handed the stocking to me.

The wool was soft in my fingertips. I passed Ben my coffee cup and put the stocking on my lap. "But I didn't get you anything."

"I don't need anything," he said. "You're here. That's all I want."

Simon lumbered up onto the bed and snuggled up beside me, taking up half the bed. Ben took a sip from my mug and then placed it on the nightstand and picked up a small remote control. A moment later, the familiar chorus of Nat King Cole singing "The Christmas Song." He nodded to the stocking. "All right, now we're set. Go on, open it."

I reached in and pulled out the first item. It was wrapped in red paper, with a gold bow. I unwrapped it with care, wanting to commit this morning to memory. Inside was a pair of knit gray slippers. I held them to my chest. "My very own *grey poupons*," I said.

"They're not"—Ben started, then laughed and shook his head. "Actually, I guess you're technically right."

I pulled my legs out from under the covers. I was wearing one of Ben's T-shirts, my legs bare. I slipped on the *poupons*. They were soft and warm. "They're perfect. How did you know what size?"

He grinned. "Guess it's all that time we've spent together." He nodded at the stocking. "Keep going. There's just one more thing, but I think *this* is the *pièce de résistance*."

This feeling. This sense of warmth. Kindness between people who cared for one another, and the solace that came from knowing, at that moment, life had slowed down to allow you to spend time together. This, to me, was Christmas. Finally, this was Christmas.

I reached in, my fingers touching the edge of a rolled-up piece of paper. I pulled it out of the stocking. It looked like the scroll Lise had handed me at the café. It was even tied with a red ribbon. I wondered if he'd highlighted things we could do together. Because late last night while we were falling asleep, we'd talked about me staying through until New Year's. So we could go skating, and cross-country skiing, build a snowman, drink wine by the fire, and do other things, too, that required *not* leaving Ben's place.

"Open it," Ben urged, rubbing my leg. I slipped off the ribbon and uncurled the paper.

I scanned the words, then looked at him, at a loss for words. "You're . . . you're giving me the film permit?" I put a hand to my mouth, my eyes filling with tears, then threw my arms around him. "Ben! Why? Why did you change your mind?" I pulled away and looked at him, taking his hands in mine.

"You're a hard woman to beat in an argument," he said. "I like that."

I pressed the film permit to my chest. "I know this is hard for you, and you have concerns, but just think how fun it will be in the town. You love Christmas, and now January will be Christmas all over again. You'll walk outside and the whole town will feel like Christmas." I was rambling. I couldn't help it.

He grinned. "I'm more focused on the fact that you'll be here."

"Well, there's that, too." I looked down at the paper again. Of course I couldn't wait to make the movie. But I also couldn't wait to be here with Ben while we were filming. To get up in the morning and have coffee with him, to go off to work while he did the same. To meet back up at night and share our days.

"There's just one thing that's unresolved," Ben said. I looked up.

"What's that?"

"Where will we stay?"

"What do you mean?" I looked around at his room. "Here. We'll stay in your house. Why wouldn't we?"

Simon sat up as though hearing something, and jumped off the bed and out of the room. I looked back to Ben, trying to figure out what he meant.

"Well, I just figured we'd be in the way. What if the actors have to do a scene in here . . ." He raised an eyebrow.

I could feel my jaw falling open as I realized what he was saying.

"You said you needed a tree farm, and the house on it, too. It didn't seem right for you to use a school football field instead. It wouldn't *feel* like the tree farm. It wouldn't feel like Chelsea. As the mayor I have a duty to the town." He said this all in a mock-serious tone.

I smiled and laughed. "Of course," I said, mimicking his tone. "I know you want what's best for the town." Then I pulled him toward me. "*I wanna thank you, baby*," I sang, totally off-key.

"Ooh," he said, his voice low. "Not a classic. But also not a challenge for this Christmas lover." He leaned toward me, his face inches away, and then nuzzled my ear. "*You make it feel like Christmas*," he sang softly, and then he wrapped his arms around me. I squealed as he rolled us

over again, our legs and arms entangled, and then pep-
pered me with kisses on my ear, my cheek, my nose, and
then finally, his lips meeting mine. I closed my eyes. I never
wanted this feeling to end.

ZOEY AND BEN'S
CHRISTMAS MUSIC PLAYLIST
(Find it on Spotify, too!)

"It's Beginning to Look a Lot Like Christmas"—Michael Bublé

"All I Want for Christmas Is You"—Mariah Carey

"Christmas on the Square"—Dolly Parton

"Silver Bells"—Dean Martin

"Christmas Tree Farm"—Taylor Swift

"Last Christmas"—Wham!

"I'll Be Home for Christmas"—Bing Crosby

"It's the Most Wonderful Time of the Year"—Andy Williams

"Let It Snow"—Dean Martin

"O Christmas Tree"—Tony Bennett

"Baby It's Cold Outside"—Holly Cole

"Merry Christmas, Darling"—Christina Perri

"Do You Hear What I Hear?"—Bing Crosby

"Jingle Bells"—Frank Sinatra

"Joy to the World"—Aretha Franklin

"Sleigh Ride"—Johny Mathis

"Don't Want to Say Goodbye to Christmas"—Jimmy Rankin

"God Rest Ye Merry Gentlemen"—Barenaked Ladies

"Everyday Will Be Like a Holiday"—Carole King

"Holly Jolly Christmas"—Meghan Trainor

"The Christmas Song"—Nat King Cole

"You Make It Feel Like Christmas"—Gwen Stefani,
Blake Shelton

ACKNOWLEDGMENTS

The idea for this book started with a long, romantic walk to the elevators inside the Penguin Random House Canada offices with my editor, the inimitable Bhavna Chauhan. Bhavna, you're a snow angel. Also on the Nice list are editor Megan Kwan and the rest of the Doubleday Canada/Penguin Random House Canada team: Kristin Cochrane, Amy Black, Val Gow, Kaitlin Smith, Chalista Andadari, Keara Campos, Maria Golikova, Emma Dolan, Kate Panek, Karen Ma, Melanie Little, and Maggie Morris; my agent, Samantha Haywood, and Megan Philipp at Transatlantic Agency; first readers and friends who offered feedback: Emily Bozik, Christie Callan-Jones, Mandi Dama, Melanie Dulos, Sarah Hartley, Janis Leblanc, Kathryn Mayor, Rachel Naud, Jasmine Rach, and Marissa Stapley. To my family—the Guertins and the Shulgans—for support, love and babysitting, and especially to my dad, who has always made Christmas Eve so special, by including our French-Canadian traditions (notably his homemade tourtière). To Chris, my partner in life, love and editing. For brainstorming this book with me, and making it come to life that weekend in Chelsea. And finally, to Myron, Penny, and Fitz—for making Christmas the most wonderful time of the year.

It Happened One Christmas

QUESTIONS AND TOPICS
FOR DISCUSSION

1. What effect do you think Zoey's childhood experiences have on her outlook on Christmas as an adult?

2. Zoey and Benoît's retention of Christmas lyrics is impressive. Are you one to know all of the words, make them up, or hum along? What seasonal song never fails to put you in the holiday spirit?

3. Who would you cast to play Zoey in the movie version of *It Happened One Christmas*? What about Benoît? And the townspeople of Chelsea?

4. From *la tire* to snowshoeing to Christmas stockings, Zoey experiences several of Benoît's family holiday traditions during her visit. Do you have a favorite? Is there a tradition that you've dreamed of bringing into your life?

5. If you could write and direct a holiday film of your own, what would it be about? What would be your dream filming location?

6. How do you think going to Chelsea, Quebec, changed Zoey, if at all?

7. Zoey encounters many more obstacles than anticipated while in Chelsea. Even so, her resilience prevails. Is there a point in the story when you think you would have acted differently?

8. Benoît and Delphine remain close despite being exes. Do you think exes can be friends?

9. Benoît continuously denies Zoey the filming permit because he is determined to carry out his late father's wishes for the town. Did learning this change your perception of his character?

10. Do you think Benoît made the right choice in granting Zoey the film permit after all? What would you have done in his shoes?

11. In what ways do Zoey and Ben complement each other? In what ways do they clash? Do you think they'll stay together?

CHANTEL GUERTIN is the author of nine novels, including the instant national bestseller *Two for the Road*, *Instamom* and *Stuck in Downward Dog* for adults and the Pippa Greene YA series. She has worked as a beauty expert on Canada's number-one daytime talk show, *The Marilyn Denis Show*, and as an editor of various magazines. She lives in Toronto with her family. Find her on Instagram and TikTok at @chantelguertin.